# GRAVE
# RESERVATIONS

# GRAVE RESERVATIONS

A NOVEL

## CHERIE PRIEST

**ATRIA** BOOKS

NEW YORK LONDON TORONTO SYDNEY NEW DELHI

ATRIA
BOOKS

An Imprint of Simon & Schuster, Inc.
1230 Avenue of the Americas
New York, NY 10020

First Atria Books hardcover edition October 2021

**ATRIA** B O O K S  and colophon are trademarks of Simon & Schuster, Inc.

For information about special discounts for bulk purchases, please contact Simon & Schuster Special Sales at 1-866-506-1949 or business@simonandschuster.com.

The Simon & Schuster Speakers Bureau can bring authors to your live event. For more information or to book an event, contact the Simon & Schuster Speakers Bureau at 1-866-248-3049 or visit our website at www.simonspeakers.com.

*Interior design by Kyoko Watanabe*

Manufactured in the United States of America

1   3   5   7   9   10   8   6   4   2

Library of Congress Cataloging-in-Publication Data
Names: Priest, Cherie, author.
Title: Grave reservations / Cherie Priest.
Description: First Atria Books hardcover edition. | New York : Atria, 2021.
Identifiers: LCCN 2020051866 | ISBN 9781982168896 (hardcover) | ISBN 9781982168902 (paperback) | ISBN 9781982168919 (ebook)
Classification: LCC PS3616.R537 F36 2016 | DDC 813/.6—dc23
LC record available at https://lccn.loc.gov/2020051866

ISBN 978-1-9821-6889-6
ISBN 978-1-9821-6891-9 (ebook)

*This book is dedicated to my sister, Becky Priest Santavicca. She didn't have anything to do with writing it and none of the characters are inspired by her or anything like that. I don't even know if she likes mysteries. But the other day I complained about running out of people to dedicate books to, and she called dibs on this one, so I told her I'd do it.*

*I bet she thought I was joking.*

# GRAVE
# RESERVATIONS

# 1.

Leda Foley of Foley's Far-Fetched Flights of Fancy cringed at her phone screen. Grady Merritt's name flashed like an accusation.

"Mr. Merritt, I was just about to call you regarding your—"

He stopped her right there. "You changed my flight?"

"Yes, sir, I changed your flight. Please let me explain—"

"I was supposed to connect in LAX and be home in time for dinner. I promised my kid! Now you've got me routing through . . ." He trailed off, checking his own phone for the updated flight notification. "Hartsfield? Why am I going to Atlanta?"

"Mr. Merritt, if you die and go to hell in the South, you have to stop in Atlanta first. I'm very sorry, but this was the next best option."

"Next to what? The original flight isn't canceled," he protested, and then the background noise drowned him out. He was hustling through some crowded corridor of Orlando International Airport, scrambling to come home from a convention.

"The LAX flight wasn't canceled, but it'll be . . . it has been . . . there were . . . difficulties."

"This is ridiculous. I know I'm running really late, but I'm almost to the gate. *The original gate,*" he emphasized, "for my *original flight.* I think I can still make it. I'm sorry, but I don't want to go through Atlanta. Maybe they'll let me change it back."

"Sir, please—if you want to get home this evening, you *have* to take the rebooked flight. Please, Mr. Merritt."

But he continued wheezing into the phone, jogging to a backbeat of someone repeatedly paged to security for a lost item.

Then she felt it: a little "pop" in the back of her head. An option had closed, and now Leda knew it in her bones—he would officially, certainly, absolutely miss that first flight. Maybe the boarding door had shut, maybe the plane had left the gate. Whatever had happened, she'd successfully run out the clock.

She exhaled, kind of relieved and kind of depressed. Maybe this guy would never hire her again, but he'd get home safely before midnight.

"Mr. Merritt, there's no way you're going to make the original flight. But that's okay! You're safely booked on the next one out, leaving in a couple of hours. I apologize for the unforeseen traffic delay and the inconvenience of rebooking."

"Delay? Inconvenience? You changed the flight I approved last week. It's not like you knew I'd get stuck in traffic on the way to the airport."

"No, sir, I did not know . . . that."

If she wanted to be completely honest with him—and she didn't, so she wouldn't be—she'd admit that she didn't know *why* she'd changed his flight. It'd been a feeling, hard as a fist in her stomach. Leda had tried ignoring those feelings in the past, but doing that had often come around to bite her in the ass. Now she didn't ignore them anymore.

He sighed. His feet quit squeaking against the floor. He was breathing hard, and he sounded wholly defeated when he asked, "So why'd you do it?"

But she'd already decided not to answer that question. "Did you make it to the original gate?"

"I'm standing right in front of it. Watching the plane pull away. Dammit, now I have to call Molly."

"I can call her for you, if you'd prefer. Give me her number, and I'll do it. You can blame it all on me."

"I *do* blame this all on you."

"It's not my fault you were stuck in traffic, sir."

"Well, not that part."

She worked hard to sound upbeat. "Let's look at the big picture, shall we? You would've missed the flight anyway, and you would've been rebooked regardless. I assure you, I've put you on the first confirmed seat assignment back to the West Coast. I even scored you an upgrade to Comfort Plus!"

He didn't fight her. Either he didn't have the energy or he sensed that it'd be useless. He'd lost this round, whatever it was. "Yeah, you're right. I'm sorry. I shouldn't have yelled at you."

Leda was touched. Usually the next step after getting yelled at was getting hung up on, so all things considered, this was going quite well. "Aw, you didn't really yell. Travel is stressful for everyone, even under the best of circumstances."

"I mean, you *did* rebook me before I even knew I needed . . . to be rebooked. I guess we would've had this conversation anyway."

"That's the spirit, sir."

He sighed again, and she tried to feel less terrible. He was really making the best of it, and she appreciated that.

"Oh, hell," he mumbled, half to Leda and half to the empty gate. "Would you look at that—they're first in line for takeoff. Those lucky sons of bitches."

She cleared her throat, and, since he was being such a mensch, she took a chance. "Sir, maybe your luck is about to change."

"For the better, I hope. I'm not sure I can take any more bad luck today."

"For the better, yes. Any minute, Mr. Merritt. I apologize again about not contacting you before I made the alterations, but I grabbed the last upgraded seat assignment on flight 3422. More leg room and free booze is lucky, right? I promised you'd be home in Seattle today, and I intend to fulfill that promise. Please believe me when I tell you this: You would have never made it home tonight. Not if you'd caught that flight."

"What do you mean, I wouldn't have made it home?"

"I don't know exactly. It's just a feeling I had. A very strong feeling."

"You changed my flight . . . because you had a feeling."

She nodded, like he could hear her head rattle over the cell connection. "A very *strong* feeling, I think I've made that clear."

A muffled thump suggested that he'd dropped himself into a seat to catch his breath. He had ninety minutes before boarding would begin for his next flight. "As long as I'm home tonight, everything will be okay. Even if I have to detour through Atlanta."

"Atlanta isn't that bad, sir. You have enough time during your layover for a massage, a drink, even a mani-pedi—if you're into that kind of thing."

He was calming down, resigned to his southbound-connecting fate. "Drink, yes. Massage, maybe. The mani-pedis, I'll leave to my daughter. She's seventeen, home alone for the first time."

"She must be a very responsible young woman."

"Generally. She has a dozen emergency phone numbers, a key to our neighbor's place, some cash, a credit card, and the dog. This was an act of faith. A leap of faith?"

"Gesture of faith?" Leda suggested.

4

"Sure, that works."

"I have no doubt that she's fine, sir."

He snorted. "Like you had no doubt that I should skip the LAX connection?"

"Yes, just like that."

"That makes me feel better. Kind of. I don't know why."

"I don't know why, either. But I appreciate the vote of confidence, and—"

She stopped. She'd heard something, loud and very close to where Grady Merritt was sitting—a hard, fast noise that echoed through the cell phone's connection. In the background, people started shouting.

An alarm went off. Then another.

"Mr. Merritt?"

He said something, a single syllable. She thought it was "God."

"Mr. Merritt? Are you all right? Is everything okay?"

With his mouth a little too close to the microphone, he breathed, "I gotta go."

"Wait—was I right? Is something wrong? Did something happen? Mr. Merritt? Are you okay?"

The call dropped.

Leda held the phone out and stared at it, blinking at her own reflection in the screen. She spun half a circle in her office chair, all the better to face her best friend. Then she said, "He hung up on me. I mean, I *hope* that's what happened."

Niki Nelson didn't look up. She smiled, though. "It wouldn't be the first time."

In high school, Niki had been Nicole-Marie, then Nickie, then Nicki, then Nikk, and then Niki—partly because she liked the look of it and partly because none of the other two dozen Nicoles at school ever spelled it that way.

Together, Leda and Niki had been the two most semi-famous

weirdos at South Lake High. Not the *only* weirdos by any means, but the only girls who got suspended for breaking into the abandoned boathouse of an old yacht club because they'd heard it was haunted. They hadn't done any damage. They hadn't done anything at all except get inside, trip over a family of raccoons, and run into the cops as they fled the scene screaming.

No charges filed. No raccoons harmed, merely startled. Best-friends-forever status, cemented. Fifteen years later, plenty of other things had changed—but not that.

A couple of weeks previously, Niki had slipped on an errant lime garnish at work, so she was on medical leave from the bar at the top of the Smith Tower downtown. Her plastic bootie was propped on the edge of Leda's desk, where it took up a lot of space and frankly smelled a little weird.

When Leda's phone rang again, a chorus of chipmunks singing Sia's "Chandelier," Niki laughed. "You need a new ringtone."

"I do not. But, hey, look. It's Mr. Merritt again." She accepted the call. "There you are, sir. I'm sorry, but we seem to have gotten disconnected. Are you all right? Please tell me you're all right."

In reply, she heard sirens, and people hollering, and something that sounded like radio static—but wasn't. After waiting another minute or two, she ended the call.

"I think he butt-dialed me."

"Where did you say he is?"

"Orlando International."

"Um. Leda." Niki frowned and refreshed her timeline. "Hang on. There's a . . ."

"What? Give me your . . . What are you looking at?" She reached for Niki's phone, but Niki swatted her hand away.

"You're not going to believe this. A plane in Orlando skidded off the runway on takeoff just now. It . . . it's on fire. Everything's on fire." She turned her phone around to show Leda a grainy video shot by somebody in the airport.

"Holy shit," Leda said. She closed the booking site on her laptop and opened a new window. Five seconds of searching and there it was, flight 2661 to LAX. No doubt delayed indefinitely due to its giant fireball status. Leda leaned back in her chair and put her hands over her mouth. "Oh my God."

"That was his flight, wasn't it? The one he was supposed to be on in the first place?"

Leda nodded. "Yup."

"Did you know that was going to happen?"

"No! Obviously!" She pushed her chair back until it hit the wall behind her, but it wasn't far enough to escape the live footage of the burning plane. "If I'd known, I would've told everybody. I would've spray-painted it on the side of the airport, I would've gotten a bullhorn, I would've maxed out my credit card with sky-writing!"

"No. You wouldn't have." Niki knew Leda was only talking. Her friend had learned the hard way that warning people about tragic misfortune could lead to restraining orders, at best—and at worst (just the *one* time), a ride in the back seat of a cop car. Because sometimes a frantic heads-up sounds like a threat. Apparently.

"I would've at least called in a fake bomb threat or something."

"Now you're talking. Keep it low-key." Niki put down her phone and put her heavy, plastic-bound foot back on the floor with a thud. "So what happens next? What are you going to do?"

"What *can* I do? The plane's already crashed. I can't undo it; I can't fix it; I can't save anybody."

"You saved that dude."

"Accidentally!"

"Still counts," Niki insisted. "You did a good thing. Stop freaking out."

"But hundreds of other people might be dead because I'm ninety-nine percent worthless as a psychic!"

"And one percent *super useful.* If it weren't for you, this Merritt guy would have been on that plane. I bet he's feeling pretty good about being in the one percent right now."

"Oh God, what if he tells people that I saved him? What if he goes on TV to talk about his close call and the cops come arrest me because they think I did something to the plane? What if somebody calls Homeland Security? What if they think I'm some kind of domestic terrorist? They're going to send me to Guantánamo." She scooted her chair forward again, all the better to collapse face-down onto her desk.

"I don't know if Guantánamo is even open anymore, and you need to calm the hell down." Niki knew better than to try a more formal intervention; Leda's freak-outs ran hot and loud, but they burned out quick. "You haven't been anywhere near a plane in the last two months. I'm sure somebody, someplace, can prove it."

Leda raised her head. "I sure as hell haven't been anywhere near Florida," she said thoughtfully. "I haven't even talked to anybody in Florida, except for the rental-car place. Mr. Merritt's boss wanted him to have a rental car so he could come and go from the event without running up an Uber bill. Mostly I dealt with someone on this end from"—and here Leda's voice ticked back up again—"*the crime lab.* Oh my God, I think he's a cop. He must have hired me with cop money."

"Are you sure?"

"No." Her hands fluttered over her desk. "But that conference had something to do with modern forensic methods in law enforcement."

"Okay, so he might be a cop. The question is, did he sound like a crazy person to you? Because if he goes on TV and tells the world that a psychic travel agent saved his life, he's going to sound like a crazy person to literally everybody else—and he will not be a cop for long."

"Even though it's true?" Leda squeaked hopefully.

"Especially because it's true. Untwist your knickers, babe."

Niki hauled her purse up from the floor. It was a big purse, the kind you could carry a toddler in, if you really had to. "I have a suggestion." She reached over and smacked a button to turn off the monitor. "Log off and look away, would you? Let's call it a day. We can get poké around the corner. First bowl's on me."

"I have to stay here and work."

"Work on what? Do your other clients need anything right now?"

"No." Leda sulked. "The other two are on their Alaskan cruise. They should be fine."

Niki frowned. "Three clients total? That's all you've got?"

"Small business is hard, Nik."

"A small *travel* business even harder, I guess," she said in a pointed fashion. "In this day and age where anyone can do anything on the internet."

Leda sighed. "Not *everyone* does everything on the internet. Corporations use travel agents. Conventions and conferences use travel agents—and so do people who attend them, like Mr. Merritt. Older people who hate the internet and couldn't use Expedia if you held a gun to their heads . . . they use travel agents. But real-life human travel agents are getting harder and harder to find." Then she added, halfway between defiance and surrender: "It sounded like a good idea at the time."

"Then you've really got to scare up a few more of those, and fast. How much does this office cost you every month?"

Leda reached down and picked up her own purse. It was stashed under the desk, next to her feet. "So much money, you don't even know."

"I could help."

"You can barely keep yourself afloat, and I'm supposed to be the responsible one," she said, except neither of those things was exactly true. "I cashed out my 401(k) from that couple of years I worked at Amazon, got a small-business grant, and took out a loan. Don't worry about it. I can keep the lights on for another three months, at least, before I default and the bank takes . . . whatever it can."

"You don't have a house. Your car is a thousand years old. What will they come for, your fish?"

"God help them if they come for Brutus," she said solemnly. "I will lay waste to them."

"You spoil that fish."

"Yeah, well. Maybe in my next life, someone will spoil *me*." Leda slung her bag over her shoulder. "Screw this, you're right. I can't deal right now. It's too late for breakfast, it's too early for lunch, and I don't want poké anyway. I can't tell if I'm hungry or nauseous, and I'm too freaked out to go home and take a nap."

"Does that mean it's alcohol time?" Niki stood on her good foot and let her busted foot hang like an anchor. "Because, honey, this day was made for mimosas. Let's go to Geraldine's for calories and adult orange juice. We'll pretend that none of this ever happened, until we can't remember that it did."

"You're terrible, and I love you."

Niki grinned and held the door open. "Yeah, well. That's what friends are for."

# 2.

etective Grady Merritt of the Seattle PD stood by the window at gate thirty-six, staring at the giant marshmallow roast at the end of the runway. The fire was bright, but the smoke was dark as it billowed across the tarmac. Visibility was low and sketchy for the wailing emergency vehicles, the scrambling luggage carts, the men and women in vests with neon orange guide cones in hand, the security personnel, and everybody else who had some reason to be running back and forth outside the safe, smoke-free confines of the terminal.

He watched as sooty ex-passengers careened down the emergency chutes. Some tumbled like dolls. Some were carried. One guy clutched a pet carrier, checking its contents repeatedly.

A twinge of concern for the mystery pet penetrated Grady's stunned, baffled fugue. His own dog was home with his daughter, and he would've never fit inside that little carrier. *Note to self*, he thought, *never fly with Cairo in the cargo hold.*

The dog's name was Molly's fault. She was the one who claimed the yellow mutt they'd found in a Target parking lot. At the time, Molly was thirteen years old and the pup was maybe six months of gangly, dirty, lost, adorable puppy. It was love at first sight. Now she was a senior in high school, and the dog was four. They were both at home in Seattle, in the north end neighborhood of Ballard.

Safe.

Waiting for him to come home.

On cue, his phone began to ring, and Molly's junior-class picture appeared, demanding a response.

"Oh shit." He fumbled for his phone. "Hey, baby," he told her, before she could get a word in edgewise. "I was *just* about to call you."

"Dad!" she shrieked. "I saw the news! From the airport! The plane blew up! Dad, it's all over the news!"

"Yeah." He struggled to sound cool and unharmed. Unrattled, even. Thank God she wasn't standing right there in front of him. He'd never pull off the bluff that way. With his best and most practiced calm, responsible, authoritative law-enforcement voice, he said, "Honey, I missed the flight. I made it to the airport just in time to see it explode without me."

Just this once, Molly was *not* trying to sound cool. She was chattering on the razor's edge of hysteria. "You weren't on board? You didn't even get inside it? You didn't escape down the big yellow slide? I'm watching it on the news, Dad. I was looking for you, but I didn't see you come down the slide—you didn't come down the slide. Where are you? What happened? Are you dead? Oh God, *please* tell me you're not dead."

Before she could cram in another question, he said, "This is not a recording, and I am not dead. I swear to God, I missed all the action. I don't even smell like smoke, all right? Anyway, it only just now happened. How did you even hear about it so fast?"

"A friend of mine got a news alert on her phone. She said there was a plane crash in Orlando, and you were flying back from Orlando today . . . and then I got my phone out to check your schedule, and . . ."

She was about to start crying. He could hear it in her voice. "I know, I know. But don't worry, okay? I never made it to the plane, and hey—I can see the whole thing from here. A bunch of people survived. Maybe everybody."

"Everybody?"

"Don't quote me on that, but I'm watching them take people away. There are ambulances and everything. I've seen plenty of people coughing, and a few limping, but I haven't seen any bodies yet."

"They're probably still inside the plane! Dead people don't get to ride on the big yellow slide, Dad!"

Jesus, sometimes he wished she wasn't quite so smart. "Like I *said*, I see a bunch of people who are definitely alive. Don't panic, all right? Stay cool, and I'll be home as soon as I can. Listen, I'm already booked on another flight, connecting out of Atlanta later this afternoon."

"Atlanta?"

"Apparently, if you die and go to hell in the South, you have to stop in Atlanta first."

She laughed, short and too loud. "Who'd you steal that joke from?"

"The travel agent. And the point is, I'm safe. I will do my absolute best to be home tonight. It'll probably be late. I might not get in until after midnight, I don't know. But I *will* get home. I'll forward you my new flight info when we get off the phone, and if anything changes—if my outbound flight is canceled because of the crash, or anything like that—I'll call you immediately."

"Immediately?"

"Yes. Immediately." His eyes were damp. He wiped them with the back of his hand. "Now I should go check in at my new gate. You can go ahead and get back to work, and don't worry. I'm safe, you're safe, we're all safe."

"I already clocked out."

"What?"

"I told them my dad was in a plane crash and I had to leave. I'm on the bus, headed home."

"You heard that my plane blew up, so you left work and caught a bus, and *then* tried calling my phone?"

"*In my defense,*" she told him, "I saw the bus coming, right when I threw my apron down on the counter. I started crying, and my boss Krista started crying, too, and she sent me home. I mean, by then I was running out the door, so it was either cut me loose for the day or fire me."

"She's a good manager. You owe her a pickup shift, or something."

Molly laughed again, still wound up tight and a little sniffly, but calming down the longer he kept her on the phone. "I'll cover for part of her honeymoon. Dad?"

"Yes, baby?"

"I'm *super* glad you're not super dead."

"Me too," he agreed. "Go home, take a hot bath, watch some Netflix, whatever. Order some food. There's extra petty cash in my closet."

"In the shoebox on the top shelf?"

They both were quiet for a few seconds.

Then he said, "Yes. There should be cash in there, if you need it. If you left any."

"I only took a few bucks, just one time! I had to tip a pizza guy."

"Right." He was flashing her the unibrow of deepest suspicion, even though she couldn't see it. "What were you doing in my closet?"

She didn't answer right away. "You remember when we had that junior-senior prom last year, and I got the Betsey Johnson dress, and you said it looked like one that Mom used to wear? Well, if Mom had a dress like mine, she probably had shoes that looked good with it, right? I wear about the same size she did."

His throat was almost too tight to squeeze out a single word, but he managed. "Right."

"That box in the closet was made for ladies' shoes, so I opened it. I wasn't looking to steal anything. You said you put some of her things in storage, but I didn't want to bother you about it." She sniffed hard and coughed to cover the sound.

"It wouldn't . . . you never bother me. You can ask me anything you want, whenever you want. About your mother or anything else."

"It seemed too hard." Whether she meant it was hard for him or hard for her, she didn't say. Candice Merritt had been gone for almost four years. Sometimes it felt like a long time ago. Sometimes it didn't.

Great. Now they were both crying.

"Hey," he said, trying to say something else and not knowing how to begin it. He tried again. "Hey, I know I had a close call today. I'm so sorry I didn't call you the moment the plane caught fire. I should have. I screwed that up, and I'm really sorry."

"No, it's okay. I bet there was a lot of stuff going on."

"Yeah," he said with the world's grimmest laugh. "It was just so *sudden*, you know? I'd been stuck in traffic, and I knew I was cutting it close, so I was running to the gate as fast as I could. But I got here just in time to watch the plane leave and I was so *mad* about it."

It was her turn to laugh. She did it with a snort, followed by the loud honking of a world-class nose-blow. "That traffic saved your life, Dad."

"Either the traffic or the travel agent." Now that he'd said it out loud, he turned the thought over in his head.

"The one with better dad jokes than you?" Molly asked.

"Yeah, her. She changed my flight, before I got here. I don't know why," he added before she could ask.

"Hell of a coincidence."

Or something else, but he couldn't say what. "Hell of a coincidence," he echoed. He heard the bus creak to a stop and the doors squeal open. If that wasn't Molly's stop, it'd be coming up soon. They didn't live far from the Starbucks where she worked, and if the weather wasn't too bad, she usually walked. "I'll text you when I hear something, okay? I love you, and I'll see you soon, and . . . and . . . just help yourself to whatever's in the shoebox and go buy something trashy and delicious. Call me if you need anything, or even if . . . if you just want to talk."

"I will. All of those things, I will. I love you, too, Dad. Please be careful."

"I always am."

Then he hung up, feeling somewhat less shaken but no less eager to get home.

He thought about what's-her-name. Foley. The travel agent who'd had "a very strong feeling." *A very strong feeling* . . . what did that even *mean?*

# 3.

Niki was a little hungover, and Leda was trying to work, ignoring the intermittent moans and the occasional rustle as her friend shifted, rolled over, and tried to get comfortable on the second-hand IKEA love seat that sat along one wall of the tiny office. It wasn't made for sleeping—it was barely made for sitting—and Niki's plastic-bound foot kept falling off the arm, landing with a *thunk* on the floor.

"Oof. Ow."

"Stop doing that," Leda grumbled. "You're going to hurt yourself even worse."

"Worse than the Jägermeister?"

"Nothing hurts worse than Jäger, but that was your own damn fault."

"They had dollar shots. In test tubes. It was amazing. Some dude was just . . . passing them out. What was I supposed to do?" she asked, sitting up with no small degree of effort. "*Not* drink any?"

"Abstinence might've been the right call, considering," Leda mused.

"It's not like I'm bothering you. You're not even working."

"I am *too* working."

"On what?" Niki asked.

"Targeted Facebook ads. I'm trying to research and . . . um . . . budget. I'm also thinking about Craigslist and the newspaper, but is that too—I don't know—tacky? Does it make me sound sketchy? How else do people even find travel agents these days? I'm already in the phone book, and I have a web page and everything. I'm easy to find! Hire me!"

Niki pointed her encased toes at the entrance. "Tacky, sketchy. Whatever gets people through that door."

On cue, a shadow darkened the frosted glass that made up the top half of the agency's door. After a brief hesitation, somebody knocked.

Both women sat upright with a start.

"Client!" Leda hissed. "Look professional, or something."

Without giving Niki time to do anything but put her other foot down on the floor beside the busted one, she called out, "Come in!"

The knob turned, and the door cracked open slowly, revealing an ordinary-looking gent in the regional uniform of casual clothes topped off with a puffy vest. He was in his mid-forties, Leda guessed. Average build. Clean-cut, with dark hair and light eyes. Something about his posture suggested military or law enforcement, unless he just had a full-time stick up his ass.

"Hello!" Leda said brightly. "Welcome to Foley's Far-Fetched Flights of Fancy. I'm Leda Foley. How can I help you?"

Her guest froze, one hand still on the doorknob. "I . . . um. Hello."

"Please, come in and have a seat. What can I do for you today?" She waved at the pair of mid-century office chairs she'd found at the Fremont Fair for ten bucks apiece the year before. They were positioned across from her desk, looking reasonably official.

The man peered around the small office, taking in the framed travel posters, the struggling succulents, the blue curtains that were patterned with little yellow pineapples, the coffee cup that read I'D RATHER BE TRAVELING THE WORLD full of mismatched pens . . . and the random brunette in a cast who was sitting on a love seat against the wall.

He cleared his throat and said, "Hello, Ms. Foley. We've never exactly met—but we've spoken on the phone and exchanged a few emails. I'm Grady Merritt, from the other day?" The question mark at the end said either he wasn't sure how long it'd been since they'd spoken, or he wasn't sure what he was doing there.

Leda's stomach sank. It didn't know what else to do.

Because holy shit, it was the guy from Orlando International.

She tried to stay chipper. "Mr. Merritt! I'm so glad to see you made it home safely."

"Yeah, well. You had something to do with that, didn't you?" He closed the door and took a seat in one of the Knoll knockoffs. "I was hoping we could talk about . . . about what happened on Tuesday."

Leda and Niki exchanged the briefest, most panicked glance. "Absolutely, we can talk about Tuesday. Oh, I'm sorry—I almost forgot." She stalled by gesturing at Niki, who clearly would've rather been left out of the conversation. "This is my friend and associate, Niki Nelson."

He bobbed his head at her and said, "Nice to meet you."

"She helps around the office when she's not busy at her own job, you know how it goes. Since she broke her foot, she's been keeping me company here." Leda was rambling. She knew she was rambling. She still couldn't stop herself. "I really appreciate it, to be honest. This little business is my first time working alone, and

I'm not sure I care for it much. Maybe one day I'll just hire Niki outright, or get myself an assistant if she gets the cast removed and wants to go back to bartending. There's probably more money in bartending, come to think of it."

He glanced at Niki again, like he was sizing her up. "Okay," he said. "I guess this isn't a particularly . . . private conversation. Just a weird one."

Niki laughed, and Leda forced herself to smile. This was her nightmare scenario, wasn't it? The man had shown up at her office, probably to accuse her of witchcraft or something. He could call the local news, go viral on Twitter, and get articles written about the nut with the travel agency who kept him off an exploding plane. She'd be laughed out of Puget Sound.

She took a deep breath through her nostrils, past the rigid smile. "All right, hit me! What exactly would you like to talk about?"

He took a deep breath, too.

Then he got right to the point. "The plane crash, Tuesday morning."

"Oh, yes, that terrible accident. Some kind of mechanical failure, I heard? It's a wonder more people weren't killed, instead of just a handful. Not that a handful of people dying isn't a tragedy!" she added quickly. "Only that it could've been so much *worse*, and I'm so glad that it wasn't. Also, I'm glad you weren't on board. What a lucky coincidence *that* was, am I right?"

"Yeah, five people didn't make it out, but everybody else was safe. Even the only dog on the flight got out okay."

"Dogs are awesome! Do you have any?" she asked, on the off chance it might derail the whole thing and they could sit around sharing pictures of their pets. Brutus was a very attractive fish. She had a number of piscine portraits in her phone, just waiting to be shown to random semi-strangers.

"One."

"What kind?"

"Yellow mutt," he said with a crisp note of finality that said he was finished with this particular line of conversation.

"Not me. My apartment's barely big enough for me and a fish. I *do* have a fish . . ." she tried one last time.

"Fish are great. Not dying in a plane crash is even better, and that's why I'm here."

Leda swallowed. "Right."

"Here's the thing," he said, gesturing. His fingers were long and slender, and they moved like he was accustomed to holding things when he talked. A pen, or a notebook, maybe. "I've played that day over and over in my head. One thing stands out above everything else that happened."

"What's that?"

"*You.*"

"Me?"

"You. I don't know how, but you knew about the crash. You knew it all along, and that's why you changed my flight."

"Mr. Merritt!" Leda exclaimed. "I certainly did not know about—"

He stopped her right there. "Yeah, you did. Maybe you didn't know exactly what was going to happen, but when you went on about having a bad feeling and not having any concrete reason for changing the flight for me . . . you *knew* something bad was on the horizon."

Leda had a bit of experience protesting this sort of accusation. It was familiar turf, and it almost made her more comfortable with the conversation, now that it'd arrived. Leda slid into "nuh-uh mode."

"Sir, I assure you I had *no* idea. More likely, as I was clicking around on the internet I saw something, somewhere, out of the corner of my eye about the big truck that jackknifed on the inter-state in Orlando and my subconscious filled in the blanks. People do that kind of thing all the time, and they call it intuition. I've been booking travel for many years," she exaggerated wildly, con-sidering it'd been only a month or two, "and after a while you . . . you get a *feel* for it."

He shook his head and locked his hands together, letting them sit atop his thighs. "Nope. That's not what happened. The more I thought about it, the more certain I was. You weren't working on intuition—you were too confident for that. You changed a customer's approved reservations against his will, and you're not an idiot. It could've cost you business in the future, and you're too meticulous for that."

"Meticulous?" Niki was incredulous. "She's a one-woman crap-shoot."

"Not when I talked to her on the phone, after the lab put me in touch with her." Then, to Leda, he added, "When I first called to set up the trip, you asked all the right questions." He kept Leda's eyes fixed with his own. "You steered me away from layovers that were too short, and made sure that I had a seat near the front of the plane to shave a few seconds off my connection. You were the picture of professionalism. You were not the kind of woman to throw caution to the wind and drop a grenade into a guy's travel plans."

Niki laughed out loud. "That's where you're wrong, my dude. I mean, um, sir."

He turned around, leaning one elbow on the back of the chair so he could see her better. "How's that?"

"All I'm saying is, you think *Professional* Leda is the real Leda, when in fact, *Crapshoot* Leda is usually the one running point."

Leda narrowed her eyes. "Thanks, Nik."

"I'm here for you, babe. I mean, um. Ma'am."

Grady rotated back to Leda and gave her the ol' stink-eye. "I don't buy it. You took action deliberately and thoughtfully, even though you knew it might upset me. You acted on information that you didn't want to share, and I want to know what it was."

"Mr. Merritt . . . or . . . or . . . Detective Merritt . . . I . . ."

"Call me Grady."

Leda opened her mouth. She closed it. She opened it again, sucked in a deep breath. "Mr. . . . Grady. Did you make it home that night, like I promised you would?"

"Barely, but yes. You were right about that, too. The Uber pulled up to my house at eleven fifty-seven p.m. My daughter was on the front porch in her bathrobe and bunny slippers, waiting for me."

"Okay." She held out her hands and then pressed them flat upon her desk, hard enough to hold it down in case of an earthquake. "Since you *want* the truth, and I *have* the truth, and it all worked out in the end . . . I changed your flight because I *did* know something was wrong—but I swear to you, I didn't know what it was. I might've been vibing off the traffic you were stuck in, or I might've been vibing off the cosmic certainty of the plane crashing. Either way, I knew that you couldn't get on that plane because if you tried, you wouldn't make it home that day."

"Wait. Vibing? Like . . . psychic vibes."

It was almost a relief when he said it first. She exhaled all the deep breaths she'd taken for a week, all over her desk. "Yes. *Exactly* like psychic vibes. It's not something I tell the whole world about, and it's not very precise or reliable, but I've learned the hard way over the years that I can't just ignore it when I feel it. When I ignore my feelings, bad things happen."

"Like customers dying in plane crashes?"

She hesitated. "Well, *that's* never happened before."

"Then what?" he pressed.

"Then people get hurt in other ways," she snapped. "Man, you really *are* a cop, aren't you? I said, 'bad things.' Isn't that clear enough?"

"I've been a detective with the Seattle PD for more than a decade."

Leda felt her neck go warm and her ears go hot. "I haven't broken any laws."

"I never said you did. This is a social call, more or less."

"You're not here to arrest me?"

"For what? Keeping me out of a burning plane?"

She chuckled weakly. "When you put it that way . . ."

"I'm just here to have a lighthearted conversation with my friendly neighborhood psychic travel agent."

Niki snorted. "Just a lighthearted conversation about people dying inside airplanes, got it. Or are you just looking for reassurance that your next flight won't go down in flames?"

"Not now, Nik."

Grady smiled. "Oh, I'm not flying again anytime soon. But next time I do . . . yeah, I'll probably check with you first. I think you might be my travel agent for life."

Frustrated, worried, and ready to get this over with—whatever it was—Leda finally put her foot down. "But that's not why you're here, so what do you want? Why did you really come today?"

He sat back in the chair and seemed thoughtful, like he was considering how much to tell her, or how much to ask her. Then he crossed his arms and started talking.

"When my daughter was born, my wife and I thought it was an honest-to-God miracle. Candice was in a bad accident back in college, and some doctor told her she'd never have kids. Molly was born anyway, and we never took it for granted. Every now and again I'd wake up at night and my wife would be gone from the bed. I'd get up and go looking for her and find her in the nursery, either holding Molly or feeding her, or just looking down at her with ... this light in her eyes, you know?"

Leda glanced down at his left hand and didn't see a ring.

He saw the glance. "I took the ring off a year after she died, if that's what you're wondering."

"I'm so sorry to hear that. Wow, you notice everything."

"Yeah, so do you. Anyway, you want a detective who notices everything," he said offhandedly. "So one night I got up to use the restroom, and when I was done, I noticed a light in the baby's room. I figured Candy must've gotten up to check on her, but when I got back to bed ... she was right there, dead asleep.

"Something about the light in the nursery bugged me, so I went back to see Molly. Just to check. Just to see." He stopped, staring into space.

"What did you find?" Leda asked, very nearly in a whisper.

"I saw a woman standing over the crib. She was small and thin, and the light ... it was ... not coming from her, exactly. But it was around her, it was part of her. I don't know what I'm trying to say," he said quickly, trying to move on. "But she was looking at the baby and making little cooing noises, so soft you could hardly hear her."

Niki asked, "Well, who was it?"

"My mother," he said. "She died when I was in the police academy twenty-odd years ago, but there she was. Standing in my house. Cooing at her granddaughter. After a few seconds, she looked up and saw me. She winked, and she was gone."

Leda said, "Just like that?"

"Just like that. I suppose she wanted to see the baby, and she came all the way back from the other side to do it."

He was quiet for a minute, but Leda had always had trouble with silence. "Detective Merritt ... Grady ... I'm not that kind of psychic. I can't talk to the dead, if that's why you're here."

If he was disappointed, he didn't show it. The look on his face said he'd either expected that much or he was fine with it. "I'm not looking for a séance, Ms. Foley. I'm just telling you that I know there's more to the world than what we can always see right in front of us. And I believe you when you tell me that you had a premonition, or a bad feeling, or a bad certainty—if that's more like it. I believe you saved my life. Saved me a hell of a story and some smoke inhalation, that's for damn sure. And now I want to hire you. Not to book any travel, and not to talk to my dead mother. I've got a case I've been beating my head against for a couple of years, and I'm all out of leads. I'm ready to try anything, which means I'm willing to try a psychic. Ms. Foley, I want you to help me solve a murder."

# 4.

Leda sat aghast behind her desk. She stared at the cop, who calmly unfolded his arms and assumed a relaxed position in the chair across from her. "You want my help? Like . . . psychic help?"

"Correct," he informed her.

"Even though I just told you two minutes ago that whatever abilities I have are not very precise or reliable? I don't know anything much about police work, but I'm reasonably confident that 'precise' and 'reliable' are two of the more important components."

"In a perfect world, sure. Hell, in a perfect world I'd be able to pay you as a police consultant, but 'we don't do that, here.'" Something about the way he said it told Leda that he'd brought it up before and someone had shot it down.

"So when you said you want my help, you meant . . . you want my help for *free*."

"I'd love to have your help for free, but I'm not an asshole. I don't have a lot of money to throw around, but I can afford your agenting fee. We can call it a trip of a different sort, right? I'll pay another booking fee, and you can kick around with me for an afternoon. What do you say?"

"This can't possibly be legal, that's what I say."

"Why not? I won't divulge any sensitive police information, you won't tell anybody I invited you out for a consultation, and maybe we're just a couple of pals, sightseeing around the greater Puget Sound area. Bring her, if you want." He cocked a thumb at Niki. "If she helps, or if you just feel better with a friend present. I realize I'm some random dude you don't know, and I won't take it personally if you don't want to be alone in a car with me."

"Woo-hoo!" Niki chirped. "It's a ride-along!"

But Leda wasn't there yet. "No," she protested, without really knowing why. "No, that's a terrible idea. Sir. Detective. Mr. Merritt. Grady," she tried at last. "You have to understand, this is *not* a science. It's not even an art. Like Niki said, it's a crapshoot. My time is a waste of your money."

"This time it's my own personal money, not precinct travel funds—and I'll waste it however I want. I promise I won't get mad if nothing pans out, and I'll never say a word about this to anybody, ever. Believe me, I don't want the rest of the guys at the precinct knowing I hired a psychic, no offense. They give me enough shit for being vegetarian." He sat forward, a gleam in his eye. "What do you say?"

What *could* she say?

*No* was always an option, but did she really want to peeve a policeman? He didn't seem like the petty sort, not that she was a particularly good judge of that kind of thing. She'd saved his life, hadn't she? She could probably get away with telling him no.

Instead, she said, "I don't want to look at any dead bodies."

"No dead bodies, swear to God."

"You know I'm probably going to get it wrong."

"Your instincts are imprecise and unreliable, got it."

"Then why do you even *want* them?" she asked, exasperated.

Firmly, insistently, he said, "Because this case has been driving me crazy. I have to believe that it's solvable, but I need a hint, or a nudge, or a clue—and I'm willing to take any half-ass, foggy, wayward clue I can get."

"Even if it comes from a psychic travel agent who's never actually helped anybody, not even once, in her whole entire life?"

"You helped *me*."

She sighed hard enough to blow out a birthday cake. "Okay, you got me there. But that was an accident! I've never done anybody any good before. Not on purpose. Not when it really counted."

"Don't you want to . . . I don't know. Help your fellow man? Contribute to the net good in the world? Fight crime? Everybody likes to fight crime, right?"

Leda and Niki exchanged a look.

They were both thinking about the same thing: a guy who nobody saved and whose violent death had never been explained. Leda didn't want to go anywhere near that subject, so she asked Grady a question instead.

"I am no fan of crime or criminals, but you're not hearing me. Let me try to explain from another angle. Do you ever watch *Saturday Night Live*?"

He shrugged. "I used to, but I haven't in years."

"That's okay. The skit I'm thinking of aired back in the nineties, I think."

"Were you even alive back then?"

She smirked. "Flattery will get you nowhere. I saw the skit on YouTube when I was in college, and it stuck with me. Here's why," she added fast, keeping the anecdote moving before he could derail it. "I don't know if it had an official name, but me and Nik always call it the 'Inconsequential Psychic' skit. There's a psychic who goes

29

around warning people about silly stuff. Tells them they're going to spill coffee in their car on the way to work, that kind of thing."

"Okay?"

"Well, I'm the *real-life* inconsequential psychic. Nothing I ever see or feel or whatever . . . none of it is actually very important. Usually my, um, flashes of insight, if you will, they're super pointless."

"For example?"

Nik interjected. "The gazpacho."

Leda pointed at her. "Yes. The gazpacho. The other day we were headed to this lunch place we like, over on Capitol Hill. On the way there, I had this powerful feeling that there would be no gazpacho soup, and that was exactly what I wanted, so I said we should go someplace else. Nik wanted the polenta, though, and she was all, 'Noooo . . . I want to do Shirley's anyway. . . .' So that's what we did."

"And you were right?"

"I was stuck with the quiche, yes."

Niki rolled her eyes. "It's good freaking quiche, Leda. Jesus."

"It's not as good as the gazpacho!" Leda insisted. "What I'm trying to say is, even when my oddball clairvoyance is reliable, it isn't useful to anybody. Ever. Except for you, that one time."

He dug in his heels. "Maybe I'm special. Come on, what have you got to lose? You don't look very busy . . ." he said, his eyes scanning the room for signs of other clientele. The phone didn't ring, the email alert didn't chime, and no text messages buzzed in to anybody's cell. "I'll pay you double your rate."

Slowly, methodically, and with great drama, Leda began to bang her head up and down on her desk. "This. Is. The worst. Idea. Ever."

"Great!" He reached into a pocket and pulled out his business card. "We'll do it this weekend. Text me with whichever day and time work best, and we'll meet wherever you like."

"Castaways!" Niki suggested.

"No," said Leda immediately. "Not Castaways."

"What's Castaways? And what's wrong with it?" Grady wanted to know.

"It's a bar. Or a venue. It's . . . all things to everyone, but it's closed on Sundays, and it doesn't open until four on Saturdays." Then to Grady, she said, "Listen, I'll think about it, okay? Give me a day to decide."

He rose to his feet and offered her his hand, now that she wasn't banging her head on the desk anymore. "I can do that. Thanks for your time, Ms. Foley."

She accepted the handshake and added wearily, "It's Leda. Just Leda."

"Leda, then. I hope to see you soon."

When the door had shut behind him, and the last echo of his footsteps had faded down the stairs, both women flailed their arms at each other.

Leda's voice was high enough to summon dolphins when she squeaked excitedly, "What am I going to do? A cop wants to take me clue-hunting!"

"You're a bloodhound. You'll be awesome!" Niki replied in kind. Then she took it down an octave to add, "You should totally do it. He's a paying customer, and this is a travel agency without a surplus of travelers to agent. He's already promised not to be mad if you suck at this."

"Oh, I am *going* to suck at this."

Niki grinned. "Is that a psychic prediction?"

"That's a non-psychic certainty." She put her head back down on her desk and left it there, her forehead smearing the surface with makeup. Her voice was muffled when she concluded, "But I don't actually have a bad feeling about it."

"You don't?"

She picked her head up and pondered what she'd just said. "I don't. I don't know how useful I'll be, but I don't feel any apocalyptic doom or anything. At worst, I'll be useless. Right? Even though . . . I mean . . . *you know.*"

Neither one of them wanted to say it out loud. Niki tiptoed around it. "I know, but maybe this is a good opportunity. You're making friends with a cop—a cop who isn't weirded out by your psychic stuff. Even if you can't help him with his case, maybe he can help you with yours."

"Don't talk like that."

"Like what? Like you're not still looking for answers?"

Leda shot her a warning look. "Tod is gone. It's been three years, and the police haven't been ultra helpful so far."

"It's not like they had a lot to go on. You weren't a lot of help."

The warning look went sharp.

Niki walked it back. "*No one* knew why Tod was in the back seat of his own car, or why he was all the way out past Renton, or why anybody would want to hurt him. Not even you."

"Stop it. Just stop talking."

"All I'm saying," Niki persisted, "is that it can't hurt to be friendly with a police detective. He could dig up the case, take another look at the evidence. He seems pretty sharp; he might see something the other guys missed."

"Nicole."

It was like she'd used a safe word. Niki closed her trap and waited to see if this was going to turn into a fight or just a round of sad bickering.

Leda sat back in her chair. She pressed her hands flat on her desk, then used her palm to rub away the sweat smudge she'd left with her forehead. "One psych-curious cop with a stale cold case isn't going to change what happened to Tod. It might not even be Grady's jurisdiction, or however that works."

Carefully, Niki said, "That's no reason not to help him, if you can."

Leda thought about it for a minute, and then waved a white flag. "Okay, fine. You're right. If I can help, awesome. If I refuse to try, then I'm a jerk. Screw it. I'm in. But I don't want to go alone. Are you in?"

"Yes, but not if you want to do it Saturday. Me and Matt have plans. We're going to Snoqualmie for a train thing. You know Matt and trains."

"Dammit. Saturday is the only day that makes sense for me."

"Go on without me; you'll be fine. No really bad feelings, right? Meet him for coffee, or meet him here, or whatever feels good to you." Niki picked herself up off the IKEA love seat, adjusted her stance with the plastic boot, and said, "Come on, it's almost five o'clock. Clock out or sign off. Now that I've said it out loud, I'm feeling Castaways."

"You just want to go see Matt." Her boyfriend was the manager there.

"Come on. Let's get some drinks, and if you feel like a little *klairvoyant karaoke*, nobody will stop you."

"Now's really not the time."

"I'm sorry I brought up Tod, but you know I'm right about this." Niki picked an oversize sweater off the rack by the door. "You always feel better after you sing. It's like exercise, or eating your vegetables, or mediation. But with glitter and the occasional high note."

"I'm *not* doing any klairvoyant karaoke."

She flung the sweater over her shoulders. "Suit yourself. Get a nice grown-up slushie and watch *me* do some karaoke of the non-psychic kind."

"You have a terrible voice."

"It's Thursday. Nobody will be there to hear it, and I am not ashamed."

Leda got up, too. There was no escaping Niki's gravitational field of forced fun times, even when the afternoon had gone a little dark. "You sound like a crow being strangled."

"Only until I've had a couple of drinks."

"Then you sound like *two* crows being strangled."

"I love you, too." Niki collected Leda's jacket, balled it up, and tossed it to her. "Get a move on, girlie. Rush-hour traffic is upon us."

"Let's take the light rail."

"The station is four blocks from Castaways, and I'm not exactly in hiking shape at the moment. If you'll recall." She held up her booted foot for emphasis.

"Fine," Leda sulked, feeling like a jerk because she hadn't thought of Niki's bum foot. She picked up her purse and fished out her car keys. "I'll go get Jason."

"Jason" was a baby-blue Accord that Leda had bought on a Friday the thirteenth. Sometimes Leda wondered if she shouldn't have named it "Jamie Lee" instead, but it was too late to turn the habit around now. Grumpily, she stomped past Niki and down the corridor, then out the side door that promised an alarm if opened. There was no such alarm.

"I'll bring the car around front."

Niki promised, "I'll be there!" and locked the door behind herself.

Five minutes later, Leda pulled up, and Niki secured herself in the passenger seat. Castaways was only half an hour out if the traffic was good.

# 5.

Leda and Niki were going against the flow of rush-hour traffic, thank God. Even on a Thursday afternoon, the city core was a still life of cars—with a soundtrack of horns honking and people swearing in a dozen languages. They'd started out a little south of town, in a neighborhood called Columbia City; Capitol Hill was only a few miles north, but any road closures or wrecks could stretch the drive to an hour, if luck wasn't with them.

Jason the Accord made it up the hill in thirty minutes, and he was successfully parked in another ten. The parking wasn't metered after six. It was a quarter till then, but Leda and Niki decided to risk it rather than spring for the paid lot down the block.

The hill was crawling with cars, bicycles, jaywalking pedestrians, homeless people with signs, rats, hipsters with tiny dogs in neon harnesses, street musicians with open guitar cases, preachers wearing sandwich boards, skateboarders, and the occasional drag queen. Cap Hill had once been known as the city's main "gayborhood," and it still had a few clubs and bars that catered to the old clientele. These days, Niki called it the "stayawayborhood" because she'd been priced out of the apartment she'd shared there with Matt for a couple of years. She was still sore about it.

But Castaways was still there, so they didn't stay away as much as she pretended.

In truth, Leda and Niki found their way to the dark little club at least two or three nights a week, and often more frequently than that. It wasn't the strong drinks that brought them back again and again, and it wasn't even Matt—a lean, good-looking guy who was a couple of years younger than his broken-toed beloved.

The main appeal of the place was, as Niki had suggested, the klairvoyant karaoke.

Leda walked slowly so Niki could keep up, thumping that plastic boot as she scaled the steep sidewalk. "I told you, you should've kept the crutches."

"They rubbed my armpits raw. Forget it. I'll stick with a really loud limp."

"Doesn't your foot hurt from doing that?"

"Not as bad as my armpits did. Crutches chafe, Leda. They chafe."

When they reached the entrance, Leda held the door and Niki strolled in like she owned the place, because being the girlfriend of the manager had its privileges. They were small privileges, like one or two free drinks and a front-row seat if there was a good act for the little round stage, but she was happy to take advantage of every single one.

"Tiffany!" she called to the bartender.

Tiffany toasted her from halfway up a very tall ladder, where she was adjusting the stock on the high-stacked shelves. "*Ladies*," she said with a wave. "Come on in and make yourselves at home. You've got the place to yourself for the moment."

"Hey!" a guy at a corner table protested.

Tiffany went back to teetering on the ladder and topping off the booze. "Except for Justice, over there. He's on his third glass of fizzy water," she said in his direction.

The man's real name was Justin, but he didn't like it—and he'd gone full anarcho-communist after the 2016 election. He used the bar as a base of operations for his zines and newsletters due to the free Wi-Fi and generally tolerant management. But as long as he left the other customers alone—and as long as he paid for his nachos and the occasional Shirley Temple—he was allowed to stay.

Sometimes he was low on cash, and then it was fizzy water until someone took pity on him and bought him something else.

Matt would let almost anybody hang out, if the hanging out was peaceful and quiet. Homeless folks who wanted water on a hot day? No worries. NIMBY protestors wanting to put something in somebody else's backyard? As long as they didn't make a stink, but no, they couldn't post their signs—no matter how meticulously they explained that their newest opinions totally weren't racist, this time. Eager college students collecting signatures for ballot initiatives? Don't interrupt the show, if there is one—but knock yourselves out.

Festive SantaCon drunks? Lock the doors, flip the sign, and turn out the lights. Pretend it's the Purge, and pray they leave without breaking anything.

Castaways was a hole-in-the-wall in the old-school Cap Hill tradition: neither bright nor clean, but cozy and often crowded after 8:00 p.m. The decor was loosely "golden age of Vegas," which was fitting—for it'd been named for a long-gone casino on the old Sin City strip. Showgirl feathers, neon lights, mid-century modern fixtures, and blown-up photos of the Rat Pack rounded out the setting. If you looked real close, you could see famous gangsters in the background of some of the pictures. Once upon a time, pointing out grainy figures that were supposedly Bugsy Siegel and Meyer Lansky had been Matt's favorite flirting move, and that's how he'd ended up with Niki. Now it was just a thing to talk about, because he was officially locked down.

Leda dropped her purse onto the far side of the bar, where she knew it was safe with Tiffany. "Anybody cool on deck tonight?" she asked.

The bartender was a curvy, brown-skinned, green-haired member of Generation Z who was barely old enough to hold the job she rocked on a nightly basis. Nobody knew where she'd learned her impressive hooch-slinging skills, but the day she'd turned twenty-one she'd shown up with an application in hand, and her timing had been good. Matt had sprained his wrist trying to Tom Cruise it up, *Cocktail*-style. He'd needed the help. She'd needed the gig. It was a match made in heaven.

She came back down the ladder again, picked up a bar rag, and tucked it into her apron. "Nobody's scheduled for the stage, if that's what you mean."

Niki flopped into her usual seat at a tiny round table, just to the right of the stage.

"Can I get you anything? It's almost six o'clock," Tiffany hollered. The music was on, but it wasn't turned up all the way. Leda thought it sounded like last decade's dubstep, but Tiffany had weird tastes and Matt was nonconfrontational enough to let her run the playlist. It wasn't too loud to talk, but it was too loud to talk across a room.

"Can you make me a mai tai?" Niki called back.

"I can, but I won't. You can have . . ." She peered around the shelves beneath the bar. "You can have a rum and orange juice. I'm still setting up."

Enthusiastically, Niki declared, "I'll settle for it!"

"How about you, Leda?" the bartender asked. "What's your poison tonight?"

Leda climbed onto the nearest stool, one butt cheek at a time. "I don't know, Tiff. It's been a weird day. Just give me a rum and Coke and let me think."

"You want to read me? Do an easy one, to get started?"

Justice looked up from whatever antifa site he was annotating at the moment. "Ooh! Do me! Do me!"

"She's not *that* desperate," Niki told him from the peanut gallery.

Leda waved her hand in the trust-fund punk's general direction. "Later, dude. I'm not working tonight."

The bartender asked, "You're not singing?"

"I wasn't planning on it."

"Yeah, right."

"What? I don't have to do it every single time I come in here."

"But you pretty much *do*. I mean, come on." Tiffany gave her a coaster and a glass to sip on. Something about Leda's slouch or maybe her frown gave the bartender pause. "Are you okay? Because you don't look okay. Your weird day must not have been a good kind of weird."

"Meh." Leda drew the skinny brown stirring straw around to her mouth and sucked on it without any joy. Then she sneezed and shook her head. "Damn, Tiff! How much Coke did you put in this rum?"

"You looked like you needed the booze more than the caffeine."

"You're an angel, Tiff."

"Thanks, Leda. You're a good customer."

She grunted again. "I guess. But I'm a real shitty psychic."

"Says who?" Tiff leaned forward on her elbows, showcasing an award-winning bosom that was covered in tattoos. She credited that outstanding rack with half her tipped income, and she went to snug, low-cut lengths to keep it visible.

"Says everybody."

"Nah. You're just having an off day. Is it something about Tod?"

A pang hit Leda in the torso, just above her belly. It never stopped being strange, hearing his name. Even after all this time. How much time? Not that much, now that she thought about it. Three years? Some days it felt like thirty minutes. She stared down into her very strong drink. "Kind of."

"Anything new? A break in Tod's case?"

"No, nothing like that." She took a sip that was too big to really call a sip. If the straw had been any bigger, it would've drowned her. "He came up, that's all. And I mean, come on. Elephant in the room, right? If I were worth a damn as a psychic, I would've totally seen his murder coming."

"Aw, *hell no.*" Tiff shook her head and pulled a bottle of Captain Morgan onto the counter. She pushed the bottle into Leda's space. "That's garbage, and you know it. None of that was your fault, and you have to quit beating yourself up about it."

"No, I don't."

"Well, you *should.*"

"I'm trying! That's why I'm here." Leda took the rum and topped off her drink that was already 80 percent alcohol. "That's why I'm usually here, anyway."

"I thought you were usually here to practice."

"That, too. The karaoke is actually helping, I think. When I get flashes now, they're often a lot stronger. Or else they're a lot clearer. It must be like a muscle—and the more you work it, the better it gets. Unless I'm fooling myself. I've been doing this for what, six months? Honestly, there's no strictly empirical evidence that my psychic abilities are improving."

Niki appeared at her side. If it hadn't been for the too-loud dubstep, Leda would've heard her clomping across the club, and she wouldn't have jumped half out of her skin. "She's *not* fooling herself. She's obviously upping her skill set. Leda, go on. Tell her about the cop."

Leda slumped down on the bar, her chin atop her hands, and her drink looming large in front of her face. "I don't want to tell her about the cop. You do it."

Niki was all too happy to oblige. She laid out the tale in graphic, unlikely, exaggerated detail—but she nailed the gist.

When she was finished, Tiff's eyes were wide. "This is great news! You're going pro with your parlor trick!"

"Not really. I feel like I'm taking advantage of him."

The bartender shrugged. "He knows what he's in for. Do your best and see if it helps. Hey, look." She tilted her head toward the door, where a party of three was coming inside. "More people for the audience."

Leda balked. "I didn't come here to sing."

Tiffany waved away her protests. "Yeah, but we know you will. Go ahead and get the sound set up. You don't want to do it while the place is packed."

Niki looked around and asked, "Where's Matt? He can check the sound levels for you."

"He went to the bank for a cash drop before it closed. I'd say he'll be back any second, but you know rush hour." Tiffany slipped Niki another drink before she even asked for it.

"Thanks!" she said, swiping it into one hand and lurching back to her seat, spilling only a few drops on the way.

"Go on," the bartender gently pushed Leda. "Settle in. I'll see what these new folks want, and then I'll turn everything on. The boss'll show up sooner rather than later. Take a couple of items from the audience, do your psychic thing, select a meaningful song for someone . . . and see if it doesn't make you feel better. If you still feel like garbage after a request or two, then call it a night."

Leda surrendered to the inevitable and nodded glumly. "Fine.

You win. You *all* win. Everybody wins, except for me." She glanced at the trio who had just come inside. Two men, one woman. She recognized one of the guys as a regular and shot him a head nod. He returned it and flashed her a wave.

She didn't know his name, but she knew he was thinking about proposing to the woman beside him. Not that he'd told her out loud, but when she'd been up on the stage—holding a plastic bobblehead from an anime she didn't recognize—she'd closed her eyes, concentrating on the contours of the odd little toy, and felt the leftover warmth where his fingers had been squeezing it.

As clear as day in her mind's eye, she'd seen the woman's face, and a purple lace bra. A hiking trip. Her backpack, as she climbed some trail ahead of him. A small box in his pocket. A flutter in his heart.

But when she looked at them now, she still didn't see a ring on her left hand. He must've chickened out, right? Surely if he'd proposed and she'd said no, they wouldn't still show up together. He might still be working himself up to it. That night a few weeks ago, when she'd sat on the stool and held the microphone, the lights of the stage shining up into her face, she'd used her psychic intuition to pick a song for him: "In Your Eyes," the old Peter Gabriel number that everyone associates with the movie *Say Anything*, if anyone remembers it at all.

His lips had quivered. His eyes had been damp.

God, she hoped she hadn't talked him out of proposing on accident. Unless, of course, getting married would be a huge mistake.

That was the problem with being an inconsistent psychic who took karaoke requests like a fortune-telling jukebox. At best, you told somebody something they probably already knew. At worst, you played God and pushed somebody in a direction that turned out to be arbitrary. You never knew if you were actually helping.

Okay, you *usually* never knew. Once in a blue moon, someone would pull her aside after the stage went dark and tell her that she'd really been on the nose. They'd been wondering about what to do about a crappy day job, and hearing Leda sing "Heaven Knows I'm Miserable Now" by the Smiths had given them the push they'd needed to put in notice. Or they'd been worried about a health problem, fearful of a damning diagnosis. But when they'd given Leda their reading glasses to hold, she'd launched into "I Feel Good," even though it was way out of her range and she was no James Brown.

Every now and again, it meant something.

It might've been her imagination, but she was increasingly convinced that yes, her instincts were steadily improving. So perhaps it was true, what Niki had so strongly implied—her "exercises" were honing her skills, and that's why she was able to keep Grady Merritt from becoming part of an airborne fireball.

Unless she was overthinking it.

It wouldn't be the first time.

By the time the microphone and sound system were ready to go, and enough people to call a crowd had wandered in, it was around eight. It was late September and the time hadn't changed yet, so eight was only kind of dusky—a hint of gray and purple still highlighting the overcast skies. Leda could barely see it through the windows that faced the street, and she let it distract her from the stage lights down at her feet. She liked those lights. They made it harder to see the audience, which made it easier to pretend she was alone up there, nobody watching, nobody making her nervous.

The door opened, and a party of four strolled in. They'd take the table beside the hallway where the bathroom was—but it didn't take a psychic to see that coming. It was the last open table.

Grady Merritt had said that people wanted a detective who noticed everything. Leda was beginning to suspect that it went the same way for psychics. The more she noticed, the more puzzle pieces she picked up—plus whatever woo-woo vibes came along for the ride.

Niki was beside the stage, running point on the sound equipment with Matt—who had come back from the bank with burgers and fries from Dick's. They were still picking at the last of the fries.

They each flashed her a big thumbs-up.

She brought the mic to her mouth and sat up a little straighter. "Good evening, everyone. My name is Leda Foley." A smattering of applause went around the room. "Some of you have heard of me. Nice."

From what little she could see past the lights, at least half a dozen faces were familiar, and they'd brought friends. Word must be getting around. Was that a good thing? She couldn't decide, and it was too late to bail tonight.

"Well, thanks so much for coming out, and thanks of course to Matt Cline for letting me commandeer his stage for a little while. I'll let this run for an hour or two if I'm feeling it, and cut it short if I'm not. Does that sound fair?"

The crowd murmured in response.

"Good. For all you new folks, here's the drill: I'm a thirty-two-year-old travel agent, born in Tacoma, Washington—"

Which got a solitary whoop from somewhere toward the back.

She pointed toward the sound. "Tacoma! Represent. Just the one guy, though? No other fugitives from the Tacoma aroma?" That got a few giggles. "We moved when I was about ten years old, but it'll always be home. I guess. Okay, it's just us, then. Let's start with you, shall we? Stand up back there, Mr. . . . ?"

"Cory!"

"Mr. Cory from Tacoma, okay. Mr. Cory, do you have any loose objects upon your person—anything you'd be willing to let me hold for a minute or two? I've got a touch of what some people call 'clairsentience,' which means that sometimes I can pick up information by touching objects. Or call it psychometry, if you like that better. It's a fiddly, silly, inconsistent superpower, but I'm doing my best to develop it. Practice makes perfect, right?"

The audience murmured agreement, and Cory from Tacoma shimmied around the tables until he made it to the foot of the stage. He was a cute young black guy, probably lured to town by a tech job. His clothes said *business casual,* his beanie hat said *it's getting colder,* and his shoes said *I was a skater boy, and I'm not ready to give it up yet.* He had a great smile, big brown eyes, and a flattened penny from a novelty machine in the palm of his hand. He held out the penny, and she took it.

"Thank you, Cory. I appreciate your trust in this ridiculous performance, and I hope it will not go unrewarded. Are you familiar with how this works?" She leaned down, to better hear his answer.

"Yeah, my friend Debbie brought me. She said you're amazing."

"Wow. Thanks, Debbie!" She waved to a nebulous spot in the back of the room, from where a faint "woo-hoo!" had come. "And for everyone else, this is what happens next: I'm going to stand up here looking real thoughtful for a few seconds, maybe a minute, while I hold this souvenir penny from . . ." She squinted down at it. "The Woodland Park Zoo. Then I'll choose a song just for Cory. If I do it right, the song will mean something to him. It might just be a line or two of lyrics, or it might be a tune that he heard with his one true love, years ago, on top of the Ferris wheel down at the pier, I don't know. But if it's meaningful for him, he'll tell me. He doesn't have to say why," she added quickly. "Just . . . tell me if I'm reading him right."

Cory gazed up at her, beaming. He was a true believer, she could see it all over his face. She hoped she wasn't about to disappoint him.

"All right, here goes nothing," she said softly, her voice barely registering in the mic.

She closed her eyes and rubbed her thumb gently over the penny. It was warm in her hands. The scene on one side was from the bears exhibit. On the other side, she found the logo for the zoo. It was the same kind of smooshed penny anyone could get from any turn-crank machine in any theme park, zoo, national monument, or roadside attraction. Nothing to mark it as special.

But she thought about Cory, smiling and young and feeling strong. Yes, that was it. A feeling of strength. Not just physical strength, but something else. Something survived, something overcome. Something in the pit of her stomach that said he'd had a near-miss with something dire.

A tune welled up in the back of her mind, a song she didn't know that well. She recognized it from a few years ago but didn't know much more than the chorus. That was okay. That's what the scrolling karaoke lyrics were for.

"Got it," she said. "Nik, hand me the catalog?"

It was a hefty thing, the catalog that went with the karaoke equipment. It had something like five thousand songs in it, and Matt checked for new downloads once a week, to keep it current.

"Here." Leda tapped her finger on one song, and showed it to Niki and Matt. "This one. Cue it up."

When the music came to life and the lyrics appeared on the big screen at the back of the room, Leda started to sing. She wasn't the world's greatest singer, but she could carry a tune in a bucket with a lid on it; and if she wished to flatter herself, she would've admitted that these Castaway exercises were improving her singing, along with her weirder abilities. She didn't struggle so hard with the highs or lows, and she was faster to nail a quick key transition.

She made it all the way through "Helena Beat" by Foster the

People, then took a little bow and returned the penny to Cory—whose eyes were full of tears. His smile was wobbly but bright when he said, "Thank you, Leda Foley from Tacoma. That was lovely."

Over the chatter of the crowd and the filler music that played in the background between songs, she asked, "Did it make sense to you? Or was I way off base?"

He put one foot up on the stage, to hear her better—and all the better for her to hear him. "It's the bit about the poison and taking a sip but holding on tight. I finished chemotherapy this week. I have that album, and I blared it through my headphones on the bus, on the way to and from the cancer clinic in Ballard. That's been my fight song."

"Oh my God, congrats on the not-having-chemo anymore!"

"Thanks, it was brutal. But it's over now, and my odds are good, and you made my night. I wanted to say that." He offered up his hand, and she took it.

They exchanged a half squeeze, half shake, and he took his penny back to his seat.

Leda exhaled hard, relieved. The first one of the night was on target, and that boded well for the rest of the evening.

Next up was a woman with a tube of lip balm, and she got a rousing rendition of "Walk the Line." Then came an older man with a war medal that she didn't recognize. He got "Violet" by Hole, surprising everybody and exhausting Leda with all the Courtney Love scream-singing—but drawing a big thumbs-up from the man with the medal. After that, a strung-out-looking punk girl offered her a patch off her jacket, a white anarchy symbol on a black background. She received "It Will Come Back" by Hozier, and Leda didn't know if that one had worked or not. The girl had left the club hastily, as soon as she got her patch back.

After that, Leda took another couple of requests, and then

ceded the stage to anyone else who wanted to take a turn at the karaoke machine, but about a third of the audience left right away.

Matt joined her at the bar and put his hand over her purse when she went for her wallet. "No way, lady. Your money's no good here. You've become our star attraction, and it's not like we're paying you."

She laughed and tried to swat his hand away. "Come on, man. Let me support my favorite independent business!"

"Nope! I won't have it. That was a great set you did just now, so consider it payment—if you'd rather do it that way. The boss would never forgive me if I took money out of your pocket."

"I sing for my supper! Or my booze, at least. But I feel like I ought to be paying you, for the use of your stage."

"Girl, you know nothing about how the freelance creative professional world works, do you?"

"No, I do not."

"We're gonna have to get you an agent, aren't we? A talent agent for a travel agent, right?"

She cackled and accepted the drink that Tiffany slipped down the bar with the grace of a Hall of Fame pitcher. "Your lips to God's ears, as they say." Then they toasted each other, and Leda downed her drink in a set of long, deep swallows.

Day-job business might have been slow and Tod was still dead, but she had klairvoyant karaoke and the folks at Castaways to keep her company—and maybe, if she gave herself a tiny pat on the back, everything might not be completely hopeless after all.

# 6.

Come Saturday, Leda wondered what she was supposed to wear to go meet a cop and talk about crime. Usually, she dressed in "professional adult-lady drag," in case any clients (or potential clients) showed up at her tiny Columbia City office. Or if she was headed to Castaways, maybe she'd wear something with a touch of bling. A shimmery top, to glisten in the stage lights.

In her downtime, it was usually leggings and tees with boots and a jacket. The weather was cool enough for jackets again, and not too wet just yet.

She was overthinking this.

If Niki were there, she would've agreed, and then whipped out something from her own wardrobe for Leda to borrow. She was a little taller, and a little more "blessed" in the torso real-estate department, but they could swap back and forth on most things. They even wore the same size shoe, which was convenient.

But Niki was off at some train thing in Snoqualmie, because Matt was nerdy for trains and Niki was nerdy for Matt.

"I'm not trying to impress this guy."

No commentary from the absent Niki, who might or might not have agreed.

"I want him to think I'm a civilized professional, but I'm not actually a professional psychic or anything. I'm only a professional clairsentient if you count Matt paying me in free drinks. That counts, right? Does that count?"

She shot Brutus a look.

Brutus stared at her from his tank, looking much like a tiny, damp Grover puppet. He was blue with red highlights on his fins, and he was generally a laid-back sort of betta fish—contrary to the "fighting fish" reputation. Leda had picked him up on a whim at a street fair, along with a half-gallon bowl—which had swiftly been replaced with a gallon bowl with rocks and a small plant inside it. Then came a two-and-a-half-gallon tank, about the size of a toaster. At present, he was swimming in a five-gallon fancy-pants tank with filters and hoses, a veritable forest of live and silk plants, plus a couple of snails that Leda had not expected (and had not yet named). They'd come in with the plants, that's what a pet shop girl had told her. No big deal, as long as they didn't multiply too much.

Leda did not know how she felt about the volunteer snails. She did not know what she would do if they multiplied too copiously. She didn't want an army of snails, but she also couldn't imagine just . . . swiping them out and flushing them down the toilet.

The snails were a conundrum.

Brutus had not yet voiced an opinion on them either way.

She held up two black T-shirts that were more or less identical. "Give me a hand, Bru. What do you think? Which one?"

Brutus declined to venture a preference. He'd figured out that she wasn't going to feed him, and he wandered off to tuck himself beneath his favorite leaf.

"Thanks. You're a big help."

She went with a long black T-shirt over black leggings with gray pinstripes—so nobody could accuse her of wearing all black. Even though she did top it all off with a long black sweater and black knee-high boots. It wasn't really cold enough for the boots, but they were very comfortable and she didn't know how much walking she could expect to do.

She grabbed her purse and went out the door.

She and Grady Merritt had spent half an hour on Friday arguing via text message about where to meet and how. They'd finally settled on a hotel bar out in Shoreline, which was a bit of a drive for Leda—but she'd refused Grady's offer to pick her up, so she was stuck in traffic and arrived twenty minutes late.

"Sorry about that," she said as soon as she saw him. "I guess it was my turn to get stuck in traffic."

"Hey, it worked out for me—maybe it'll work out for you, too." He stood to greet her, hand outstretched. "Welcome to the crime scene. Sort of."

He was stationed by a window with a copy of the local magazine *The Stranger* and a cup of coffee. It probably wasn't good coffee. The bar's carpet was clean, and all the furniture matched, but this hotel was half a step up from a Motel 6, at best. He was drinking the coffee anyway. Maybe he was desperate. Maybe his taste buds had been shot off by bad guys.

She shook his hand and slipped into the seat across from him. "I meant to text you when I left the house, but I forgot. Sorry."

He sat down. "It's fine."

"I know, right? It's a *big* fine, if a cop sees you texting and driving. And you're a cop, so . . . I'm sorry."

"No—I meant that I don't care. I can entertain myself for half an hour, no big deal. You're here, that's the important bit. Stop apologizing."

"Oh, good sir—I have not yet *begun* to apologize."

"Then I look forward to hearing the rest."

She couldn't tell if he was joking or not. She let out a short, relieved laugh. "I've never done anything like this before, and I'm nervous."

"There's nothing to be nervous about, I promise. If this works out and I get a fresh lead . . . awesome. If it's a bust, I'll pick up the pieces of my shattered life and move on. The case is stalled anyway. It's not like you're going to hurt anything."

"Of course I could hurt something! I'm very good at screwing things up," she protested. "What if I point you to the wrong person? What if you arrest the wrong guy and the real killer goes free!"

"I'm not going to arrest anybody based on any psychic findings you may provide. I swear."

That made her feel a little better. "All right, then. How do we do this?"

Grady hesitated, and Leda had the very strong non-psychic feeling that he'd never done this before, either. "I can't just give you a bunch of insider police information about the case in question, but plenty of details made it to the media. I can give you that much, and a little bit extra if I decide that you can keep your mouth shut." He fiddled with the magazine in his hands, then folded it in half and set it aside. "I thought about bringing you in cold, just to see what would happen. Then I thought that you might make better connections if you had more information. If you have a basic framework of events to draw from, you might recognize the significance of any random details you pick up. That's my thinking. My daughter didn't agree, but she's not the one with a badge."

"She thought I should come in blind?"

"Something about giving you too many opportunities to bluff. She gave me a lecture about how TV psychics glean details about people with microphones and research, that kind of thing."

Leda nodded. "Cold readings are notorious for that—I know exactly what she's talking about."

"Have you ever done a cold reading?" he asked, his head cocked to the right.

"What? God, no. Until very, very recently, almost nobody knew about . . . you know. *This.* My parents figured it out when I was a kid, but they didn't exactly advertise it. Dad even gave me this gentle, firm speech about being careful not to frighten people. He always acted like he thought somebody would burn me at the stake if word got around, so I kept it to myself."

"But your friend knows."

"Niki? She knows everything. And now that I've started doing my thing at Castaways . . . I guess everyone else will find out eventually."

He frowned. "Castaways? Where your friend suggested we meet up?"

"Yeah, it's a bar on Cap Hill. Her boyfriend is the manager."

"Wait, you have an act? In a bar? Is it like . . . a singing thing? Stand-up comedy? Magic show?"

"A little of all three, if I'm really on my game. Anyway!" She clapped her hands together. "This is a whole new ball game for me, and I'm nervous about it, and I hope I don't screw it up."

"Then let's get started." He reached into a messenger bag down by his feet and pulled out a folder with some newspaper clippings. Everything was carefully labeled and fastened together with paper clips. He pushed the folder across the table.

Leda glanced through the clippings. "Oh, hey . . . I think I remember seeing something about this on the news. This happened a couple of years ago, right?"

"About eighteen months ago."

"Right. Some guy got murdered in a hotel room . . . oooooh. . . ." She looked up, looked around. "Was it *this* hotel? Is that why you wanted to meet here?"

"Yes, but don't holler about it. The hotel would prefer that everyone forget about the whole thing, and I promised the manager that if he let me into the room again, neither one of us would say a word about it."

"Gotcha. So . . . no blogging about this very cool thing I'm doing today."

"You don't have a blog."

She narrowed her eyes and stared at him. "You googled me."

"Yes, but it was a very *light* google. It's not like I ran a background check. You didn't google me?"

She hadn't thought to. She'd taken him at his word. He was a cop! And a client! Why would she google him? Oh, yeah, because he was a strange man she barely knew who'd invited her to check out a crime scene. Maybe that should've tripped a few red flags. Too late now.

"I have your name and address, plus all your credit card information on file for billing purposes. I felt like that was enough."

If Niki had been present, she would've given her a high five for such a clean save.

But Niki wasn't there. Leda couldn't tell if Grady believed her, but he acted like he did, bobbing his head in a mildly impressed nod. "I suppose that's fair."

"Damn right it is." She looked down at the clippings. "Huh, so this is where Christopher and Kevin Gilman met their end. Like I said, I recall the case but I'd forgotten their names."

"No reason you should've remembered them. Their deaths were on the local news for five seconds, then everybody forgot it when the next thrilling murder occurred, maybe forty-eight hours later.

But here's what we know for sure, all public information: Christopher Gilman was the CEO of an internet start-up called Digital Scaffolding. He established the company with his brother, Adam, back in 2012—so he really beat the spread. Most start-ups like that fold within a year or two."

"What did the company do?"

"Consulting work for Amazon, mostly. As I understand it," he qualified. "Look, I'll be honest: tech is not my strong suit."

"Mine, either. I'd like to say that the details probably aren't important, but we don't really know what's important right now, do we?"

"Well, I know more than what I've got in this folder, but I can't discuss it."

"Okay, so just the public facts, then." She scanned a couple of columns, picked up the next little clump of newsprint, and scanned that, too.

"Chris was found shot to death in his hotel room, and his son was found in a similar state, out in the parking lot. Conventional wisdom says that the dad was probably killed first, then the son walked in on the murder. The killer chased him out to his car and shot him. Forensics couldn't tell for absolute certain, but our working theory suggests there were no more than a couple of minutes between the two killings. It all went down around three in the afternoon, so nobody was coming and going for lunch, or dinner, or drinks yet. The place was pretty quiet."

"Do you think Kevin was running for his car?"

"They found his body on the ground beside it. His hand was in his pocket, reaching for his keys—but the murderer had a gun, and he was either lucky or a decent shot. He only missed once, and the bullet struck the car. The second shot is what killed Kevin. It caught him in the back, right below his neck."

"I, um . . . I don't see any mention of that in this paperwork."

He shrugged. "So I gave you a smidge of extra info. Don't tell nobody."

"I most definitely will not. But this was eighteen months ago? Plenty of people must've come and gone from the room since then."

"They left it shut for a while, then hired a trauma cleaner to bring it up to snuff again. It's empty at the moment, and I have"— he tapped the messenger bag beside him with his foot—"things I'm not supposed to share . . . that I'll definitely show you anyway."

"You're really going out on a limb here, aren't you?" she asked.

He shook his head and gazed balefully at the clippings. "This case has never made any sense, and we've never had any real leads. Something about it just . . . stuck in my craw, as they say."

"Who says that?"

"My late wife's family, in North Carolina. They have a wide selection of colorful expressions in circulation out there." He used his index finger to move a few of the paper scraps around. "Consensus is that the murders were part of an interrupted robbery . . . but that explanation never felt right. This isn't *that* kind of hotel, you know what I mean? We're in the wrong part of town for a cheap shakedown, and this isn't the kind of place that a tech CEO would choose for legitimate business activities."

The restaurant manager sauntered by with a plate of pungent chicken wings and a lifted eyebrow.

"No offense," Grady called over his shoulder.

When he was gone, Leda asked, "You think he was running something else on the side?"

"Oh yeah, definitely. But I can't prove it. Since the case is cold now, nobody gave a damn when I checked out some old evidence. So here's some stuff for you to . . . look at, or hold. Or whatever it is you do."

Perfect! The only skill she'd been practicing might prove useful to somebody after all. Then she realized how cautious he'd been with his phrasing. "Wait a minute. Nobody gave a damn that you were leaving the precinct with evidence . . . or were you just real careful, and lucky that nobody noticed?"

He grinned. "I like you. You're quick."

She grinned back. "Like you said about cops, you want a psychic who pays attention to details."

"Damn right I do. Are you ready to give it a go?" He whipped out a key card.

"As ready as I'll ever be."

He stood up, closed the folder, and handed it to her. Then he collected his bag. "Great. Let's do this."

# 7.

Leda followed Grady out of the bar and through the lobby.

As they walked, Grady quietly filled in a few more details that probably weren't in the official, public, totally-legal-to-share-with-friends version of the files.

"Christopher Gilman specifically requested a room with disability accommodations, but there was nothing physically wrong with him, as far as anyone knew. Either he was hiding some problem, or as I privately suspect, he knew that an ADA-compliant room would be located on the first floor."

"Why would he want a first-floor room?" Leda asked.

"Proximity to the parking lot via a side door for a hasty getaway is my guess, because his car was parked right over there." He jabbed his thumb in a direction that didn't mean anything to Leda, since they were walking down a windowless corridor. "He'd checked into the room four days before he died, under his son's name—but he paid cash in advance, so nobody looked too closely at the reservation."

"That's weird."

"Even weirder: He left a Do Not Disturb sign on the door the whole time, and except for the employee who checked him in, none of the hotel staff could recall having ever seen him before. If he came or went, he did so quietly. Probably through the exit at the end of the hall." Now he waved toward the light-up green Exit sign. "All the better to bypass the security cameras at the front desk."

"Were there cameras in the elevator or stairwells, too?"

Grady turned and aimed his pointing finger right at Leda. "Yes. And that's one more reason to ask for the ADA room." He stopped at room number 118 and held up the key card. "I think he scoped the place out. He chose this hotel, this room, this place."

"To get murdered in?"

Grady sighed through his nose.

"I mean, for *what*?"

He unlocked the door and held it open for her. "That's the big question, isn't it? If we knew that, maybe we'd have some idea who killed him."

Leda stepped slowly inside.

Room 118 was virtually indistinguishable from a thousand other hotel rooms in King County alone. It smelled faintly damp and vaguely moldy—stinking also of cheap and overly scented soap, plastic wrap, bleach, and an air conditioner that needed its filter addressed. The single king-size bed was covered in a polyester bedspread that probably used to be a brighter shade of blue, and above it hung a framed ocean print that seemed to be missing its inspirational poster text. A large cabinet held a commensurately large television, an old CRT the size of a storage ottoman. A coffee maker covered in dust stood sentry over a tray of white and yellow sweetener packets, red stirring straws, and a single-use package of Folgers.

Grady came inside, letting the door swing shut with a heavy click. "So . . . what do you think?"

Well. What *did* she think?

She thought that she was shut inside a hotel room with a cop who she didn't know very well, after he'd made it very clear that this was an excellent place to get murdered—especially if someone never wanted anybody to find out what had happened. She did not say so out loud.

"Here," he said, as if he'd suddenly remembered something. He dropped his messenger bag on top of the bed. He removed a plastic bag and retrieved the items inside—a series of smaller items, individually sealed in their own baggies for maximum recycling bulk. "See if this stuff rattles anything loose. But do me a favor and leave it all sealed. Unless that matters? Does it matter? I have no idea how psychic procedures work."

"That makes two of us, buddy." Leda quit scanning the small, bland, entirely nondescript hotel room and sat down on the foot of the bed. "Let's see what you've got here. Is it okay if I ask questions?"

"Ask away."

She started with the nearest baggie. It was sealed with a red piece of tape that read EVIDENCE in big white letters. Inside, she saw a wadded-up bit of yellow fabric. "Okay, what's this?"

"It's a tote bag. Came from a big tech convention called E3. It's held in LA every year. Gilman and his wife went there together, more often than not."

"To represent their company?"

He shook his head. "Nah. E3 is a big entertainment expo. Mostly video games. It seems like just about the only thing Gilman and his wife had in common—they both liked to play. When we interviewed her, she said the tote bag might've been hers, or he might've picked it up last time they went. No idea what was inside it; it was empty when we picked it up."

Leda held it up to see it better. "Got a little blood on it, though."

"How do you know it's blood?"

She squinted at it. "If it's not, what are these brown splatters? Blood is kind of brown when it dries, isn't it?"

"Yes, but that's just coffee." He nodded toward the brewer on its tray. "He made a pot within half an hour of the shooting. Didn't drink most of it, and one of the bullets went through him—shattering the carafe."

"Okay, that's less creepy, good. Let me think."

She squeezed the plastic bag, feeling the cheap cotton canvas underneath. Massaging it, she turned it over and examined the logo for "Electronic Entertainment Expo." She closed her eyes and took a deep breath that turned into a cough. One more deep breath then.

She pretended she was at Castaways, sitting on the wood stool with a microphone. She imagined that a customer had handed her this tote and requested a song. What would she sing? What would she tell Niki and Matt to call up on the karaoke machine?

A flash.

Bright white, and the smell of something burning. Loud noise.

Her eyes shot open.

"You got something?"

Her forehead wrinkled. "Give me a second." Was it the gunshot? She closed her eyes again and saw the flash again—not as bright. More like an echo of the first one. Then motion. Yelling. Another man present, but she didn't see him. "He was arguing with somebody. A man."

"What did he look like?"

"I don't know, but he sounds like . . . an adult. Not an old guy, not a real young guy. Maybe in his thirties or forties, hard to say. He's angry, and Gilman . . . I guess it's one of the Gilmans at any rate . . . he's very calm. He's the one in charge. Or he *thinks* he's the one in charge."

"Was he meeting an employee? Some underling?"

"That feels right. This guy . . . he . . ." Her voice faded.

The fight was loud, and Gilman was telling the other guy to keep his voice down.

" 'Keep it down, asshole,' " she said out loud. " 'The walls have ears, even in a dump like this.' "

The words had flown right out. She hadn't expected them, and she clapped her hand over her mouth.

Grady held out his hands. "No! That's great. Keep going. What else did he say?"

She jammed her eyelids together as tightly as she could and removed her hand from her mouth. "Oh my God . . . that's never happened before."

"Don't take this the wrong way, but *I don't care*. Keep going."

"Um . . . Gilman wanted the other guy to do something, and the other guy didn't want to do it."

"What? What was the thing?"

She was at Castaways. Holding a microphone. Casting her psychic net around, hoping to catch a song. Whatever that mental muscle was, she struggled to use it without an electronic beat bouncing along and a screen with all the lyrics at the back of the bar.

"I don't know. Something bad," she finally said. "Something he didn't want to do."

"Something illegal, I assume."

Eyes still closed, she shrugged. "You said totally ordinary, above-the-board deals are made every day in dumps like this." Then she cracked one eye. "I'm kidding, of course." Whatever flare of information had lit up in her brain, it dimmed and died altogether.

She opened both eyes, excited. "It worked! It kind of worked! I actually got something!"

"You sure did," he said encouragingly. "Now have another piece

of evidence and tell me if you get anything else." He foisted another bag into her hands.

This one was smaller but heavier. Inside, she saw a torn en-
velope with more splashes of coffee. Unless it was blood. "Is this
blood?"

"That one's blood, yes."

She didn't let herself cringe. She wasn't actually bothered by it,
now that she was holding it in her hand—with a sanitary piece of
clear plastic between her and the dried-up bodily fluids. She tried
again, fondling the paper and hearing it crinkle.

"Any chance you can tell me what used to be inside it?"

"Photographs," she said without hesitation. "One showed a man
and a car. There was an address on the back."

He lit up. "An address!"

"Don't get too excited, I only saw it for a second—and not very
clearly, at that. The car was silver, and expensive. A Mercedes, I
think. The man was in his fifties or thereabouts. Maybe his sixties,
if he takes good care of himself. A real silver fox."

"Hm . . ." he said, as if it made him think of something.

Leda was on a roll. A rickety, intermittent, half-assed roll. "It's
not like anyone took out a hit on the guy. I think it was something
else. Insider trading?" she guessed wildly.

"Nope. Something a little bigger than that."

Her eyes snapped open. "How do you know?"

"Because I think I know who the silver fox is. I can find out
with a phone call if he drives a Mercedes, but I'd be stunned if he
didn't. I'll find out when I get back to the precinct."

"That's not fair!" she complained. "I want to know what's going
on! Details help me, just like they help you. Remember?"

"Yeah, but this conversation puts my job at risk. It would even
if we weren't having it at a crime scene."

"It's a very old crime scene."

"It's not *that* old. Here, try something else." He handed her a plastic-wrapped pen that was broken in the middle. "How about this?"

Leda took it, and immediately received an image. A foot, stepping on it. Tripping, almost—then recovering on the way out the door. "He slipped on it."

"Who?"

"The killer. He was leaving, and this was on the floor. He smashed it with his shoe, stumbled, and kept going. Opened the door." She held out her hand, like she was reaching for a phantom knob. "The other guy had barged in on them."

"Kevin."

"The son, yeah. I think it's him. He's younger and better-looking than the first guy."

"But you're not sure?" Grady pushed.

"Man, I'm not sure about *any* of this. This was your idea, and you promised you wouldn't get mad if nothing came out of it."

"I know, I know. I'm just . . . eager."

Leda was eager, too, but she had the very distinct feeling that whatever she'd tapped into was out of juice. She didn't feel even the slightest tingle, twitch, or flash. "I know, but I'm afraid that's all there is for today. I'm not getting anything else."

"Does that mean you *won't* get anything else or that you aren't getting anything else right *now*?"

"Holy Moses, dude. You're trying to apply a rigorous scientific standard to something that kind of . . . comes and goes, and mostly sounds bugnuts insane if I talk about it out loud. I don't know what to tell you. It comes. It goes. It comes again later, unless it doesn't. I can't pull clues out of my ass just because you want them really, really bad."

"Yeah, I got it. And I'm sorry. I don't mean to put all this pressure on you."

Her shoulders slumped, and she dropped the last piece of evidence. It joined the others in her lap. "It's not your fault. I honestly appreciate this exercise. If I'm going to have some special gift, or talent, or whatever you want to call it, I should maybe put it to some use other than karaoke."

"Karaoke?"

"Um . . . I do this karaoke thing." And while he collected all the evidence bags and stuffed them back into his messenger bag, she explained klairvoyant karaoke.

He tried not to laugh but laughed a little regardless. "That sounds amazing. I love it. When do you do it?"

"Whenever the fancy strikes me. Maybe . . . several times a week?"

"At Castaways? On Cap Hill?"

She nodded. "Niki's boyfriend runs the place; I think I told you. I know it sounds dorky, but it's been my only outlet for this psychic stuff, until this. I really feel like I flexed some new muscles today. So if you, um . . . if you have another case or anything, or if you get any good hits off anything I said . . ."

"You will absolutely be the first to hear about it," he vowed.

He closed the flap on his bag while she climbed to her feet and brushed imaginary dust off the top of her thighs—as if the dried blood or bits of coffee had managed to escape their sealed plastic packages. Then he opened the door and held it for her, and together they walked to their cars.

Leda reached hers first. "Thanks again," she said.

"No, thank you for your time." He held out his hand for a good-bye shake.

She took it, shook it, and had the most blinding flash of woo-woo psychic shit in her whole entire life so far.

And then.

*Then* she passed out cold.

# 8.

"I don't know!" Grady Merritt said, waving his hands at the hotel manager and the EMT like he was trying to claw his way out of a spiderweb. "It was like I'd accidentally tased her or something—which I did *not*. She was fine; we were saying goodbye. I shook her hand; she shrieked and fell over!"

"Did she hit her head?" asked the EMT.

"No, she didn't hit her head. I caught her, and set her down, and called nine-one-one. Now you know everything I know, I swear. I have no idea what happened."

On that note, Leda—who was on a gurney—sat up straight and shrieked again. "*Oh my God*. What is this? What's happening? What just happened? Grady?" she asked, catching a glimpse of him. "What are these people doing here? Why am I strapped down on a table?"

"Leda! Yes. Right here." He darted to her side. "It's not a table, it's a gurney. And you're not strapped down, exactly. You're secured so you don't roll off and break your neck."

"I'm not gonna break my neck," she said, writhing and testing the straps. She yanked at the one around her waist, swung her legs off the side of the gurney and began to hop off.

The medic barked, "What are you doing? Stay where you are."

"No, no. I don't need this. I don't need any of this," she protested.

Grady put a hand on her shoulder. "Look, you passed out, okay? I called for help. Let the helpers *help*."

She pushed the medic away and jumped down to the ground, grabbing the gurney to steady herself. "I didn't pass out. Or if I did, it wasn't a normal passing out. It was a . . ." She squinted at everyone in the vicinity, then aimed her squint hardest at Grady. "*Special* passing out. Related to what we were talking about inside."

He shooed the EMT away. "Give us a minute, would you? She's okay. She says she's okay. Believe women, would you?"

The guy shrugged and walked away, probably happy to go help some other person who wouldn't be such a dick about it. The hotel manager went back inside, looking bored to death with this entire event. From where he was standing, the whole scenario could only lead to more bad press.

When they were gone, Grady turned to her.

"Did you see something else? Anything new that might help?"

For a split second, Leda's face froze. But her glazed expression of horror passed quickly, sliding into something more like shrewdness. He didn't know what it meant, and he wasn't sure he liked it.

"It wasn't like that," she said, keeping her voice down. "It had nothing to do with you. Unless I'm wrong. But I think it doesn't. Except it might. Look, the flash I saw . . . it wasn't about your case, okay? Definitely not about *this* case, or else it's a bigger mess than I thought."

Carefully, he said, "None of that made any sense. Do you want to back up and take another run at it?"

"I do *not!*" she shouted back. She made a clumsy effort to compose herself, patting down her shirt, her pockets, and then shouting to whoever might be listening, "Where the hell is my purse! I had a purse when I passed out, and I want it back!"

Grady looked around, spotted it, and swiped it off the back of the ambulance before they could close the doors and leave. "Here. It's right here, Jesus. Calm down."

She snatched the bag from him and tucked it under her arm. "*You* calm down! No, no. I'm sorry," she said abruptly. Her eyeliner had smudged so completely that one formerly sleek black wing now zigzagged toward her temple; her hair was a hopeless brown tangle that had halfway left its original ponytail and hung down toward one shoulder. She looked like she'd fallen down an elevator shaft.

"I have to go," she concluded. "I'm sorry, I'm really sorry. It's not you; it's me. I *seriously* have to go."

"But what happened?" he begged. "What did you see?"

Then, because it occurred to him that he ought to, he asked, "Are you all right?"

"I'm fine! So fine. The finest I've ever been, no, seriously."

She shoved her hand down into her purse, retrieved her phone, and sprinted for her car. The last thing Grady heard before she shut herself inside and peeled away was, "Niki? Oh my God, Niki, you won't believe this...."

Grady stood in the parking lot, wearing a messenger bag full of evidence that he was absolutely not supposed to have in his possession. The ambulance and EMTs were gone; they'd left as swiftly as they'd arrived. The hotel manager had skedaddled. Leda had fled.

It was just him—confused and alone and very, very afraid that he'd colossally screwed this up.

He took a deep breath, let it out, and made for his own car.

He should've never involved a civilian in the case. It had been a boneheaded move from the start, and now he regretted it more thoroughly than he'd ever regretted anything, at least since his high school Juggalo phase. Christ, what was he going to do now? He needed to get the evidence back to the locker without anyone knowing that it'd ever left. There was now a 911 recording of him sounding absolutely bananas, begging for help with a woman down. He hadn't identified himself, had he? He couldn't remember. He didn't think so. It had happened so fast.

The key fob beeped, and Grady opened the door wide enough to throw his bag onto the passenger seat. He climbed inside behind it and sat behind the wheel. "This was a bad idea," he said to his own reflection in the rearview mirror. "The worst idea. Literally the worst. In the world."

It hadn't even seemed like a good idea at the time, when he'd first gotten a bug up his ass to look up the travel agent. It had always been a terrible idea, which was why he hadn't told a single soul about it, except for his daughter.

He shoved the key into the ignition.

According to the clock on the dashboard, he still had a couple of hours before Molly got home from work, but Cairo would be happy to see him—and that was the number one perk of having a dog, wasn't it? No matter how bad your day, how terrible your choices, how ridiculous your risks, a dog would never tell you how stupid you were.

"Only because they don't speak English," Grady grumbled to himself.

Indeed, Cairo understood refreshingly little English, and he was predictably face-licking happy to see Grady home at the unusual hour. The pooch had a doggy door so he could come or go from the house to the backyard when no one was home. If the nanny cam Grady had installed a year ago could be believed, the dog kept close to home, listened for his people's car to pull into the driveway, and mostly snoozed in obscene crotch-upward positions all day.

Grady dropped his bag on the coffee table, paid a bit more attention to the dog, and turned on the TV with a flick of the remote's power button. Then he sank as far into the couch as he was physically able.

It wasn't far enough. It didn't swallow him whole.

Cairo hopped up onto the cushion beside him, having long ignored the "no dogs on the furniture" rule that no one tried to enforce anymore. He flopped his head on top of Grady's thigh and gave him an expression so pathetically optimistic that Grady couldn't help but scratch his ears and tell him that yes, of course everything was all right.

"It's all right for *you*, at least. You didn't risk your job and your sanity to sneak a psychic into a crime scene."

The dog didn't argue. He rolled over on his back and flashed his no-longer-existent balls at the ceiling.

Grady reached over Cairo's fuzzy, warm head and retrieved the bag with all its illicit contents—dragging it onto the couch, beside the leg that wasn't occupied by a dog's sprawl. The Gilman case had been driving him batty ever since it'd been more or less abandoned by the PD almost a year before. Nothing about it had ever made sense.

"Eh, that's not quite true," he argued with himself.

Cairo raised an eyebrow. Grady patted his noggin and continued.

"Here's the thing, see? Chris Gilman was a garbage human, and he was probably killed by *another* garbage human, over some garbage deal gone garbagely wrong. But Kevin . . . he wasn't so bad," he explained to the dog in a voice that teetered perilously close to baby talk. "He'd been making changes to Dad's company while Dad wasn't looking. Offering parental leave, better health insurance, all the stuff that helps you keep quality employees. He even dabbled in philanthropy. He was in the process of establishing a scholarship fund at UW in memory of his mother. All of which begs the question . . ."

Molly poked her head into the living room. "Begs what question?"

Grady yelped, and Cairo jumped, and the contents of the messenger bag went scattering across the table and floor. "The hell? You're supposed to be at work!"

"I got a nosebleed, and they sent me home."

"What? Are you okay?"

"I slipped and fell, and hit the espresso machine with my face." She did a quarter turn left, then right, as if to show off some tragic injury, curiously absent. Her shift at Starbucks was supposed to start at two. It was presently three thirty, and she shouldn't be home until after five. If she'd gone to work, then she had not spent very much time there.

Grady didn't see any signs of black eyes or a broken schnoz. "Well, you can't tell at all, so congratulations. You've successfully weaseled out of your gainful employment yet again."

"Nobody's weaseling, Dad. It was gruesome. Blood and snot everywhere. Stray boogers flying around like tiny droids. Customers don't want to see that, or so I was told."

"Now I *know* you're full of it, but I'm glad you're okay," he added, in case that part wasn't clear. "Wish I'd known you were home, though."

"I was taking a nap, and you disturbed me. You probably owe me a pizza or something."

"Yeah, I'll get right on that." Instead, he scooped up his sealed plastic bags covered in brightly colored warnings and began to stuff them back into the bag.

Molly came to sit beside him, reaching across his lap to pet Cairo, whose butt was shaking like a paint mixer. As if she were giving the dog her full attention and had only the most casual, innocent interest in knowing the answer, Molly asked, "How'd it go with the psychic? Should I gather from your mood that this little adventure went . . . poorly?"

He nodded, then shook his head, then shrugged. "She does this trick where she holds things and she can tell you something about them. Sometimes. That part was pretty cool."

"Did she give you any good clues?"

"About eighty percent of what she had to say . . . it fit the facts; I can say that much for certain."

"And the other twenty percent?" she pressed, leaning forward.

"The other twenty percent was either nonsense, or useful—and I don't know which one yet."

"But you're going to find out?"

This time he nodded firmly. "I'm definitely going to find out. She said this one thing that really stuck with me, about a silver fox . . ."

"A fox? An actual fox, like the adorable mammal? Or like a sexy old guy?"

"More like . . . an attractive older man. Please don't use that phrase, for the love of God."

She laughed and threw a pillow at his head. "You're ridiculous."

He caught the pillow, startling the dog—who leaped down off the couch and wandered away. "Maybe, but that doesn't mean I'm wrong. Or that Leda was wrong. See, there was a guy on the periphery of the case, named Richard Beckmeyer. We interviewed him as a person of interest but never really considered him a suspect."

"Are you rethinking it, now that a psychic brought him up?"

"Slow your roll, kid—you're jumping to conclusions." He held up his hands and counted off a few of the variables. "I believe that Leda is legit, but I don't know it for a fact. Even if I assume she knows what she's talking about, I don't know if the silver fox she described is Beckmeyer, I don't know if she's right about his involvement, and I don't know why she wigged out on me before she left."

"She wigged out? Did she attack you or something?"

"Not exactly. We were finished with our little meetup, and we shook hands . . . and she lost it. She shrieked and fainted. I called nine-one-one, and there were medics, and the hotel manager yelled at me because he was doing me a favor by letting us inside the room again, and the whole thing was just . . ."

"A shitshow?"

"Yes, dear. It was a shitshow."

"Was the psychic okay?"

He hugged the pillow and wished the dog would come back. No wonder therapy animals were so popular. "She came around, screamed at me again, ran away from the ambulance, and drove off in her own car. If you want to call that 'okay.'"

"Oh, wow."

"Wow, for sure." He let his head fall back on the couch, so he was staring up at the ceiling when he said, "I wish to God I knew what happened."

Molly considered this, pouting her lower lip and tilting her chin back and forth like she was thinking. "You said she gets her info from touching objects, right? Do *you* count as an object?"

"Me?"

"Uh-huh. What if she got a vision or something when she shook your hand?"

"God, I hope that's not it." Once again, he wished that the couch would eat him—thereby sparing him from further embarrassment. He wondered what she saw. Whatever it was, it must've scared her to death."

"Maybe you just creeped her out," his daughter suggested oh-so-helpfully.

"Thanks. That's even worse."

"I'm full of great ideas."

"Always, yes."

"I've got another great idea, right here on deck," she hinted.

"All right, fine. Hit me."

Molly pulled her feet up underneath herself, in order to sit cross-legged on the cushion beside him. "Why don't you suck it up and ask her what happened?"

"I *did* ask, when she was standing in front of me having a meltdown."

"Ask later. Ask tomorrow. Text her, and ask her to call you back."

He turned to face her. "You don't get it. She *fled*, Molly. She didn't want to look at me for another second, much less answer any more of my questions."

"Thus my suggestion that you send her a *text*. Listen to us kids, old man. We know things about how to communicate when the world is super awkward. Text messages are your friends. She can answer whenever she feels like it, or not at all. You have her number, don't you?"

"I do. It's not a terrible idea, and I appreciate you for being the voice of reason during this difficult time."

"Don't give me any avoidant-cop speeches. Just text her, find out what freaked her out, and quit worrying about it. Maybe she'll talk to you again and you'll learn the details, maybe she won't and you'll never hear from her again. That's life."

"That's pleasantly wise of you."

"I'm a pleasantly wise person."

"That you are, kid." Grady pulled his cell phone out of his pocket and pulled up Leda's number. Then he spent half an hour composing a handful of words, hoping he wasn't coming off like a jerk or a creep.

Thanks for meeting me today, and I'm sorry about whatever happened at the end. Please call or shoot me a text to let me know that you're all right, and I swear I'll leave you alone. If that's what you want.

He pressed Send. Then he finished packing up his pilfered evidence and went online to do a little surreptitious info-hunting. He had questions about Rick Beckmeyer, and although some of those questions would have to be answered in person, more than a few answers might be found on the internet.

# 9.

Leda drove Jason the Accord like she'd stolen him, all the way back to the south side of town and her tiny, adorable bungalow she rented from a retired couple who were presently traveling the country in an RV. She flung herself inside, slammed the door, and immediately apologized to Brutus—even though he surely hadn't heard the commotion. But she'd gotten into the habit of apologizing to him, and asking his permission, and telling him how handsome he was—even though Brutus was about the size of a stick of gum, and with the same allotment of brain cells.

Not all of Leda's interactions with her piscine roommate made a great deal of sense, and she'd be the first one to admit it.

But Niki hadn't answered her second frantic phone call, dialed on the interstate, against Seattle local laws (and risking a hefty ticket, like that was going to stop her this time). Niki also hadn't responded to the subsequent frantic voice mail, but in Niki's defense, it'd been only about twenty-five minutes since Leda had abandoned a cold crime scene and the perfectly nice cop who'd persuaded her to meet him there.

She'd never made such good time crossing town before, but she was entirely too rattled to be excited about it. Instead, she paced and fretted, shaking her phone as if doing so would persuade Niki to magically dial in and hear all about it.

Leda was almost desperate enough to call her mom in Spokane when Niki somehow heard the psychic Bat-Signal (or else she'd finally listened to the voice mail) and reached out to learn what the big emergency was.

Before Niki could even say hello, Leda was in full "marbles mode"—a state they'd coined together that one time when they were on the run from a security guard in a golf cart while fleeing the allegedly haunted yacht club boathouse of high school infamy.

People can scatter like marbles. Sometimes their thoughts do, too.

"The cop Grady Merritt had something to do with Tod's death," she blurted. "I don't know what and I don't know how, but when I shook his hand I got a flash—a crazy flash, like, the strongest flash I've ever had—and I saw a moment of . . . of . . ." She was hyperventilating now. "Of Tod's body in the car. I saw Tod, shot and drowned in the back seat; that's what I saw when I shook Grady's hand!"

"Whoa, whoa, *whoa*," Niki replied. "Hang on, now. He's not the cop who investigated the case; I know he's not. It was an old dude and his partner, a younger woman. She died a year or two ago in a shoot-out at a liquor store, right?"

"Whiteside, yeah, that was the old guy's name. It was practically his last case before he retired, and he half-assed it. He never took me seriously, and he avoided me, and he didn't want to answer my questions, and he was a big fat jerk, and—"

Niki interrupted. "He was a perfectly nice old man who didn't have any answers. It's not his fault that Tod got murdered."

"Tod got murdered," she echoed back, phlegm in her throat and tears in her eyes. "Tod got murdered, and I didn't see it coming. It's the only thing I actually know how to do, Nik. I can see things coming, and then one time, I didn't. Not when it counted."

"It's not your fault." Niki kept her voice level and calm.

With despair and a snot bubble, Leda cried, "It's *somebody's* fault!"

"That's a fact, babe. But it's not *your* fault; it's not this cop's fault. It's not the old cop's fault, either, and it probably wasn't even Tod's fault. Maybe, though . . . maybe your woo-woo vibes are trying to tell you to work with this new guy. What if they're trying to point you in the right direction and chase you toward some actual answers?"

Leda slumped into an overstuffed recliner that looked like it belonged in the office of an elderly rich man who smoked cigars and sipped brandy in his downtime. She tucked her knees against her chest and clutched her phone tight to her ear. She brought her voice down a few decibels and at least one octave when she said, "Maybe it's Tod's ghost."

"You don't believe in ghosts."

"I've never seen one or talked to one, but that doesn't mean they don't exist. I've never talked to a billionaire, either. Or . . . or a treasure hunter. Or a lion tamer. For that matter, I don't know what ghosts sound like when they try to communicate. What if they sound like flashes of light and terrible visions? What if they sound like migraines? Anything could be a clue, Nik. Anything."

"You had vibes and visions for years before Tod died. His ghost is not the source, and now you're grasping at straws."

"Then what *is* the source?" Leda asked the universe at large.

"Sweetheart, if we knew that..." Niki didn't finish the thought. She didn't need to.

"If we knew that," Leda grimly agreed. It wasn't even a question anymore, because the answer probably didn't matter.

"Listen, I'm on my way home from the grocery store. It's hard to hold this phone and"—she shifted something around—"three bags of heavy crap while I'm working with a boot cast and a limp, but I'll be done in another ten minutes. We only just got back from Snoqualmie. You want me to head over?"

"Yes."

"Okay, then. Give me half an hour."

"Twenty minutes," Leda bargained.

"I've got ice cream here. Other things I need to put away, too. But I'll be there as soon as I can, I promise."

They hung up, and Leda clung to her best friend's vow. She had to survive on her own, with no one but Brutus to cry to, for only half an hour. Likely a little longer than that, knowing Niki. Niki always ran fifteen to twenty minutes late, unless Leda was flogging her with the Guilt Whip of Punctuality.

Forty-five minutes, then. She could hang on that long.

She bounced out of the chair and went to the tiny dining nook beside the kitchen, where Brutus's tank was sitting on a vintage buffet near the window. She was careful to keep him from getting too much direct sunlight, and careful to keep him from getting too cold, and careful to keep him from eating too much. And while Leda could survive on Rice Krispies treats and beef jerky, left to her own devices, her single small pet ate the most expensive fish food she could find, on the grounds that it was surely the highest quality.

She'd tasted it once—putting one tiny pellet on her tongue—and then wished she hadn't for the next six hours. It'd been like a wee breath mint in "concentrated tide pool" flavor, and the aftertaste had lingered.

"Bruty-boy, what do I do?" she asked, staring through the glass and spotting him chillaxing—tucked under his favorite leaf.

He flicked his tail to acknowledge her presence but didn't offer any useful advice.

"Tod is gone. Somebody killed him, and I still don't know who. I don't know why. *Everybody* loved Tod," she assured the fish. "Not just me. Even Niki liked him, and she never likes anybody I date. It's been that way since tenth grade."

Tod Sandoval had died three months after proposing to Leda Foley at the top of the Ferris wheel on the pier. It was a cornball proposal, with a little box and a pretty ring, and a short speech about how great they were together. Tod had been six feet even, with curly black hair and green eyes. Tod had a bright laugh that could light up a room, and a quick hand if anybody needed help. Tod was almost perfect, and in his absence even the faintest rough edges had been sanded away smooth. Now Tod was an angel.

But Leda didn't believe in angels any more than she believed in ghosts, and the more time passed with no breaks in the case, the less she believed in justice, either.

But, wonder of wonders, Niki was prompt for once.

She arrived in twenty-eight minutes flat and let herself inside. She found Leda crying to the fish in the dining room. "I'll open some wine," she declared.

Shortly thereafter, both women sat on either side of the little bistro set that served as a dining room table: Leda, red-eyed and still shaking, and Niki, topping off the glass of pink wine every time it seemed necessary.

"I know it feels like a lot right now, but when you calm down a little . . . I think you should call the cop and explain yourself."

"I didn't do anything wrong," Leda snuffled.

"No, but he's probably worried about you. You fainted and ran away screaming. If I were him, I'd be concerned."

"I know, I know. He's concerned. He already sent a text."

"A text?" Niki nodded approvingly. "Good call. You can respond whenever you want. If you don't, he might swing by the office, or look you up here, at home. Jesus, Leda . . . I only heard about your afternoon secondhand, and I'm worried enough as it is. That guy must be freaking out."

"His text didn't sound too freaked out." Leda pulled out her phone and showed Niki the message that had landed about ten minutes before Niki'd arrived. "It sounded politely interested in my well-being."

"I'm sure he's holding back for the sake of propriety."

"He's a homicide detective who brought a fragile psychic to a gruesome crime scene. He has no sense of propriety."

Niki rolled her eyes with vigor. "Girl, he didn't drag you out there at gunpoint. He barely even twisted your arm. Don't be a dick about this. Tell him you're okay and let him off the hook."

Leda glared down at the screen. "Fine. I will." She retrieved her phone and pounded out a text like she was mad at it. Thanks for the adventure, and I'm sorry I passed out. I'm okay now, don't worry. She tossed the phone aside, but Niki caught it before it flipped onto the floor.

Since it was still unlocked, she added a second text—so quickly that Leda almost didn't notice. We should probably talk later.

"What are you doing? Nik, what did you do?"

Leda flailed for the phone, and after hitting Send, Niki passed it back to her.

"I'm helping."

"That's not helping!"

"Yes," she insisted. "It is. You're planning to avoid this man for the rest of your natural life—and don't you act like I'm wrong about that. We both know you're already wondering if the rent is any cheaper on the dark side of the moon because you're embarrassed and you never want to see him again. But if there's any chance at all that this guy can help you get answers about Tod's death, you *have* to follow up with him."

"You don't understand. I saw Tod. *Dead.*"

"I *do* understand. I've been watching you process this for three years, and I know that one reason you've been beefing up your skills at Castaways is that you've been hoping to see Tod in a psychic flash ever since you got the phone call that he'd been found. You admitted it once, last year. When you were, okay, *super* drunk."

Leda folded her arms on the small round table and laid her head down on top of them. "I feel stupid about it now."

Niki patted her nearest elbow. "There's nothing to feel stupid about. You saw something terrible, and it scared you. You ran away from it. That's normal."

"Grady Merritt didn't think it was normal."

"Only because he didn't know the context. You should tell him. Talk to him, explain the whole thing about Tod, and you might have a new ally in the hunt for his killer."

Leda's response was a mumble, spoken into the crook of her arm.

"C'mon, take the rest of the day off. It's the weekend, right? Do you want to go to Castaways?" Niki offered, since Leda usually treated the bar like it was base in a cosmic game of tag. She was safe there, if nowhere else in the world.

But Leda surprised her. "Not tonight. I don't want to do anything tonight except finish the second bottle of pink wine and cry."

"Netflix and swill?"

She considered it. "I'd rather PlayStation and complain. While swilling, yes."

"Are both controllers charged up?" Niki asked. When Leda nodded, she said, "Good. Ready player one, bitch. Let's get this cheer-up show on the road."

# 10.

The next day, Leda gripped a mug of hot chai so that her hands would have something to do other than shake from a combination of nerves and a slight hangover. Niki sat beside her in the small, narrow coffee shop around the corner from the travel agency office, serving as emotional support while Grady Merritt settled into his seat across from them both. He placed a to-go cup of coffee down on the table.

"Thanks for coming," Niki said, since Leda didn't.

Then Leda added suddenly, "Yes! I'm so sorry, and I appreciate you coming all the way out here again."

"No problem. I'm just glad to see that you're all right. You really had me worried yesterday."

"I know, and that was entirely on me. I owe you an explanation, and I intend to give you one. But first I have to give you a little background," she said carefully. She hadn't yet decided how much she was going to tell him about Tod.

Niki already knew. "She's going to give you a *lot* of background. All of it, I bet."

Her shoulders drooped. "Come on, Nik."

"Do you want me to get the ball rolling?"

"No!" Leda insisted, and sat up to full attention. "No, of course not. It's not your story to tell."

"It's kind of my story."

"Okay, but only kind of."

When Niki nodded to accept this compromise, Leda began to talk.

"So . . . five years ago, I met the love of my life."

Niki jumped in. "He thought he saw an otter off the side of the pier, and when he leaned over to look, he lost his glasses."

"He couldn't see very well without them, and he was new to the city, and he needed help. I helped him call an Uber to get home. When I put him into the car, he slipped me a business card with his number."

"And the rest was history!"

But Leda shook her head at Niki. "No, it wasn't history. That's what people say when somebody gets a happy ending, and we didn't." She sniffled, but it might've just been the wildfire smoke that was hanging over the city. Usually it cleared out by fall. Sometimes it stuck around. "We got almost two whole years together, and I got an engagement ring in a box that I now keep in a drawer, because I don't have the heart to wear it."

"Why's that?" Grady asked, a polite prompt, since she appeared to need one.

"Because one day, Tod went missing. Eventually they found his body in the back seat of his car. It had run off the road, and it sank in a culvert."

"It was completely submerged," Niki added. "Some kid with a drone spotted it and called the cops."

"Right. He'd been underwater for . . . for a while. Like, a few days, I mean."

Grady nodded, gently sympathetic. "Did you have to identify him?"

"No, his mom did that. She came in from Spokane, and she . . . I think she saw him through a video monitor. I don't think they let her see him in person. They did a DNA test and everything, since he was pretty waterlogged. His mom said he didn't even look like a person, much less her son."

Leda's voice caught, and Niki picked up the thread. "After that, Leda and his parents cleaned out his apartment. About six months later, his mom died."

"Yeah, and I haven't heard from his dad since Tod's birthday, a year after. We'd tried to stay in touch, but you know how it goes." She took a deep breath to make up for all the shallow ones. "At any rate, Tod's gone and nobody knows what happened to him."

"Was it some kind of freak accident, or not an accident at all?" Grady asked.

Leda grunted down into the chai and took a big swig before answering. She'd been quietly hoping Niki might jump in again, but no such luck. She had to do the hardest part herself. "It *was* pretty freaky, but it wasn't an accident. Tod was shot through the stomach, and then he drowned."

"Shot? In the back seat of his own car?"

"They think he was shot outside the car, then stuffed inside it, then the car was pushed into the water," she said. "But it gets even weirder. A few days later, while the cops were dredging the culvert and the streams that fed it . . . they found a woman's body. She was shot, too. With the same gun, or that's what they learned when ballistics came back."

"Wait a minute . . . wait. Hang on." Grady tapped one finger against the edge of his cup. "This rings a bell. You said this was about, what? Three or four years ago?" When the women nodded, he said, "Okay, I didn't come to homicide for another year after that, but I *do* remember hearing about it."

Leda asked, "So you didn't work the case at all? Not even in a supporting role?" She and Niki exchanged a look.

"No, back then I was still doing car thefts and break-ins."

Niki shrugged. "Must be some other connection, then."

"Wait, what do you mean, *connection*?" Grady asked.

Leda pushed her chai away. She didn't want it. "When you and I were parting company yesterday, and you shook my hand . . . I got a flash. It was so bright I couldn't see anything at all for a few seconds. Sometimes it happens like that, like an ocular migraine. Not usually so hard and sudden, though. Then I saw Tod, underwater in the back of the car. His eyes were open, but he was dead. He still looked like himself, at least."

"If she'd seen him all grody and decomposed, she'd still be holed up in her house, drinking," Niki explained solemnly.

"I didn't mean to shriek at you, and I'm sorry I didn't stick around to explain myself. I was really thrown for a loop, and I needed to . . . to collect myself. Now you're all caught up, and now you understand why I fled the scene of the crime. I mean, the crime scene you took me to visit—not the one I caused. Since I didn't cause any. As I've established."

"I guess?" he replied without conviction. "Except, why did you flash on your dead boyfriend when you shook my hand? It wasn't the first time we'd touched; I shook your hand at the office the other day, too."

Niki said, "We don't know. We thought you'd maybe worked the case and that was the connection that set her off."

"No, I never had anything to do with it. Who was the detective, do you remember his name?"

"Whiteside," Leda said confidently. "He was old and mean."

Niki disagreed. "He wasn't mean. You were just mad because he didn't solve Tod's murder."

"And he didn't exactly hustle to do so, now did he?"

Grady held up his hands. "Wait a minute, Jim Whiteside? He was a friend of my dad's, back in the day. Jim's all right, but I'll grant you—'hustle' was never a big part of his vocabulary."

"I think he retired a little while ago," Leda said grumpily.

"Couple of years ago," Grady supplied. "He lives out in Lake City with, like, a thousand little dogs."

Niki jacked up an eyebrow. "Really?"

"Half a dozen, at least. Dachshunds. Yippy ones. They're cute, but it's basically an army of short things with sharp teeth that reach halfway up to your knees. They're not even his late wife's— they're *his*. It always blew my mind. At any rate, I can run past his house and have a word with him, if you want. Maybe he'll be game to talk about an old case with another old cop."

"You'd do that? For me?" Leda asked, her eyes as big and wet as a dog staring through a meat-shop window.

"For you, sure. But for me, too. I want to know why the Powers That Be think I'm connected to your old case."

Niki nodded. "It could always be something else. It could be a sign that you're supposed to help Leda find out what happened to Tod, with your fresh eyes and your younger-dude hustle. Hell, for all we know, you could be the murderer."

Leda gasped. "Nik!"

But Grady only laughed. "I'm not too worried about that." Thoughtfully, he concluded, "Then again, it might not be anything like that at all."

"Then what do you suggest?" Leda asked. The look on his face said he was still thinking. So did his tapping fingers, drumming a little tune on the paper coffee cup.

He quit running his fingers. "Here's a thought: What if this isn't about me personally? What if your flash was prompted by the work we did, on the case at the Shoreline hotel? The first time we shook hands we'd only just met—and it was a neutral location, your office. The second time, we were standing at a crime scene."

"Keep talking," Niki urged.

"That's it," he admitted with a shrug. "That's all I've got. Playing by the rules you've given me, there's a chance that I'm not the one connected to Tod's murder. It could be this other case."

Leda bobbed her head, thinking. "The cases do have some similarities."

Grady Merritt eyed Niki cautiously. "We should probably keep the details to ourselves," he said.

Niki cackled. "Oh, honey. She told me everything as soon as I got a half bottle of wine in her. There's a key to the Leda brain vault, and it's about twelve percent alcohol."

Grady rolled his eyes and clutched his coffee. Leda apologized, immediately and profusely—but he cut her off. "No, stop it. This is my fault for looping you into the case in the first place. All I can do is ask you not to blab any further, please?"

Leda mimed locking her mouth and throwing away the key.

Niki mimed tipping back a glass, then waved her hands to show she was kidding. "Don't worry! Anything you can tell her, you can tell me—and it won't leave our cone of silence. If anything, you should think of me as her backup brain."

"External hard drive?" he tried.

"Right! Except better. I'll stop her from telling anybody else. I'm an external hard drive that comes with insurance. It also comes with Mace, and I'm not afraid to use it."

Grady's slowly shaking head suggested that he wasn't in love with the idea, but he was resigned to it. "You understand that we could *all* get in a lot of trouble if word gets around that we're looking into these cases together. Don't you?"

It was a grim prediction, but Leda lit up like Christmas. "We're looking into these cases together?"

"Sort of. Between us, we might be able to scare up information that might not have been . . . let's say 'readily available' in the immediate aftermath of the murders."

"And the Seattle Police Department won't be super thrilled with this?" Leda asked, but it wasn't really a question.

"No, they will not," Grady admitted with another shake of his head. "I'll even have to leave my partner out of it."

"You have a partner?"

"Sure I have a partner," he told her. "I've left him out of everything so far; I can leave him out of whatever else happens. We've only been working together for a few weeks, and he's got his own problems—namely a new baby at home. We don't hang out much, outside of work. As long as I keep all extracurricular investigating to my personal time, he shouldn't hear anything about it. What he doesn't know won't hurt him."

"I like the cut of your jib, Detective," Niki said.

"I just want to solve some crimes, and I think you . . . you two"— he adjusted on the fly—"can help me do it. Leda already gave me a hint I'm planning to chase for the hotel killings; all I have to do is take a step back, you know? Look at the big picture. If I step back far enough, maybe I'll see how the cases are connected."

"*If* they're connected," Leda said carefully. "We're still shooting in the dark here."

Grady shrugged. "Then we'll shoot in the dark, and maybe we'll hit something. Give me a day or two to chase down the new lead, and I'll report back."

"You mean the silver fox, right? You're going to talk to him?" Leda asked.

"The alleged silver fox. Right."

"Cool. Can I come, too?"

"What? No."

"Why not?" she demanded. "I can't help you if I can't see what you're doing."

"It's police business."

"It's my business *now*. If the hotel case is connected to Tod's case, you *have* to keep me involved. I deserve to know. I have a right to know."

Grady picked up his coffee cup and took a long swill of the cooling brew. "First of all, that's not strictly true. And second, there's always a chance that you won't like the answers, if you find them. You're aware of this, right?"

"Yeah, I can't possibly hate the answers even more than I already do—and Tod needs justice."

"You need justice," he corrected her.

She didn't like it, but she couldn't argue. "Fine. I need justice. If I can get some by tagging along with you, then that's what I plan to do. Like it or not, you're stuck with me. With *us*."

Grady Merritt smiled and downed the last sip of his coffee, then tossed the empty cup into the nearest trash can via a tidy three-point shot. "Okay, ladies. But if we're going to do this together, we need to establish some ground rules."

"Like what?" Niki wanted to know.

"Like if I share information with you, you can't go running off doing your own investigating without me. And sometimes, I'll have to give you a hard no when it comes to police-work ride-alongs. I don't want to lose my job, and I don't want you to get arrested for interfering with a case. If we do this together, we do it together. But I'm the one calling the shots."

Leda sulked. "Just because you're the cop."

"Yes, because I'm the cop. My badge can open doors, and your psychic powers can open . . . I don't know, windows or whatever. But the whole world believes in my badge, and maybe a handful of people believe in your psychic powers. Is that fair? No. I won't tell you how to do whatever it is you do. You have to loop me in, though. If you get a big hit, you call me before you go free-diving in any culverts, or breaking into any buildings, or stalking any suspects. Can you live with that?"

Leda wasn't 100 percent thrilled, but she understood. Furthermore, she was prepared to disregard him if the situation called for it. What he didn't know wouldn't hurt him. "I direct you to the clues, and you protect me from the consequences of sharing them. That's . . . fair."

He held out his hand. "Shake on it?"

She held hers out more slowly. "Shake on it."

They did. This time, absolutely nothing happened.

# 11.

"I've been putting together a murder board," Leda solemnly informed Grady. They were riding in his low-key cop sedan, wending through a posh and hilly neighborhood alongside Lake Washington called Leschi—dodging cyclists and dog walkers and skateboarders and random joggers wearing earbuds.

His eyes audibly rolled. "A murder board? You don't say."

"It's a whiteboard. It's only about the size of a poster, but it does the job. I've got *Tod Sandoval* written on one side, and *Gilman Murders* written on the other. Below that, all the clues for each case."

"You have basically zero clues for the Gilman case. Except for the one you gave me, and we haven't even talked to that guy yet."

"But we're about to, so I put him up there anyhow."

Curious, he asked, "What did you put under Tod's name?"

She adjusted her seat and accidentally kicked her purse. "The basics. The name of the woman who died by the same gun, where the car was found. You know. Stuff like that. I'm just trying to do what you said—take a step back and look at the big picture. See if there's any place where the two cases overlap, or meet up, or whatever."

"That's not a bad idea. Visualizing all the details in one place can be helpful."

"Thus the concept of a murder board. Don't cops have them all over the station? I've seen probably thirty years' worth of *Law and Order*, and I swear—it's like you work in these little rooms that are just one murder board after another. A veritable labyrinth of murder boards, from wall to wall."

"You watch too much TV. Seattle isn't New York City, and nobody has that many murder boards." He pulled into a driveway in front of an impeccably kept craftsman home, and he pulled the parking brake. "Anyway, we're here. You know the drill, right? Please, before we knock on this man's door, I'm begging you: Assure me that you know the drill."

"Keep my mouth shut and don't volunteer any information. If I get a flash, I keep it to myself until we make it back to the car."

"Attagirl."

"I'm not in middle school. I know how to behave like an adult."

He opened his door and climbed out. Leda did the same.

Once she was free, and they looked at each other across the top of the car, he said, "I know you're an adult. But there are *so many* fiddly police rules, even though we're doing this on our own time."

"You don't want me to jeopardize the case. Either case. Both cases. Whatever."

"Right. It's not personal. Let me do the talking, and everything will be fine. Beckmeyer is expecting us."

They climbed a paver path up to the house, then a short stack of stairs to the front door. A curtain that covered one of the sidelight windows fluttered.

"Detective Merritt." He greeted the cop with a smile and a handshake. "Good to see you again."

"This is my associate, Ms. Foley," said Grady. "I hope you don't mind her joining us."

"Not at all," Beckmeyer said brightly. He was a tall pink fellow with a vivid shock of snow-white hair and the healthy glow of a man who can't see himself retiring anytime soon, even though he was free to do so a decade ago. Was this the silver fox from the photo she'd briefly glimpsed? Maybe. Probably. He reached for Leda's hand to shake it, but she hesitated.

"I'm sorry, it's very nice to meet you—but I'm recovering from a bit of the flu. Best to play it safe."

"Absolutely, absolutely," he said with a short, shallow bow. He held the door open wide for them to come inside. "Thank you for your consideration. Please, come on in."

The house was as lovely inside as outside, with high tray ceilings and antique decor that was tasteful without being dull. All in all, Leda gave the place two thumbs up, and she said so out loud. Richard politely gave all the credit to his wife, who was presently at work.

"She's on the board of directors at Swedish," he said, meaning the medical center. "She's the designer, and the shopper. Always, she's had such an eye for quality, and for bargains. So many people have antiques and simply don't know what they're worth, or how to take care of them—but not Sheila. Once in a while I raise an eyebrow, like the time she shipped *that* thing home." He pointed at a lovely art deco buffet with a bar setup on top. "It only cost her a hundred dollars, and she paid three times that to ship it here. Then we had a fellow who specializes in these things appraise it at three times the total, so I was forced to eat my words."

He led them to a seating area that once might have been a parlor and offered them drinks.

"I never partake during the day," Leda lied through her teeth.

"And I have to head back to work after this," Grady said. "But thanks for the offer. We're here as part of the . . . let's say 'ongoing conversation' about the Gilman deaths."

"It's been ages, and we don't have any resolution yet."

"Oh, it hasn't been that long—and plenty of murders go even *longer* without being solved," Leda noted. "Some of them never are, right? A lot of them, probably."

Grady gave her a look that said he'd happily, swiftly elbow her if he were sitting any closer. "But we do our best with every case, and yes—even after this vast epoch of eighteen months, we're still working on this one. They don't always come together neatly."

"Ain't that the truth." Richard Beckmeyer poured himself a bit of Scotch and took a swallow. "Nothing much ever went neatly when it came to the Gilmans. Why should their deaths be any different?"

"I have no idea," Leda answered, and Grady gave her another look. She remembered she had agreed to stay quiet.

He pulled out a little notebook and returned his attention to Beckmeyer. "I know we've been over some of this before, but I hope you don't mind refreshing my memory. How long had you worked at Digital Scaffolding when Chris and Kevin died?"

"I was never really an employee," Beckmeyer said. "Sheila does a bit of angel investing, here and there. She put up some money and managed the books. They let me hang around and help them with their in-house digital tools, mostly as a courtesy to her, I think."

Leda opened her mouth to ask what that meant, but a sharp side-eye from Grady stopped her.

"What kind of in-house tools?" he asked.

The older man hesitated, holding up his hands like he was trying to describe the shape of something—and words weren't quite cutting it. "Digital Scaffolding helped smaller companies interface with larger companies, like Amazon, Google, and Microsoft. They had a number of in-house tools that made it easier for these corporate systems to talk to one another, help them sell one another's products and hire consultants and monitor their money. I did some of the design, fiddling with the user interfaces and making them more"—he hunted for a word, his long fingers still swaying, like he could pluck one from the air—"user-friendly. I was really a consultant, more than anything."

Leda piped up, "Same here." And offered him a fist-bump.

He returned it with a grin. "But to answer your question," he continued, "I'd only been with them a few months—and at the time, I didn't see myself staying much longer. It was a toxic work environment, let me put it that way. Usually Sheila's nose is on point, and she sniffs out the creeps before getting involved . . . but Christopher Gilman was a hell of a salesman. I'd give him that, if nothing else. He was a grade A asshole, but it took people a little time to figure that out."

Grady nodded and jotted something down. "Yes, I seem to recall that you didn't like him much."

"Nobody who worked with him longer than a month liked him. But Kevin was all right. I think the young man honestly wanted to do something good with his father's money. He saw the same potential that Sheila did, and the two of them got along smashingly. But Christopher . . . well, he was a bit of a con man."

"Do you think he was actually involved in any illegal activities, or was he just an asshole?"

Richard held out his hands, palms up as if he were weighing something in each one. "Eh . . . a little of column A, little of column B. Wait, he's dead, right? It's not like he can sue me for slander."

"Correct."

"Then I'm *confident* that the man was a full-blown crook. Couldn't prove it, but it wouldn't surprise me in the slightest. He was a terrible fellow, with terrible impulses and terrible attitudes. Honestly, his death is the only reason I stayed on as long as I did with that company. I'd been on the verge of quitting when he died. Oh my, wait—that doesn't make me a suspect, does it? I'm sure I have an alibi."

Grady grinned. "You were cleared in the original investigation. You were in the hospital with kidney stones when the murders occurred. The hospital confirmed it."

He snapped his fingers. "That's right. The kidney stones. I knew there was some reason I couldn't have done it, but it's been so long that the details escaped me. I'm definitely not the murderer, so I have no reason to lie to you: Nobody liked the guy. His own wife went out of her way to avoid him. She's probably someone you should talk to, if you're revisiting the case."

"Janette," Grady said, checking his notes. "Yeah, she's on our list."

"She seemed like a cool lady, though it's hard to say. I only saw her a handful of times, mostly with Kevin. Neither one of them was Christopher's biggest fan, and I don't know why she stayed married to him—except, one must assume, it was cheaper than a divorce."

Leda nodded vigorously. "I would put up with a lot of garbage for a lot of money." Then she saw the stink-eye Grady was giving her. "Probably."

Richard smiled and gave her a wink that was intended in a grandfatherly manner, she was pretty sure. He reminded her of Joe Biden, without all the hair-sniffing.

Grady shook his head slowly. "At any rate. Mr. Beckmeyer, off the top of your head—and remember, this is just between us—do you have any thoughts as to who else we ought to speak to?"

Beckmeyer hemmed and hawed, leaning his head left, then right. "I suppose if you forced me to make some guesses, I'd start with Janette. Isn't the spouse usually the guilty party, in this kind of situation?"

"More often than not, but you don't think she murdered her son, too—do you?"

"Kevin was her stepson, but now that you mention it . . . no, I don't. She and Kevin seemed to get along pretty well; they were more"—he hunted for a descriptor—"from the same planet, if you know what I mean. But no, I don't think she would've hurt him. If anything, I might have suspected the pair of working together, if poor Kevin hadn't bitten the dust along with his dad."

"So do you have any second-tier suspicions?" Leda prodded.

"I'd take a look at . . . well, let's see. You should probably talk to that fellow, Abbot somebody. He was a low-level consultant, newer to the company. Supposedly he and Christopher had some kind of in-office row, and nobody knew exactly what it was about—but Chris didn't fire him, and I remember he laughed off any suggestions that he ought to. Then there was Brian Doherty, the old CFO, but wait . . . he's dead now, isn't he? I heard he died of a heart attack or a stroke, a few months back. I saw something about it on Facebook, maybe."

"I hadn't heard that," Grady mumbled down to his notebook as he scribbled away. "But I'll double-check it when I get back to the precinct. Any other names you want to hit me with?"

"I can only think of one more: Kim Cowen. She was Christopher's secretary, but that really undersells her position. She was his right-hand woman. Nothing happened in that office without her knowing about it. I heard through the grapevine that she was up all night after the funeral, shredding documents in his office."

"Ooh," Leda exclaimed softly. "Juicy!"

"Dear, if you want juicy . . . *well*. There *was* a rumor going around that Kim and Kevin had something going on, out of office, if you get my drift."

Leda said "Ooh!" again with a little more oomph behind it.

Grady looked up like he'd been thinking about rolling his eyes yet again in response to this nonsense, but now he was just thinking. "Good to know, thanks. I'll see if I can't confirm or deny it. I don't remember hearing anything about it at the time."

"It was only office gossip—you know how that goes. I'm not even sure that it's worth checking out. It might not mean anything at all. Sheila had access to everything Kim had, too . . . so you might want to swing back around and talk to my wife."

"You know what, we'll be sure to do that. Listen, I want to thank you for your time," Grady said, folding his notebook away and stuffing it into his pocket. "We all know you didn't have to sit down with us today, and I appreciate it."

They exchanged parting pleasantries, and Grady and Richard shook hands before Grady and Leda left.

Back inside the car, still parked on the steep driveway in front of Richard Beckmeyer's house, Grady asked Leda, "Did you get anything? I didn't see you throwing up any time-outs; and if you had any psychic flashes, they must've been more low-key than the ones I've seen so far."

"Not a thing," she told him. "But Mr. Beckmeyer seems lovely."

"Nice guy, yeah. And probably not the murderer, so that's always a plus."

"So what happens next?"

"Next?" He put the key in the ignition, started up the car, and left it in park for a few seconds. "Next, I drop you off at the destination of your choosing, and I go back to the precinct to poke around in the files a little more. That Abbot guy . . ." He brightened and threw the car into gear. "Keyes, that was his name."

"Abbot Keyes? Sounds like a Victorian orphan."

Grady chuckled. "I guess, but he was an exceedingly normal-looking guy, maybe five foot eight or nine. Dark hair that didn't want to lie down right. I remember the whole time I talked to him, I wanted to offer him a comb and a tub of hair gel."

"Did he have an alibi?"

"Almost everyone had an alibi. Abbot was at a funeral. His brother's? Half brother's? Something like that. Pictures put him there. He showed up in the background of the church shots, and he was present for the reception later that night."

"So not our guy, either."

Grady looked over his shoulder and checked for traffic, then pulled back into the street. "Yeah, but here's the thing about alibis: anybody can get one—even someone like Beckmeyer, who seems so . . . how'd you put it? Lovely. His alibi wasn't rock-solid, either. The only rock-solid alibi is being dead, in my experience. Not sick, not injured. *Dead.* All others vary. You can buy one, you can make one up, you can bribe friends into giving you one. You can even fabricate one, if you know what you're doing. There's almost no such thing as an airtight one."

She frowned. "You mean we can't even check that nice old man off the list?"

"He's moved down the suspect list, but no. He hasn't escaped it entirely. Nobody has, until we've got a confession or a smoking gun."

"What if, while somebody was being murdered, the suspect was in the middle of a live TV broadcast? In front of a live crowd?"

"That would be pretty airtight, but there's always the chance the suspect paid somebody else to do it. Those are always the trickiest cases, when people have enough money to outsource their murder needs."

"Sounds like the wife would have had enough money to pay a professional."

"Maybe, maybe not. Christopher Gilman was rich, but our investigation turned up evidence that he was also richly in debt. I don't know how much of the estate was left when he was gone."

Leda nodded. "Right, but what if she didn't care about inheriting all his money and stocks and things? What if she just wanted him gone? Even if it meant she'd be broke? Some people are just that terrible—it doesn't matter how you get away from them, as long as you get away."

"I've rarely seen it play out that way in real life, except in cases where there's a lot of abuse. But anything's possible. I'll talk to her again, if she'll agree to see me. I'm not sure where she is right now. She left the country for a while—I believe she had family in England—but I think she's back in town. I'll find out for sure—"

Leda interrupted. "Once you get back to the precinct, I know, I know. You'll go do all the *real* detective work downtown without me."

"Yeah, I will. And don't take this the wrong way, but you're not a real detective."

She folded her arms and sank back into the seat. "Says you."

"Says literally everybody, including the city of Seattle, King County, and the great state of Washington. Don't get all huffy on me. I let you come along for the interview, didn't I? Even though I said no way, at first."

"Yes, but come *on*. You're as close as I've ever gotten to any answers about what happened to Tod. You've put actual vengeance on the table for the first time, and I don't want to just . . . walk away and let you do it all yourself. This is my murder, too."

He looked like he really wanted to beat his head on the steering wheel, but traffic was too bad to allow it. "Okay, first. This is not *your* murder, Leda. This is a murder to which you might possibly have a tangential connection. And second, vengeance? Is that really what you want?"

"Justice, whatever. I deserve justice."

"I never said you didn't. I just don't know how much I can help you find it if I get fired from the force and you go to jail for obstruction of justice."

"I'm not obstructing it, I'm hunting for it!"

"That's not how the authorities will see it. What you're doing looks like meddling, you understand? It looks like interference, to a certain sort of district attorney. I've enabled it. I am trying to keep you as far away from trouble as I can, while still keeping you involved. You're just going to have to get okay with that."

Her posture in a full-body sulk, she stared out the windshield. "I'd be okay with you letting me go meet the widow."

He squinched his lips and said, "Hmm." He straightened them out again. "We both know that I shouldn't let you, but I probably will—if for no other reason than having another woman present might put her at ease. I remember her being jumpy, but that might have only been the timing of our introduction. I got the impression she didn't like or trust most men, me included. Maybe she was always high-strung, or maybe Christopher really did a number on her psyche."

"Why don't we go see her next? Like, right now? Today?"

"No."

"Why not? We've got momentum, baby!"

"For a variety of reasons." He tapped them out on the steering wheel. "One, like I said—I have to go look her up. Two, I don't know if she'll agree to an informal conversation about her husband's death with an unknown third party in tow. Three, it's already, what? Almost three in the afternoon? By the time I can scare up her contact information, call her up, and show up in person, it'll be a little late in the day for police business."

"Okay, I get it. Why don't we go to Detective Whiteside's place instead? I want to talk to him again, but with you there this time.

I never felt like he took me very seriously. He might actually tell *you* something useful."

"I know what you mean. He had a bad habit of calling his fellow officers 'little lady,' if you know what I'm getting at."

"Then let's go to his house. I want to pet his dogs."

He sighed wearily and sang the same tune as before. "We can't just show up on his doorstep unannounced. I don't even know where his doorstep is, exactly. I know you don't like it, but your investigatory work is finished for today. We'll circle back around to retired Detective Whiteside and widowed Janette Gilman another day."

"Which other day?"

"Whichever one is convenient for them, for me, and for you."

Leda batted her eyelashes slowly, sweetly, ridiculously. "You swear to God you won't go see them without me?"

"Nope. But I'll try, and that has to be enough right now. I have other work to do, too. You *do* realize that I'm an active-duty police officer. I have open cases to work, and you have travelers to shepherd through airports, and visas, and travel vouchers, and rental-car agreements. I already paid your fee the other day, and you volunteered for this particular run. This is now an unpaid side hustle for both of us."

"Right. You're absolutely right. I do have clients. I have a job. I earn money."

He hit a stop sign and took the pause to give her some stink-eye. "Now that you put it that way, I have to wonder."

"Okay, it's a fairly new enterprise," she said with a touch more defensiveness than she liked to hear in her own voice. "My job is both taking care of clients and getting more clients to take care of. You're right. I have work to do. You can drop me off back at my office, and we can both return to being full-time professional adults."

"Yes. That's exactly what's going to happen."

She dipped into her best Captain Picard impression, which was terrible—but it got the job done. "Make it so, Number One."

He banged the back of his head gently on the seat rest. "I will, but not because you told me to. And not because you called me . . . Number One? What?"

"It's a *Star Trek* thing. You must not be a fan."

"More of a *Star Wars* guy, to tell you the truth."

She groaned. "This is never going to work." She said it half joking, but the words sank into her soul regardless. If they couldn't agree on which sci-fi memes to deploy in conversation, how could they work together long enough to fix anything? Solve anything? Save anybody? "We're never going to solve these murders—Tod's, or the Gilmans', or anyone else. We are wasting our time, and we're going to get each other in trouble, I can feel it."

"Like, *feel it* feel it?" he asked. But something about the look in her eyes must've told him no, and she didn't answer otherwise. Her frown declared that this wasn't the time to ask. This was the time to agree. So he agreed, for practically the first time all day. "You're absolutely right. We haven't got a chance in hell."

# 12.

**G**rady dropped Leda off at her office door, gave her a wave, and disappeared back into traffic. As soon as he was out of sight, she wandered around the corner to get some coffee. She didn't really want to sit down and work. In fact, she didn't have any work to sit down and do. She hadn't sprung for the Google keyword ads yet, or the Facebook ads, or even the Craigslist ads for Foley's Far-Fetched Flights of Fancy, even though they were all queued up and ready to go. It seemed like a waste to run them this late in the afternoon. It did not seem like a waste to go visit more suspects, but she'd made a deal with Grady when it came to investigative work—none without him, period—and she had to respect that deal. For now.

She really wanted to get back to her murder board, but it was kind of early for that.

Wasn't it?

She checked her phone. Well, it was almost four o'clock. The doors at Castaways opened at four, in case of a happy-hour crowd. By the time she could get there, it'd be closer to four thirty. It wouldn't be *super* weird if she showed up so early.

Would it?

While she stood against a wall and waited for a barista to hurry up with that pour-over already, she texted Niki. Where you at?

A minute later, she got a response. With Matt, getting early dinner. You lost?

Not lost. Just wondering when you'd be at Castaways.

Another hour or two? Tiff's there. So's Ben. They're opening tonight.

Okay, Leda typed. I'll see you there later.

Her coffee finally arrived, approximately a hundred years after she'd ordered it. It was good and hot, though, and it smelled like it'd been roasted sometime in the last week, which was nice. She took the to-go cup and went back outside, where it had begun to drizzle.

"Screw it," she declared to the world at large. "I'm going to the bar."

She'd parked Jason around the corner from her office, on a side street where the free parking was only for parkers who needed two hours at a time, not that it ever stopped anyone. Almost nobody ever got a ticket, and Leda had been lucky this time, too. She climbed inside, stuffed the coffee into the cup holder, and headed north into the city, then up Cap Hill—where parking was considerably trickier, even when someone knew all the tricks.

By 4:42, she'd finally found a place to leave the car and sauntered inside.

She shoved the door open and whipped off her sunglasses. "I've arrived," she announced. "Let the games begin!" The door shut behind her. She blinked until her eyes adjusted to the lower light. "Anyone? Are there any games to be had? Anywhere?"

"Hark! Who goes there?" called someone from behind the stage.

"It's me!" she called back.

Benjamin Kane popped his head out from between the black stage curtains and beamed like an angel. "Be thou Leda? That's a fair name. I'll have no psychic, if you be not she!"

"What's that, Shakespeare or something?"

"Or something!"

Ben was a sharp, gay Asian man in his fifties. In another ten years, he'd be a silver fox. For now, his thick dark hair had only two streaks of silver—streaks that contrasted nicely with whatever black velvet outfit he was wearing at the time, unless it was summer. Then it was black linen all the way.

It was Leda's opinion that he always looked a little like a friendly vampire, but she never said so out loud. She didn't know him well enough to know if the comparison would offend or delight him. Sometimes he could be a tad fussy, and although Matt managed most of the day-to-day operations, Castaways belonged to Ben. She didn't want to piss him off.

"You're here early," he noted.

"I try not to make a habit of it, but what can I say? I found myself at loose ends."

He climbed out onto the stage and then hopped down off it. He wended his way between the tables and clutched her in a big, crisp hug. "We're always happy to have you, of course. Will you do a set tonight?"

"I haven't decided."

"Yes, you have, you just haven't committed," he argued. "But that's fine for now. You *do* know that Matt and Niki aren't here yet, right?"

She nodded and stepped back out of the hug. "Yeah, I know."

"Leda!" Tiffany shrieked. She bounced out from the employee entrance beside the edge of the bar, smelling like cigarette smoke and cheap pizza from down the street. She delivered Leda's second hug of the last ninety seconds, and immediately asked, "Do you want a drink?"

"No. I don't know yet. Okay, yes, but I don't want to impose."

Ben waved his hand like he was swatting an errant wasp. "Oh, honey, we had our highest-ticket night ever last time you did your little song-and-dance routine. For God's sake, Tiffany. Make the woman whatever she asks for."

Leda scratched at the back of her neck and laughed awkwardly. "It's more like a sit-and-sing routine, really. But thanks, Ben. You're the best."

"Nonsense! Another night or two like the last one, and I'll start booking you outright. I can't pay you much, but I can pay you enough to show up and show off."

Tiffany whacked him on the arm as she walked to the bar. "*You're* the show-off, Ben."

He made a coy face and shrugged. "Anyway. I'll haul out the karaoke getup, and you have a little gin fizzy or whatever floats your boat. Once the evening crowd rolls in, you can do your thing. But from here on out," he said more sternly, "you need to give me a heads-up. Or give Matt a heads-up, whoever's around. I want to start advertising your *psychic songstress* nights."

"We've been calling it klairvoyant karaoke."

He frowned, his perfect eyebrows dipping toward the bridge of his nose. "I don't get it."

"Like . . . *clairvoyant* but with a *k* you know?"

"Ah." He nodded. "Like a Kardashian thing."

"What? No, it's just—"

"Yes, it is," he protested. "I get it now. It might be hard to fit on a flyer . . ." he said, mostly to himself as he walked away. "*Psychic song-stress* works better, if you ask me, and it has such a pleasant assonance to it. We'll see. I'll play it by ear, when I get back to my computer."

"But . . ." Leda began to protest, but he was already behind the stage again. Tiffany was calling up something that required some martini-shaker stylings, so she said her thoughts out loud to the bartender instead: "If you spell *psychic* without the *p* it looks weird."

Tiffany worked the stainless-steel shaker like a pro, bobbing her head to the rattling mixture of ice, booze, and whatever else she was whipping up. "Oh, I'm with you. Klairvoyant karaoke is the hands-down winner in my book, but he's the boss. And I think he doesn't want to . . . he's not going to take off the *p*. He wants to add one. To *songstress*."

"He's not *my* boss. And that looks ridiculous in my head. I'm sure it looks ridiculous on paper, too."

Tiffany stopped agitating the beverage and strained it into a martini glass. "Until you find someplace else to do your thing, I mean, it is *his* bar."

"Yeah, I know. And he seems like good people." Leda pulled up a barstool and parked on it. "I'm not mad. I just really like the *KK* thing. Oh, wait. One more *K* and we've got a problem, don't we?"

"So, don't add any racist jokes to the mix, and you won't have anything to worry about."

"Very funny. Very funny indeed."

"Racist jokes are never funny!" Tiffany slapped down a cocktail napkin and put the glass on top of it. "Now try this. See if it doesn't perk up your day."

"What's in it?"

"Try it first."

Leda squinted at the glass. Its contents were yellowish, with light bubbles and an orange peel curlicue garnish. It did not look especially dangerous, but that didn't mean anything where Tiffany was concerned. That girl could pack twelve ounces of fire into a shot glass and call it lemonade, right to your face without cracking a grin.

"Will it hurt?" Leda asked, poking the glass with her index finger and taking away a fingerprint's worth of condensation.

"No?"

"Well, that's good enough for me." Leda picked up the glass and didn't bother to sniff it. She tipped it up, took a healthy swallow, and set it back down again with a hard stare, as if she meant to interrogate it. "Tiffany, I'm asking you seriously, and I want you to tell me the truth: What's in this?"

"What does it taste like?"

"Like death by bananas, with a hint of eau de sunscreen."

"That's the coconut liqueur," she said. "I'm trying to make something that tastes tropical but isn't just the same old mai tai or piña colada you can get any-damn-where. I skipped the orange juice and rum, because that's too obvious. How would you feel about an orange-blossom infusion? That might give it a good bouquet."

"You just said you were skipping orange juice."

"No, I mean like a vodka infusion with orange *blossoms*. They don't smell like oranges, they smell like . . . like flowers. I don't know. I'm still working on the formula. But did you like it, that's my question?"

Leda took another sip. "Tone down the banana liqueur, and you might have a winner. Or cut it with something stronger than the coconut? I don't know, but I'm down to be your guinea pig while you work it out."

"Excellent! But yeah, banana is a hard flavor to work with. It overpowers whatever you put it in. Hmm . . ." Tiffany wandered back to stare at her assortment of booze, stacked up from waist height to the ceiling. "I'll keep experimenting. But until then, I might put it on the menu anyway. And I'm stealing your 'death by bananas' bit."

"Have at."

Tiffany picked up a piece of chalk and started to write it down as the daily special. "At least this way, people will know what they're in for—and the banana haters can try something else."

"Right. Good call. Hey, I'm going to take my monkey juice and head back to Matt's office, okay? Tell Ben, if he comes looking for me."

"Spending a little time with the murder board?"

"Since it's dead in here and all. No pun intended." The words flew out of her mouth before she could stop them. She looked away to hide a wince and took a deep sniff of the banana-y beverage.

"I'll holler if the crowd picks up, but on a Monday . . . you know. It's not really going to be hopping."

"Thanks. Hey, let me ask you . . ." Leda said quietly. "Does Ben know about the murder board?"

"He might not? Matt flipped the board over, so the bar's work schedule faces out."

"Okay, thanks. I just don't want to upset him with my creepy-ass hobby." Leda swept her glass into her hands and collected the napkin right along with it. After the third sip, the bananas weren't quite so overwhelming. They even became quite pleasant. Unless that was the liqueur talking.

It might've been the liqueur. Without it, she might actually have to consider that this wasn't a hobby but a wholly unpleasant obsession. But what could she do?

Drink. That's what. Drink, and stare bleary-eyed at her murder board.

She carried her drink around the tables and back past the audio/video booth beside the stage, then down the corridor behind the curtain. Ben was sitting at his desk in his office. She waved when she walked past.

"Hey, are you headed to Matt's office?" he asked innocently. "The one that used to be the hall closet?"

Too innocently.

Her eyes narrowed. "Yes. Why?"

"No reason. Have fun in there, with your oddball extracurricular activity."

She sighed. "You know about the murder board."

"I was looking for Matt's extra keys. I lost mine the other day. It's quite a . . . project you've got there. Very *casualty chic*."

"Do you hate it?" she asked, her voice high and tight. "I can put it somewhere else or take it home if it bothers you."

He shook his head. "Nobody goes back there except for me and Matt every now and again. Is it weird? Totally. Do I care? Not at all. I do have a question, though."

"Shoot."

"Why don't you keep it at your house? Or at your own office?"

Another blast of bananas on the tongue, and she was cleared for takeoff. "Because . . . okay, because my travel agency office is about the size of a powder room, and there's nowhere to keep it out of sight without blocking the window or the door. If I had it at home . . ." She hesitated. "Look, to tell you the God's honest truth? If I worked on it at home, I would think about it one hundred percent of the time, and I would get crazy and weird and overly focused on it, and that would be bad for everybody."

"More crazy and weird than you already are, you mean?"

"Yes. That's what I mean. I'm sorry, Ben. I didn't mean to involve your marvelous bar in my ridiculous quest for justice." It was a slight struggle to keep her tone light. Would it ever feel okay to speak so thoughtlessly of what had happened to Tod? Maybe, with time. It hadn't been so long, in the scheme of things.

Ben nodded in a sympathetic, even fatherly fashion. "No, darling. It's not ridiculous, and don't you ever apologize. You're adding to the mystique of your brand, that's how I'm choosing to see it—and otherwise I'm working hard to mind my own business, *fascinating* though all this is. Go on, do whatever you need. Maybe in another hour or two, you could . . . ?" he hinted hard.

"In another hour or two, I'll come out and do my sit-and-sing routine, yes."

He clapped happily, perhaps delighted for the change in subject. "Excellent! Do you want to see the flyer I'm working up?"

"I'm morbidly curious, sure." She walked around behind his desk to stand beside him. The flyer on his screen was neon pink with a stock-art crystal ball and black letters with black blood dripping down them. The letters read PSYCHIC PSONGSTRESS.

All she could say was "Wow." A missing *p* had sounded absurd. Tiffany was right, though, and the extra *p* was even worse.

"I know, right?" He smiled from ear to ear. "Can I put you down for six o'clock?"

She glanced at the clock on his wall. "Let's say six thirty. I want to take a minute, okay?"

"Okay," he agreed, then added the information to the flyer. "I don't know how many people will see it, but we need to grow your brand, right? Let's grow your brand. I'll help."

"I'm supposed to be doing that with the travel agency," Leda complained. "Not my weirdo singing career."

"You can do that, too. Make yourself some business cards, and we'll put them in a bowl by the door. But tonight, I'm sticking these up on every post on the block. Across the street, too. You know, people come in here all the time asking if you'll be up onstage."

"Business cards? Actually, that's a great idea—I'll get on that." Suddenly, she was mortified that she hadn't thought of business cards sooner. "I'll just be . . ."

"Down the hall. Gotcha. And take that drink with you, will you? I hate bananas. The smell makes me gag."

She saluted him with the now half-empty drink and set off down the short, narrow corridor that ran behind the stage until it hit the exterior wall and ended at an exit. (DO NOT OPEN EXCEPT IN CASE OF EMERGENCY read the red-and-white security bar mounted across it.) She stopped right before that door and opened the one to its right.

This was Matt's office, though he didn't use it much. Sometimes he tallied up the till in there, but usually he did so in Ben's office—since Ben had the good calculator and his computer was the one with the payroll software. Matt's office was Matt's office because it was a largely empty room that was otherwise used for storage, and Matt had wanted an office.

It worked out well for Leda, because like she'd told Ben, she didn't want to keep the murder board at home. The board was a midsize model that fit on the large easel in the corner. The easel was left over from Niki's last run at an art degree, and Leda had supplied her own note cards and magnets to hold everything in place. This meant that even the more gruesome details were held up by adorable novelty magnets, picked up on Leda's travels—or at her favorite coffee shops, or the neat old florist at the end of the block, or a gas station in Ballard.

The whiteboard was presently turned to the wall. The backside was plain brown corkboard, completely nondescript and perfectly uninteresting. The employee schedules had been printed out and affixed with brass thumbtacks.

But when Leda turned it around, the murder board was revealed in all its terrible, sloppy glory. The very sight of it gave her a weird, sad little pang—but also a gentle lift of hope.

She'd picked up a pack of one hundred index cards in assorted neon colors, and in the beginning, she'd had plans to color-coordinate the information. Those intentions evaporated fairly quickly, as she realized how little she knew and understood.

At the top of the board in royal highlighter yellow, she'd written: *TOD SANDOVAL, 30 years of age, RIP.*

Below that, on the far left: a tree of newspaper clippings, starting with one that declared him missing. Then another, from several days later: his car was found in a culvert, over on the east side of the city. And the next day: "Body Found in Sunken Car Believed to Be Missing Columbia City Man." That one was held up by a magnet that advertised the possibility of bigfoot sightings in Olympic National Park. The next one was from three days later, announcing that a second body had been found and the police were not prepared to state for the record that the new body was connected to Tod's in any way.

She'd left out Tod's obituary. She couldn't stand to look at it, and it wasn't like the little paragraph of smudged newsprint offered any additional information about his death.

In the next column, on index cards so bright they made her squint, she'd listed *Things We Know About Amanda Crombie, 27 years of age, RIP.*

The top card read: *Killed with the same gun that killed Tod, probably around the same time. Body was discovered later. She wasn't in the car when it went into the water.*

The next cards read, in descending order: *An accountant with a small firm called Probable Outcomes. PO was an advertising group(?) that went under a year after she died.*

*No known enemies. Survived by parents, two brothers, and a cat.* *(*Parents adopted the cat.)*

*Might have met Tod at a gas station a couple of miles away.*

Leda had argued with herself over where to put that last card, since it applied to Tod as much as it applied to Amanda—but Tod's row was getting full, so she'd stuck it down under Amanda's name.

Video surveillance at the time showed that Tod had stopped at a BP station for gas that night, about ten minutes after a woman matching Amanda's description had been hanging around it. The cashier wouldn't swear that she was the woman he'd seen, and the footage from security cameras was so grainy as to be nearly useless . . . but he thought the mystery lady had been hiding from someone. She'd never come inside to ask for help, and she was never positively identified.

Leda would have bet her life that the woman at the gas station was Amanda Crombie. It might have been her psychic senses tingling, or it might've been the coincidence, or it might've been a blind grasp at narrative straws. But she believed it all the way down to her bones.

Next column: *Things That Don't Make Sense.*

She read from the top down.

*Why was Tod in the back seat of his own car when he was found?* Police insisted that he hadn't somehow floated back there when the car sank; he seemed to have bled out there. The killer either shot him there or tossed him inside before he'd run the car into the water.

"He?" she second-guessed herself out loud. "Or she, I guess." She took a pen and added a question mark to the pronoun.

"Any idiot can fire a gun. No reason it had to be a dude," she muttered.

Next card.

*Did Tod know Amanda from somewhere?* She'd never heard him mention her, but that didn't mean they weren't acquaintances. She could've been someone he recognized from his usual bus route, or from a restaurant he frequented, or any of a thousand places he went without Leda along for the ride.

Next card.

*Everybody loved Tod, and nobody wanted to kill him.*

She sat on the edge of Matt's desk and scowled at that last card through eyes that were getting damp. She stared at it, long and hard. Every letter written thereupon was absolutely true, but someone had killed him anyway, and one way or another, Leda was going to find out *who*. Now that she had the interest of a real-life detective, she was flush with optimism and renewed determination. She was going to do it with Grady Merritt's help, or without it. He had the badge, but she had the psychic powers.

Right?

She downed the last of her death by bananas and went to the ladies' room to freshen up.

"One thing at a time," she told herself. "First we sing. Then we use our powers for more than mere good. We use them for *justice*."

# 13.

Grady Merritt had lied, but only a little.

The truth was, he'd already decided to go meet Whiteside without Leda, for all the reasons that Leda had stated and then some. Whiteside wasn't a bad guy, but he'd talk to a fellow dude more openly and honestly than he'd talk to any given woman. He was only in his sixties, but he somehow seemed older than that—like he belonged back in the 1950s from whence he came.

Grady knew Leda would not take such exclusion lightly, but he figured she'd get over it quickly—especially if he got any useful information out of the older man. So rather than ask for permission, he'd decided to beg forgiveness.

And the next day, he took a long lunch break to go see the retired detective.

The drive north to Lake City didn't take long when rush hour wasn't in play, and soon he'd found his way to the tasteful split-level house on a hillside. He pulled up into the driveway next to a fence that had been dug beneath and reinforced so many times that it looked like a WWI trench.

As Grady was getting out of the car, the house's front door opened to reveal a heavyset man in a Hawaiian shirt, with a wagging wiener dog tucked under his arm.

"Merritt!" he hollered. "Come on in, you ol' son of a bitch—it's good to see you!"

Grady pointed at the fence, with its strips of sheet metal, chicken wire, and sticks of rebar pounded around the edges. "One of the dogs is a digger?" he guessed.

"Two of them are, and goddamn them both."

When Grady reached the small porch, they shook hands.

"This one's smart enough to dig like a Virginia coal miner but too dumb to stay out of the road. Got a death wish, he does."

"Well, he's a cute little guy."

"They're all assholes, but they're *my* assholes."

An army of ankle-high canines spilled out of the house, swarmed Grady's feet like furry piranhas, and followed both men back inside—where they thoroughly sniffed the newcomer, deemed him harmless, and immediately began fighting over whose belly he'd pet first.

Whiteside said, "Have a seat, man. Can I get you a drink? I mean a soda or something, since I know you're still on duty."

"I'm on my lunch break, but no, thanks. I can't stay long—I just wanted to touch base."

"About an old case, you said. The one with that kid, dead in the back seat of his own car, at the bottom of the reservoir."

"Tod Sandoval. He wasn't exactly a kid, but he was young. Barely thirty when it happened. I think there might be a connection between his case and another one I worked a year or two ago."

"Some lead popped up, and now it's got you looking even further back?"

"Something like that, combined with a real strong feeling," Grady said, not clarifying that the feeling belonged to someone else. "I've read through the files but wondered if you might have any insight you feel like adding to the stack. Anything at all: any impressions you might've gotten that were too vague to write down, or connections that felt like connections but didn't—I don't know—connect."

Whiteside nodded sagely. "That was a weird one, I tell you what. And God Almighty, the Sandoval widow."

"His widow? I didn't think he was married . . ."

"Maybe not. You got a word for a surviving girlfriend, because I don't. I remember her clear as day: a flaky, feisty brunette who couldn't keep her voice down and had real strong opinions about every goddamn thing, if you know what I mean."

Grady badly wanted to laugh, agree, and high-five the man—but he tamped it down. "Oh, I've met her. She's something else."

"Something else—that's putting it mildly. Whole lot of personality, that's what my late wife would've said. Crazy as a soup sandwich, that's how I'd put it. I know she'd just lost her husband, but—"

"Fiancé."

"Whatever. It was tragic, that's for sure, but woo boy howdy. That girl could raise hell and make it wish it'd never shown up."

Grady grinned, despite the subject. "She'd lost someone she loved."

"Just a kid, that one. Plenty of other fish in the sea, and all. She'd only been with the guy a couple of years. How well could she have even known him?"

That wasn't a fight Grady was willing to pick, so he gently redirected. "Long enough to care that he was gone, but there's nothing I can do about that—except find whoever killed him. I know the official word was that it must be a carjacking gone bad, however . . ."

"However"—Whiteside picked up the thread—"there were a

dozen little things that didn't fit the scenario. Why was the guy in the back of his car? What was with the woman they found downstream? At first, I thought there was no way the cases were connected. Grim coincidence, that's all it was—finding two bodies in the water, a week apart, in different places. We'd found her car a couple of miles away; it looked like she'd had a minor wreck and got out to go look for help. Then ballistics came back, and I had to throw the coincidence out the window. Even if they didn't know each other, even if they never met, alive or dead, the same gun definitely killed them both."

"Yeah, I'm having that same problem," Grady admitted.

The old detective sank deeper into his easy chair. A second and third dog leaped into his lap, joining the one he still held in the crook of his arm like a loaf of bread. "There was no evidence that the two ever so much as shared a bus. All I could figure is that the intended victim was one of them—and the other got caught up in the murder by accident."

"Wrong place, wrong time?"

"A bad case of it, for sure."

"But the question is . . . which one?"

Whiteside's big round head bobbed up and down. The ambient light flashed off the top of his crown, which was quite bald and rather shiny. His remaining hair, still cropped close in traditional cop style, was mostly white with streaks of the same yellow as an old nicotine stain. "I went back and forth on that. Some days, I was sure it was the guy. Others, I was sure it was the girl."

"Did anything leave you leaning one way or another?"

Thoughtfully, he said, "If you held a gun to my head and forced me to pick, I'd say that the girl was the original target. She was young and reasonably attractive, if you don't mind them a little thick. She'd had trouble with a boyfriend, once upon a time, but he didn't pan out."

"Right, he was in Afghanistan, wasn't he?"

"Uh-huh. His CO confirmed that he was deployed a few thousand miles away when she died, so we could safely cross his ass off the suspect list. But if she had a problem with one guy, she might've had a problem with another one, that's my thinking. She might not have even known it, or known the full extent of it. Some of those creepers hide it real well, right up until they don't—and things go south."

"So all things being equal, you think it's more likely that Amanda had somebody out to get her."

"Neither victim had any known, current problem people in their lives. It was either someone with a very quiet grudge, or a totally random act of violence that caught up two strangers and a 2007 Toyota Corolla."

"Anything ever turn up at work? For either one of them?"

"Nah. Sandoval was a bottom-rung Amazon employee, ticking boxes and pulling levers, and everyone seemed to like him. The worst thing a coworker had to say about him was that he was too earnest and too quick to take on extra tasks."

"Made other employees at the same level look bad?"

"Not *that* bad. Nobody was on the verge of getting fired, and he wasn't up for any promotions in competition with anyone else. I know, because I checked. And as for Crombie, she was fresh off her master's degree in accounting. She'd only been working at her job for a few months, and everyone seemed to think she was great at it. Her boss said she was the best damn accountant he'd ever had."

"Hmm," said Grady. "Sometimes accountants find things they aren't meant to, especially if they're extra good at their jobs."

"Yeah, but I wouldn't chase that angle too hard. The company folded, like I said. I talked to her old boss again after that, it was a guy . . . what was his name . . . Elliot something."

It was Craig Elliot, but Grady didn't want to contradict him while he was on a roll. "I'll look him up when I get back to town."

"Don't bother. He was on a cruise ship in Alaska when it all went down. Left a few days before the murders happened and didn't get back until after both bodies were found."

"That's awfully convenient."

"I thought so, too—but the trip had been booked for months. If he orchestrated the killings, he must've cheaped out and hired some inexperienced nobody, because that was *not* a professional hit job. The girl was shot—what? Three or four times? Twice in the back, as she was presumably running away? And the guy, he just took the one bad hit, right in the gut. Bled out in the car, but it took some time."

Grady leaned back in his own seat and exhaled heavily—which apparently sounded like an invitation to one of the remaining dogs. A small black-and-tan girl in a pink collar with a bow put her feet up on his shin and gave him the big-eyed dog stare of *Please pick me up so I can sit on you.*

He obliged, gently lifting her up to his lap.

"That's Smidget," Whiteside told him. "She's a lover, but don't pet her ass. She doesn't like that, and she'll nip your fingers."

"Good to know," Grady said, sticking to ear scratches until she turned three circles and settled down atop his knees.

"She's a sweetheart, though." When the dogs who occupied Whiteside's own chair gave him concerned looks, he patted them all in turn. "They're all sweethearts; that's a fact. Daddy's sweet little assholes."

Grady murmured in polite agreement. Then he said, "Let me ask you something: What do *you* think happened? Nothing you can prove, nothing you even have any good evidence for . . . I'm asking for any hunch that you never did shake, or any theory that you wanted to stick to but you couldn't nail down enough proof."

Whiteside pondered this while he rubbed the head of the near-est pointy-nosed dog. "Well, first of all—I think it was definitely Crombie on the gas station surveillance video. The resolution was garbage, and the IT guys would never confirm it one way or an-other, but she fit the bill and her clothes matched up about right. I think she was hanging around, looking for help—and I think Sandoval tried to give it to her. She might've approached him as he was about to drive away, or even hitchhiked from the edge of the road as he was leaving. He left the pump alone, but his car went out of frame as soon as he'd moved away from the fill-up island."

"But it was probably her."

"I'd swear it on a Bible. She was running from somebody, and she saw this nice young man—clean-cut, friendly face, and prone to offering assistance, according to his parents. I think she was running, and whoever was chasing her figured he had to kill them both. Maybe Sandoval got a good look at him or tried to fight him off."

"A scuffle would make sense. He was shot at close range, maybe even point-blank. He'd been in the water too long to find any gunpowder residue, but the coroner said the gun hadn't been more than a couple of feet away when it went off."

"See, there you go. Knight in shining armor gets murdered for his efforts. Tale as old as time."

"It works, but there are still a lot of holes to plug."

"Yeah, and that's the problem, ain't it? If I could've plugged those holes, the case would be shut by now. The only other thing I can think of . . ." Whiteside said slowly, chewing on the words, considering every one. "Her purse turned up almost a month later. A couple of kids found it tangled up in some plastic roadwork netting and fished it out of the water."

"Her purse? I don't remember seeing anything about that."

"Like I said, it turned up well after the fact, and there was nothing in it that pointed to anything. We sent a couple of beat cops down to dredge the area, and all they ever found was an empty glasses case. Her vision was bad, and she usually wore contacts, but I guess she carried a pair for backup."

"I don't remember seeing anything about contacts in the coroner's report, but I might've just missed it." Grady added the last bit to himself.

"Well, I don't remember anymore. But even if the doc didn't find any, they might've washed out of her eyes or something. She was lying downstream from the pond, in the water runoff trench—and she'd been there almost a week. Absence of evidence is not evidence of absence."

"Again, you have a point. Still, good to know. Was there anything else in the purse?"

Whiteside shrugged. "Tampons and breath mints, stuff like that. She had a little key chain Mace thing, too. Pink, so you know it's for girls." He laughed to himself. "I don't remember what all else; I just remember that none of it was helpful. See if you can't get into the evidence locker and get a gander at it, though. It might tell you something it doesn't tell me."

On that note, Grady carefully put Smidget back down on the floor and offered his thanks, then said he'd take his leave.

Whiteside stayed put but shook his hand heartily, and cautiously—so as not to disturb the dog that was now snoring across his thighs. "You'll have to forgive me if I don't see you out. Good luck to you, though. I hate leaving a case open like that. If you can zip it up, more power to you."

"Thanks again, Jim. I'll let you know how it goes."

Back at the precinct, Grady went to his desk and pushed a small stack of paperwork aside, then removed a couple of new folders that had been left in his seat and sat down. There was always something, wasn't there? He was falling behind, but he was used to that. Before she'd retired, the previous police captain had told him that coming to peace with playing catch-up was one of the most important skills a career detective could learn.

"Every day," she'd told him, "you have to decide how to fail, and make the best of it." At the time, he'd found it cynical. Now he honestly found it helpful—if for no other reason than he knew it was normal and he knew he wasn't alone.

Every day, something was going to fall through the cracks, run late, or be wrong. If he paid enough attention, he could come back and deal with most of it later. Collect the crumbs. Run a little faster. Correct the inaccuracies. Bat cleanup.

But some days, he only had the bandwidth to do so much and try so hard.

Grady looked up at the desk that faced his own. His partner, Sam Wilco, had been out for the last couple of days with the flu.

"When Sam gets back . . ." he said under his breath, "I'll have some help again."

"Getting a little snowed under?" asked Lieutenant Le from the next desk over.

"Par for the course, right?"

"Always." Her phone rang, and she took the call before her vibrating cell could shuffle off and fall on the floor.

Grady glanced at his phone and saw a message from Molly. She was grabbing pizza with a friend after school, then heading to a short shift at Starbucks. Someone had called in, and she wanted the hours.

"Will wonders never cease?" he mumbled. If nothing else, it meant he didn't need to make dinner that night. He could grab a sandwich on the way home.

For a guy who worked in a large building surrounded by people, Grady Merritt felt weirdly alone. His partner was out of the office, his daughter wouldn't be back home until bedtime, and his conversation with Jim Whiteside had left him feeling oddly unsettled. It had unnerved him, seeing what living alone could do to a man. He could wind up in a split level, surrounded by tiny, yippy dogs who were constantly trying to tunnel out to freedom like fuzzy little prisoners of war. If it'd happened to Jim after his wife had died, it could happen to anybody.

Even Grady. Maybe even *inevitably* Grady, when Molly moves out.

Grady sighed down at his desk. He wouldn't let it come to that. No yippy dogs, just Cairo—who yipped once in a while but mostly just barked at delivery people and cried for treats. That wasn't as sad as an army of dachshunds, was it?

He popped his laptop open.

It took him a couple of minutes, but he finally found an address for Abbot Keyes, the low-level consultant Beckmeyer mentioned who'd worked for Christopher Gilman. Technically, the case was still open. Technically, he was doing his job.

"Everybody knows 'technically' is the best kind of correct."

# 14.

Leda and Niki sat on the curb in front of the travel agency office, where Leda had just sent forth several rounds of advertising through all her favorite social media sites—and one fairly extensive post on Craigslist, just to cover her bases. For the sake of the business, she'd also created a Twitter account (though she was still waiting on her fancy-pants blue check mark of officialness), a Facebook page, and an Instagram account where she posted pictures that her most recent clients had sent her from their cruise. So far. There would be more pictures to come, she was sure of it.

The ladies rose to their feet when Grady Merritt's car crawled around the corner and stopped in front of them.

"Shotgun!" shouted Niki.

Leda tried to hip-check her friend out of the way, but she wasn't fast enough. "No fair!"

"You know the rules. Tallest person gets shotgun."

"You're barely an inch taller, and most of that's because of the plastic boot."

"Devil's in the details," Niki declared, popping the latch and throwing herself inside. "Hey there, Detective!"

He looked at her with muted surprise. "Hey there . . . Nicole. So you're coming along, too?"

"It's Niki. You said it was okay."

"I did?"

"Back when you first came to the travel agency, that one time. I'm pretty sure." She found the seat belt and buckled herself in, just as Leda was scooting into the back seat.

Looking over his shoulder, he said, "Hey, Leda. You didn't mention—"

"I know, but you said it was okay."

"I guess I . . . did?" He gave in, since possession was nine-tenths of the law and now these two women each possessed a seat inside his car. When Leda's seat belt was fastened, he sighed, looked forward, and took the wheel with both hands. "Okay, then. So it's a party. I hope he doesn't mind."

"Who are we visiting again?" Niki asked.

Leda leaned forward as far as she could, so she hovered over the gear shift, right between their heads. "Abbot Keyes. Supposedly, he got into a fight with one of the murder victims a couple of days before all the killing. Right?" she asked Grady.

"Right. He's agreed to meet us at the university between classes. Well, he agreed to meet me and Leda." He shot one more look at Niki. "I'm sure it'll be fine, though."

"Obviously it'll be fine. Tell him I'm a detective-in-training or something."

"I'm not going to tell him that. I'll think of something else. How's your foot?"

"Healing by the day!" Niki declared brightly, wiggling it around on the floor—where it rattled and thumped.

Leda said, right into the side of Grady's face, "Tell him she's a forensic accountant. Or a roving lab tech. Or a crime scene investigator!"

He pulled out into the flow of traffic and didn't look at either one of them. "I'm not going to tell him that. For one thing, we're not visiting a crime scene. For another, roving lab tech? That's not a job."

"I could be a pirate?"

"Maybe stop talking," he suggested. "I'll think of something when we get there."

"Why are we going to the university?" Leda asked.

Somewhat wearily, he said, "Because that's where Abbot Keyes is."

"Why?" asked Niki. "Is he a student there?"

"Yes. He's working on a computer science degree when he's not roaming King County as an Uber driver."

Leda sat back. "So I guess the consulting gig didn't shake out?"

"Digital Scaffolding folded after Christopher and Kevin died," Grady informed them. "Either Keyes couldn't land another consulting gig, or he simply chose not to. You can ask him when we meet him. Wait—on second thought, no. Neither one of you should ask him anything. *I* will do all the talking."

"*You* will do all the talking," Leda and Niki said in unison.

Grady frowned, but he was too far along in these shenanigans to bail now. "I do the talking," he repeated. "And if this gets ugly, or heated, or anything like that, this is the first and last time you two get to do a ride-along. Got it?"

"Got it," they said in sync, though they sounded a bit deflated.

It was late enough in the morning that rush hour was over, but the trip to the U District still took half an hour. They made it onto campus and parked behind the University Book Store—where Abbot had promised he'd meet them in the café area downstairs. True to his word, he was there waiting when the trio came in.

"That's him," Grady said under his breath to Leda, his eyes flashing to a white man in his early thirties with tragic dark emo hair and a waistcoat with a pocket watch that said he visited the nineteenth century in his downtime, for funsies.

Leda tried very hard not to squeal with excitement when she whispered, "The Victorian orphan!"

Grady checked her gently with his shoulder. "Yeah, I know—but keep it to yourself." He took the lead and approached the seated fellow at his table.

Abbot popped a pair of earbuds free, looping the skinny cords around his palm until he could stuff them into his pocket. "Detective Merritt?" he asked, rising to shake hands. "It's been a while."

"Good to see you again," Grady said with a smile. "And thanks so much for taking a few minutes to talk with me. With us."

Leda and Niki loomed behind him, grinning like maniacs.

"Us?"

"Yes, I'm sorry about the surprise third . . . fourth wheel," Grady said as he pulled up a chair and urged his companions to do likewise. There were just enough loose seats to accommodate them all around the small table against the wall. "This is my associate Leda Foley, and this is Nicole Nelson—she's . . . a forensic accounting student at Pacific Lutheran. She got assigned to us as a ride-along for class at the last minute, you know how it goes."

"Sure . . ." Abbot said, without sounding sure at all. But he mustered a social smile and said, "It's nice to meet you all. This is something about the Gilmans, right?"

"Correct," Grady said. "Some new evidence has come up, and we're making the rounds again—talking to people who worked with them, trying to take another look at the big picture surrounding their deaths."

"Right, right. Well, whatever I can do to be of help."

"We *do* appreciate your cooperation," Leda said benevolently, and Niki kicked her under the table with her booted foot. Leda was careful not to look at Grady and whatever side-eye he was flashing her. She only smiled bigger.

Grady worked around her. "I have your statements from the last go-round, so I don't want to make you rehash too much of the same old information."

"I mean, there's not very much to rehash, you know?"

Abbot looked confused and a little anxious when he fiddled with his mug of coffee. Was it coffee? On second glance, Leda thought maybe it was chai. Either that, or he'd really loaded up on the creamer.

"I didn't work for Gilman very long, and I wasn't around when he died, either."

"I know, but I wanted to talk about that fight the two of you had, just..." Grady flipped open his notebook and glanced at whatever was written there. "Six days before the murders. We're taking a broad look at Digital Scaffolding, getting a little more in-depth with regards to the company's dealings. We're starting to wonder if Christopher and Kevin weren't killed over some shady business dealings. Maybe they screwed over the wrong person, or people. Maybe they were making bad deals that hurt someone, or maybe they were taking money from investors."

Keyes shot a glance at Niki. "That's what the forensic accountant's for?"

Grady said, "What?" then caught himself quickly. "Oh, yeah, right. Yes, we're exploring all possible avenues here."

Leda leaned forward and asked, "So why don't you tell us about that fight you two had, shortly before Gilman died?"

"It wasn't, like, a knockdown, drag-out thing. Nobody threw any punches, if that's what you're asking."

Grady jumped in. "But someone *did* throw a paperweight through a window."

"Ah. Well, that's true. That was me," Keyes admitted. "I was pretty pissed off. I wasn't trying to hurt anyone; I was just mad, and it was stupid. I felt stupid about it then, and I feel stupid about it now."

"At the time, you said the fight was over a bunch of credit card reimbursements that never happened."

"That's right. I didn't love being treated like an errand boy, but that was part of the job, and I did whatever Chris asked me to. But I'd run up all these toll charges, and gas charges, and all that stuff. The guy refused to reimburse me, even when I gave him all my receipts. It was only a few hundred bucks, but come on, you know? It's not like I was making big money over there, at an entry-level gig in a start-up."

Leda nodded. "Oh, no kidding. I had a gig like that, and it sucked. Who the hell can live on twenty-two grand a year in Seattle? I mean, come on." Then to Grady, she added, "There weren't even any benefits."

"Bad benefits, bad money, bad everything, got it," Grady said with a note of finality that suggested everyone except for him and the interviewee needed to back out of the conversation, right freaking now. "But is that all you did there, at Digital Scaffolding? Coffee and dry cleaning?"

"Sometimes I rotated PDFs. Once, I helped Mrs. Gilman scrape ice off her car windows with my ORCA card."

Niki laughed. "Sounds like a thrill a minute."

"Yeah, it wasn't the kind of job that I mourned a whole lot, once it was over."

Grady jotted something down that Leda didn't see. "And do

you know of anyone else who may have had any difficulties with the work environment? When I asked around last time, there was not a lot of love lost between Christopher Gilman and literally anybody he knew or worked with—which made it tricky to narrow down suspects. But everyone really liked Kevin, and no one can figure out how he got wrapped up in his father's mess."

"Kevin was all right—I didn't have any problem with him." Keyes agreed. "Nobody did, as far as I know. I assumed that he got caught up in something with his dad, or he showed up at just the wrong time. I don't think anybody really thought Kevin had anything to do with what happened, but anything's possible, right?"

Leda let out a laugh that sounded more like a snort. "Anything is *definitely* possible."

"We've looked into Kevin pretty extensively, and I think we've more or less ruled him out as the intended target. He was on the board of two charities, with an ex-wife who sang his praises and a dog-rescue group that started an adoption grant in his honor. The guy was practically a saint." Grady leaned back in his chair and folded his arms. Somehow, he looked both relaxed and accusatory.

Abbot Keyes felt it, too. He clutched his mug again and gazed down into its depths. "You know what's funny? I'd talked to Kevin about using him for a reference. I was already planning to leave when he and his dad died. I only stayed on as long as I did because . . . God, it sounds terrible to say out loud, but here you go: I stayed at Digital Scaffolding because Chris was gone. He was such a bully, I hated having him for a boss. His wife took over after the funeral—but mostly she was doing the work of shutting the company down. I don't think it made much money, and it was never her baby. She didn't want to run it, and she had money of her own."

"Speaking of Janette Gilman—any thoughts on her? You think she had something to do with it?" Grady asked.

"I mean . . . ?" Keyes replied, a slow shrug joining the senti-
ment. "She seemed like a nice lady, but I didn't know her well. I
didn't know her at all until after Chris died; I'd only seen her once
or twice in passing. After that, she came into the office a couple
of days a week—sorting out paperwork, making phone calls, I
don't know. She worked out of Chris's office. Within three or four
months, I think, she'd cleaned house and shut the doors. But by
then I'd quit to go work as a freelance writer."

"You don't do that anymore?" Leda asked.

"No. It's really hard. Even when you know people at Amazon
or have contacts at some of the consulting firms, there's all these
weird rules for tech writing when you work for big digital market-
places, and it's hard to make anybody happy, ever. I gave up on that
pretty quick."

Grady asked, "Then you went to work for Uber?"

"No, then I went to work for Starbucks. Don't laugh," Keyes
said hastily, even though no one had done so. "The hours are okay,
and the benefits are pretty good. But it was really hectic, and I had
a hard time keeping up."

"*Then* you went to Uber?"

"Yeah, then I went to Uber. It's better, kind of. I don't have
to answer to anybody, and that's something. I want to go into IT,
though. That's why I'm back here at the university, taking computer science classes. It sounds perfect—you get an office to yourself, and you help baby boomers reset their internet passwords.
Stuff like that," he said dreamily.

"That can't *possibly* require a degree," Leda said.

He shrugged again. "Sometimes IT jobs require the degrees
just to get an interview. Companies put it in the job listings, even
if you never need to know Java, or C++, or anything like that in
order to do the job. Everybody needs a job, and employers around
here get picky. You can't just apply for whatever strikes your fancy,

like, 'Hey, I'm Abbot—and I know how to do what you need done. Hire me!'"

Leda's eyes went wide, and she went stiff. She stopped breathing for a few seconds.

Grady agreed. "Nah, I hear ya. It's a competitive world. Hey . . . hey, Leda, you all right?" He nudged her with the side of his arm.

She was fine. She was just distracted. A vivid white light was creeping into the edge of her vision.

Niki put her hand on Leda's wrist. "You okay, babe?"

"I'm fine!" she said, too loudly. Everyone in the café area turned to look at her, and she cringed.

"Sorry . . ." she said more quietly. "Sorry, everyone. But yes," she added to Grady and Niki. "I'm all right. I, um . . . I thought I was about to sneeze."

"A *useful* kind of sneeze?" Niki leaned in.

Grady leaned in, too. "A *regular* sneeze, I'm sure." He took one last look at his notes, slapped the book shut, and tucked it into his pocket. He folded his hands on the table. "Now, once more, for the record, where were you again when the murders were committed?"

"My stepbrother was killed in a car wreck a few days before. I was at his funeral in Tacoma."

"I realize it's been a while, but I'm sorry for your loss. And, Mr. Keyes, I want to thank you again for your time. I know you don't have to meet us like this, and you've been a big help."

"I have?"

Grady eyed Leda with concern.

"From the standpoint of updating our records, absolutely. You've been a big help, and . . . and . . ."

Leda was already standing up, and Niki was right behind her—pushing her chair back with the plastic-booted foot she was dragging around behind herself.

"Thank you," he finished awkwardly. With a brief handshake,

he followed the women back out of the bookstore and into the parking lot.

By the time he caught up to them, Leda was doubled over—catching her breath. Her head was throbbing and there was a weird yellow halo around her vision that was so bright she could hardly see out of one eye.

"Hey, hey, Leda," he said. "Look at me."

"I can't. It's too hard." She squinted in his general direction, trying to make out the shape of his face.

"What happened in there? Did you get a flash? Did it tell you anything good? Do you think he's our guy? Are . . . are you going to be okay?"

"I think I'm having an ocular migraine," she said. "Let me sit down a second."

"What's an ocular migraine?" he asked.

"It's . . . it's a migraine that doesn't hurt, most of the time, but it . . . it's like all this *light*, and all these sparkles, man."

Niki helped her drop herself onto a concrete parking space header, where Leda sat with her knees almost up against her boobs. The header wasn't any more than ten inches high. She felt like a kindergartner.

Niki finished the rest. "Some people think that Joan of Arc had them. Like, when she thought she was looking at God, she was looking at a neural irregularity that created a light show behind her eyes. It's no big deal, usually."

"Do you often get those, when you have flashes of the psychic variety?"

"Sometimes," Leda told him. "But it's just as likely to be unrelated. I'm fine, it's really fine. It's not like I drove here. I don't need to see that well, not right this second."

"Well, thank God for that, right? But *did* you see anything?"

"Nope, just a light show." She squinted and rubbed her eyes

with the back of her hands, never mind the mascara smudge. "I'm really sorry about that. I wish I had something more useful to tell you, but that's all I've got: a real bright light behind my eyes, and ooh . . . it's starting to sparkle."

When everyone was confident that Leda was not going to fall over or pass out, they all piled back into Grady Merritt's car and headed back south, into the city.

# 15.

Leda Foley hadn't called shotgun this time, but by playing up her vision difficulties, she'd slipped into the preferred position without Niki even noticing—or at least, without Niki saying anything until they were back on the interstate.

"I *let* you have the front seat, you know," she informed Leda. "Just because I felt sorry for you and your garbage gimp-vision headaches."

"Is that supposed to make me feel bad? Because I'll take your pity shotgun and smile about it all afternoon."

Grady smirked. "You seem to be feeling better."

She rubbed at her left eye and closed them both, trying to ignore the last rings of light that spun around her vision. "Indeed I am. And that Keyes guy, he's pretty weird, right?"

He asked, "Is that your psychic sense talking, or your sense of drama?"

She shrugged. "I don't even know, anymore. He's weird, and I got a flash of light, and that's it."

"Plenty of people are weird as hell, but they never murder anybody. Besides, he wasn't *that* weird. At worst, he was kind of . . . I don't know. Pathetic. Leave the guy alone for now and save your psychic senses for the widow. We're talking to her on Thursday."

"We are?" Niki chirped.

"We . . . okay, fine. We *all* are, sure. She didn't care when I told her I'd have a consultant with me, so what's yet another consultant, right?"

Niki sat back in the seat and looked very smug. Leda could see it from the rearview mirror.

"Goddamn right," Niki said.

"But you have to swear to me, on your own graves, that you'll be quiet. That was *way* too much interrupting back there—*way* too much audience participation. That's not what we need—not what we want—and there's a chance you could screw up the case. Keep your thoughts to yourselves, please? Can you do that for me?"

"Yes, sir," they both said.

"Because if you don't, then we can't keep doing this. If you guys botch a case, we're all finished here, got it?"

Synchronized again, they said, "Got it."


After Grady dropped them off at the travel agency office, Leda and Niki went inside for the rest of the afternoon. Niki didn't have to be at work, and Leda was in a productive mood.

"Why waste it, right?" Leda dropped herself into the office chair, only indulged a single round of spinning with her feet up off the floor, and then checked her email. As soon as it loaded, she started to squeal.

"Oh my God, are you dying?"

"No, I'm succeeding!" She swiveled the monitor around. "Look, two new queries about travel arrangements! Just like that!"

"All it took was money and advertising."

"That's all anything takes, as far as I can tell." Leda reclaimed the monitor and whipped up a couple of crisp, professional emails in response, with rates and details as requested.

Niki reclined, bringing her booted foot up to the love seat's arm and letting it rest there. "Before long, you're going to need a bigger office."

"Your lips to God's ears."

"Who says that? And where?"

Leda was only half paying attention when she replied, "Somebody, someplace." She was looking at her stats for the Facebook ad, and deciding whether to spend more money to boost the signal even further. Then she pulled up her bank account and decided to try again later. Money was running too low for risky measures.

"I know that look," Niki said.

"What look?"

"The look of worry. What's wrong?"

She hemmed. She hawed. "Nothing's wrong. Usual stuff. Costs of doing business. Growing pains, budgeting concerns, et cetera."

"You're broke."

"No, not yet," she insisted. "My overhead is low, my equipment is all tax-deductible, and I don't have any employees to pay. Also, I am very fond of ramen noodles. I live cheap, Nik. I can do business cheap, too. I don't actually need *that* many clients to stay afloat."

"If you say so, girl. How close are you to meeting rent on this place, this month?"

"Super close. If either one of these two new emails pans out, then I'll have it covered," she said with confidence.

"You say that like you don't suck at math."

"I don't suck as much as you do. I've been careful. Just trust me."

Niki smiled and stared at the ceiling. "I always trust you. But I always worry about you, too." Then she shifted gears. "Hey, did you mean what you told Grady? That you were just having a perfectly normal migraine?"

"Sure, I meant it. I wish I had more for him. Maybe I should've touched Keyes. Or even his coffee cup, or . . . I don't know. I don't have a lot of control over this. I never have."

"Didn't you shake his hand?" Niki asked.

"No, I forgot."

"But still, you're getting better! I know you are. I've seen it in action myself."

Ordinarily, Leda agreed with almost anything that came out of Niki's mouth, but this time, she balked. "Am I, though? Serious question. I know we were talking about all the practice I'm getting at Castaways, but what if it's just a fluke? Keeping Grady off that plane, flashing on those objects in the hotel room . . . those were pretty high-powered events for me. What if I'm still just an inconsequential psychic, and I'm merely lucky enough to have the occasional breakthrough that's useful to somebody?"

Niki sat up again—leaving her bum leg elevated but putting her other one on the floor so she sprawled obscenely. "Okay, *first* of all, I don't think that's true. I've known you almost forever, and I've watched you learn and grow with this. If you ask me, your skills are definitely on an upward trajectory. And second, even if it *were* true—so what? It's still a gift that practically nobody on earth has, in real life. Who cares if it's a little janky?"

"Um, the people who rely on it, that's who."

"News flash, babe: Detective Merritt is not relying on you. He's bringing you along just in case you have some supernatural flash of insight. He's not actually counting on you doing so. He's a cop. A *real* cop. He's gotten this far in his career without a psychic sidekick, and he'll be fine without one in the future, too."

Leda groaned and kicked her spinny chair away from the desk. "Oh God, you're right. I'm useless."

"Nobody said that! Jesus, woman. I'm only saying you're not the lynchpin in these proceedings. If you fail to produce any psychic insights, or if you screw up wildly . . . it doesn't actually matter very much. This guy's using you as a Hail Mary, on the off chance you can help him solve a tricky old case. Don't give yourself too much credit; but also, don't underestimate yourself."

"That's, I mean, I guess it's decent advice."

"It's excellent advice, because I'm brilliant. And you trust me, I know you do. So listen to me. Believe the Nik. The Nik has your best interest at heart, and she believes in you."

"The Nik? That's what you're calling yourself now?"

She nodded. "I kind of enjoy having an article before my name."

"I'm not going to call you 'the Nik.'"

"No, of course not. You'll *refer* to me as the Nik when discussing me with others. You'll still *call* me whatever you want."

Leda dragged her chair by her tippy-toes, pulling it back up to the desk. "I always have, and I always will." She took hold of her mouse and called up a web browser.

"What are you doing?"

"Nothing psychic, don't worry. I'm googling."

"Who?"

"Everybody," Leda informed her, fingers clicking away on the keyboard.

One of the only skills Leda ever crowed about was her superlative typing speed. She could also type one thing while reading another. Niki always said it was spooky, but Leda shrugged it off. It was an ordinary talent, that's what she'd say.

"Starting with . . . ?"

"Beckmeyer. The silver fox."

Leda learned virtually nothing about him, except that he was a semiretired dilettante with money who liked to hop between gigs for giggles. Then she tried Janette Gilman and learned only that she'd recently gone to Italy to see her grandmother—if her Instagram could be believed—so to hell with her. "I don't like her," she declared.

"Why? Because she went out of town and didn't consult you first?"

"Yes. No. Because when it comes to murder, it's almost always the spouse, that's why."

"You haven't even met this woman yet."

"We're gonna meet her soon, and I want to be prepared," said Leda. "Ooh, she was married once before."

"So?"

"So . . ." Leda typed rapidly, scanning a couple of links before settling in to read. It took only half a minute. "So . . . never mind. Her first husband died of natural causes, a couple of years after they divorced. Looks like she's not a black widow."

"If she's any good at being a black widow, you won't find any evidence of it on the internet."

"All knowledge is contained within the internet!" Leda protested. "Even if it's found in rumors on Reddit, or wherever."

"Okay, are you finding any rumors about either one of them on Reddit?"

"No," she sulked. "Nothing I didn't already know or couldn't guess. Janette and her first husband were pretty rich, they traveled together a lot, and they sold the house when they split up. Looks like she married Christopher Gilman fairly soon thereafter; they were probably carrying on behind her husband's back. Ooh . . . slutty. I like it. Rich people have the most *interesting* lives."

"You don't actually know that, you conclusion-jumping maniac. Google somebody else. Try the Victorian orphan. That Abbot Keyes guy."

Leda nodded at the screen. "Good call."

She clicked around for a couple of minutes without saying anything.

Niki asked, "Well?"

"He's got a Facebook page, all locked down, so I can't see anything but his picture—but that's him. I can't tell if he ever posts to it, but a single grainy profile photo suggests that it's not much of a priority. He had a Twitter account, but it was deleted a few months ago, if the Google cache can be believed. Maybe he's just not into social media much. Oh well, that was a bust." Leda leaned back in her chair and lifted her feet so it would do a slow, thoughtful spin. After a few rotations, she concluded, "Hey, you know what? I don't want to do Castaways tonight."

Niki gasped. "Are you . . . are you feeling okay? Do I need to hobble over there and take your temperature?"

"I'm fine, I promise. I'm just . . . weirdly tired. It's probably because of the migraine. If you want to go see Matt, then go for it. I'll be fine by myself with Brutus for the evening. I think I'm going to go home and watch TV and drink the last of the pink wine that's still sitting in the fridge from the other day."

"You haven't finished it by now? Okay, now I *know* you're ill."

Leda shook her head. "Nah. Don't worry about me. I need a night to myself, that's all. I've been so *sociable* lately. Go on. Get outta here. Go snog Matt and tell everybody at the bar that I love them, would you?"

Eventually Leda talked Niki into leaving. It wasn't easy, and she didn't leave without a whole host of suspicions, but she left.

After she was gone, Leda did not go home.

When she was certain that Niki wasn't watching the door, she collected her purse. She locked the office and took too long to remember where she'd parked Jason. She wiped the chalk off his tire with her foot; it was after-hours in Columbia City, but the parking enforcement officers had been on the prowl earlier in the day—tootling around in their miniature popemobiles, doling out tickets. They wandered the blocks with a long stick that had a piece of chalk on it, swiping tires and keeping track of who parked where, and for how long.

"Screw 'em," she muttered. She threw her purse on the passenger seat and pulled out onto the main drag. She should have left the car at home that morning, really. She lived within walking distance of her little office, but sometimes she just didn't feel like making the hike.

Her true destination lay farther north, only a few feet from the interstate.

She parked underneath an on-ramp, where it was safe to do so in two-hour stints—as long as she dodged the puddles of urine and the rats who were the first on-site. The rats had seniority, unless the crows and seagulls did.

Overhead, cars zoomed. All around, vehicles idled.

It wasn't so far past rush hour that everybody wasn't trying to leave downtown, so the small roads that crisscrossed under I-5 were packed and people were honking, swearing, and demanding that Siri give them alternate routes—for all the good that would do.

Leda let herself inside the former Tully's roasting facility, a giant nineteenth-century building that the interstate bowed around. Drivers overhead zipped past so closely that they could look in the windows and see office space, hallways, and doors. Nobody roasted any coffee there anymore, but some of the old space had been set aside for lofts, in case anybody wanted to try to sleep eight yards from eight lanes of traffic.

But a large portion of the facility had been converted to self-storage units, and that's where Leda was headed.

Up too many stairs and around a few corners, she found the orange door she was looking for. She unlocked it and went inside, turning on the light and shutting the door.

"Forgot about that," she said to herself, regarding the opened can of soda she'd left sitting on a small end table beside a vintage rocking chair. She sat down in that chair and used her tippy-toes to lean the rocker back and forth. At least it was diet.

And thank God for that, or there would have been ants.

Beside the flat, warm soda was an old radio that still worked. Leda tuned it to KEXP in case there was any good indie rock left in the world. She shoved a few boxes of her own stored items aside and picked up the nearest box of Tod's personal effects. She tried not to notice how they didn't smell like him anymore. Not when she sniffed them deeply, not when she held them up to her face, and not when she used them to dry a few tears.

Not at all.

# 16.

Thursday afternoon, Leda Foley and Niki Nelson met their new detective friend not far from Castaways—in a bar that used to be a mortuary and now had barstools pulled up to the nooks and crannies where cremated remains once were housed. For the umpteenth time, Leda groused, "I don't understand why this bar isn't *gothier*. It feels like it should have black curtains, silver crosses, and more candles."

Grady shrugged. "I see plenty of candles."

"They're tea lights!" she argued. "And there's all these cutesy little martinis with cutesy little stirring sticks and umbrellas, and weird chunks of fruit on skewers."

Niki leaned forward, to talk around Leda's head. "She does this literally every damn time we even walk past this place." Then, imitating her friend's voice, she said, "I want to see vampires! Ghosts! Bats! I want to fear for my life every time I order a drink!"

"I never said that."

"Sure you did. More than once. So where is this woman?" Niki asked. "I thought she was meeting us here."

"She is." The detective glanced at his phone, sitting on the small, round table between them all. "She'll be here any minute. She works out of an office a block away."

"I thought she was rich? Why does she still go to work?" Niki's eyes scanned the scene below, where there weren't many customers yet. The floors were stone, and the ceilings were high. Every click of a woman's heels, every drop of a plate, clink of silverware, shake of a martini in progress, and friendly toast bounced off every surface.

"I don't know that she's rich," Grady said. "There's money, and then there's *money*. Maybe she doesn't have enough money to stay rich if she doesn't work. Or maybe she just likes having a job. Some people get bored, left to their own devices."

Leda asked, "What does she do?"

"She's a financial consultant with a big firm, but I think she only has a few clients. Big-name ones."

"Money," Leda said, nodding to herself. "Must be nice."

Over the echoes of early happy hour, all three heard the distinctive sound of hard-heeled footsteps on stairs. They collectively swiveled their heads, and soon there appeared a tall, attractive white woman in her fifties. Janette Gilman wore a gray lady-suit with a midi skirt and heels that were just a hair too high to call sensible. Her hair was auburn—a very good, expensive dye job in Leda's estimation. She'd been hiding her own baby grays with a box from Walgreens for years. It probably showed, but she didn't care too much and didn't have too much to hide.

Grady stood, like a proper goddamn gentleman, and then Leda hastily did likewise in order to participate in the round of handshakes that opened the conversation. Janette Gilman's hands were soft of skin, smooth of grip, and nicely manicured. But they didn't trigger any interesting insights.

"Oh, no," Janette said to Niki—who was still trying to stand, with the plastic boot stuck beneath the table. "Please, stay there. I don't want to make any trouble for you." She shook her hand, then claimed the last free seat at the table and crossed her legs tidily at the shins.

Janette told them, "Before I came upstairs, I put in an order for a pitcher of sangria, fully expecting to share. I hope you won't make me drink it all alone. I could, but what's the fun in that?"

Brightly, Leda declared, "I never say no to sangria!"

Niki smirked. "Or anything else with a detectable alcohol content."

"Excellent!" their guest said with a quick clap of her hands. "It'll be up here shortly, or so I've been assured. Now. What can I help you with today, Detective Merritt? It's been a while since I saw you last."

"More than a minute, ma'am. But these things take time, as I'm sure you understand."

She nodded and reclined prettily in the stylish seat. One arm stretched out along the back, one she left casually in her lap. "I know the wheels of justice may turn slowly, but sometimes I wonder if we'll ever know what happened to Kevin and Christopher."

Something about the way she phrased it stuck in Leda's head. Her stepson's name first, not her husband's. "Well," Leda said with more cheer than the subject required, "as you can see, we're still on the case!"

Grady gave her a look that could've rusted a bumper.

Janette Gilman smiled politely and said, "Now, what do you do again, dear? I caught your name and only that you were a consultant."

"I consult," Leda said simply. Somewhat desperately, she wanted to keep talking—to assure Ms. Gilman that she was a competent adult professional—but something about the withering look in

Grady's eye and the death grip Niki had on her thigh convinced her to restrain herself.

Quickly, Grady jumped in. "Ms. Foley is a victim's rights advocate," he offered smoothly. "She's also doing research on a graduate degree in criminology. We're trying to talk her into joining the force in something of a social work capacity. Ms. Nelson," he said, gesturing at Niki, "is a forensic accountant who we've recently added to the task force."

Leda gazed at him a little too adoringly, she suspected, but she'd always been a little too impressed with people who could lie on the fly. She aspired to be so effortless, so casual. In anything, really.

"That sounds *fascinating*," Janette Gilman said.

Then a server arrived at the top of the stairs, bearing a tray upon which was balanced a big pitcher of sangria and four glasses. Leda very much wanted to ask how she'd known to ask for the right number, but maybe the server had told her how many people were waiting upstairs. Or there was always the chance that four was the number of glasses everybody got.

When all the glasses were full, Grady reached one hand for his ever-present notebook, lying on the table beside a condensation-moistened coaster. He flipped the book open and scanned a page or two of wholly indecipherable handwriting. "I know we went over the case together a time or two, and in great depth, Ms. Gilman, but—"

"Copeland."

"I'm sorry?"

"Copeland," she said again. "I've returned to my maiden name. I wanted to put the past behind me."

Leda frowned. "You put the past behind you by going back to your original name? From all the way back in the past?"

Janette flipped her hand dismissively. "Oh, you know what I mean. I needed a fresh start. The Gilman name was never any good, to me or anyone else. If Christopher hadn't been murdered, we would've likely divorced within a year, and I would've gotten rid of the name then, at any rate."

"Really?" Niki asked. "I know a lot of divorcées, and not all of them ditch the married name."

Leda asked her friend, "Why is that, do you think?"

The older woman answered for her. "It's a great deal of paperwork, that's why. Also, some women have children, and they want the whole family to match. I don't have children, I don't mind paperwork, and I don't have much nostalgia regarding Christopher."

Grady asked, "What about Kevin?"

She hesitated, just a little. "I did like Kevin. He must have favored his mother, I don't know—she died when he was young. He really wasn't anything at all like Christopher. Such an upstanding young fellow. Always trying to do the right thing, be the right person, make the right call." She let out a small, rueful laugh. "I used to call him the Boy Scout, which he hated. But he was always too good-natured to bicker about it." She took a long drink, nearly emptying the glass. The bottommost cubes of ice tinkled together. "He was the closest thing to a son I ever had, even though I only knew him for a handful of years. I *am* truly sorry that he's gone. The world is a darker place for his loss."

Grady took over again. "Then you don't think Kevin was the target?"

She frowned. "Oh, are we back on that again? No, I don't think that—and I never have. I told you then, and I'll tell you now: Kevin wouldn't hurt a fly, and he didn't have any enemies. There's always a chance that he caught his father doing something untoward and made a stink in front of the wrong person. But whatever happened, you can rest assured that it was Christopher's fault."

Leda's hand tightened on her drink. Her eyelids fluttered, but otherwise, she did not move.

Niki noticed and gave her leg a gentle squeeze.

Grady didn't notice. He nodded down at his notebook. "You mentioned last year that you suspected Christopher was embroiled in illegal activities, but you were never terribly specific."

"I didn't say I suspected, I said that I'd bet my life on it—but I couldn't prove anything, and my suspicions were vague. The man was so crooked; literally nothing he was mixed up in would surprise me. Why do you ask? Have you turned up anything new?"

Behind Leda's eyes, fireworks were flashing. Weird, disjoined fireworks with only one word coming through clearly. She blurted it out. "Blackmail."

Everyone stared at her.

She said it again. "Blackmail." Then she added, "I'm sorry—I didn't mean to interrupt. But do you think he was involved in any blackmailing? Of anyone? In any way?"

Janette Gilman née Copeland leaned forward thoughtfully. She took the pitcher of sangria and topped off her own glass, using most of what was left. "It's funny you should say that. I know for a fact that he wasn't *above* blackmail. He blackmailed casually all the time—but you wouldn't necessarily call it that." She took a sip and held her glass close to her chest, rubbing her thumb up and down its length, smearing the condensation. "He liked to collect useful people who owed him favors, let's put it that way. I know he thought of it as leverage, really—and maybe that's all it was, most of the time. I'd say his idea of 'blackmail' was closer to other people's ideas of insider trading, except that he once . . . well, it's funny. It's definitely funny." The thoughtful look on her face suggested something less "funny" than "strange."

"Funny how?" Grady asked.

"I haven't thought of this in ages, and I don't think I mentioned it during your early investigations. Only a couple of months before Christopher was killed, he was feeling very pleased with himself about something, and I asked about it. Christopher being pleased with himself was *never* a good thing. He was never happy about anything that wasn't dirty or mean."

"He sounds like a real peach," Niki observed.

"He surely was. He could hide his true nature well, for periods of time. But it was like clenching a muscle, do you know what I mean? Even when he was in full masquerade mode—that's what I'd call it, when he was being pleasant and charming—the performance would sometimes slip. After a while, he'd have to quit pretending. Sometimes 'a while' was a few days or a few weeks. Sometimes it was even longer, but it was never perfect." To herself, she murmured, "No, it was never perfect."

Grady pressed on. "Was he blackmailing someone at the time of his death? Is that what you're telling me?"

"I guess so? I asked him what had put such a smile on his face, and he'd had enough to drink that he filled me in. He said he'd caught somebody at the company skimming. I was ready to raise hell about it," she amended quickly. "But he waved away any concerns of mine. Now he had leverage. He could get this person to do whatever he wanted, all he had to do was snap his fingers. That man, I swear. He treated the real world like his own personal RPG. Role-playing game, I mean. We used to play together. I don't have many fond memories of our time together, but that's one of them."

Grady leaned back, leaving his barely touched drink on the table. "That leaves us with a big question: Who was this skimmer?"

"Two questions," Leda piped up. "What did Christopher blackmail the skimmer into doing?"

The detective pointed his pen at her. "Good point. Two big questions. Can you help us with them, Ms. Copeland?"

"Not as much as I'd like to," she admitted. "I don't know who the employee was; I'm not even sure if it was a man or a woman. But he referred to them as 'kid' once or twice, so at the time, I thought it might be one of the underlings. But then I thought it might be Kim. I'd assumed he was sleeping with her, and that's why she was so fast to step and fetch at his command."

"Kim . . . Cowen." Grady found the name in his notebook. "His assistant."

"Assistant, sidepiece, whatever. Now, *she's* the one you really ought to talk to. She knew every little thing, about every little thing he did."

Leda nodded enthusiastically. "She's definitely on our list."

"Good, good. She can probably be of more help to you than I can."

Niki asked, "Really? You were the one who was married to him."

"Trust me, she saw more of him than I did. And in the end, that was fine with *me*." She finished more of her drink and eyed the empty pitcher. "God, my life would be so much easier right now if I'd just divorced him."

"Easier than him dying, and leaving everything to you?"

She laughed. It wasn't a happy laugh, or a pretty one. "Honey, he didn't leave anything to anyone. It turns out, the selfish dick didn't have a will. Every time I think I'm just about done with probate court, there's some new wrinkle, some new piece of paper they want . . . I don't know." She sounded tired of the whole thing. "It took a few months for me to close the company. It never really made any money, and I couldn't even sell it off for parts. Christopher had some money, but he also owed some taxes—so until that's sorted, I can't touch a dime of it. Thank God I have my own."

Leda opened her mouth to ask but hesitated.

Grady went ahead with the rude follow-up. It was less rude coming from a cop, that's what Leda figured. Better to let him do it. "Your own?"

"I got my money the old-fashioned way: I married it. My first husband was loaded, he was a cheater, and he died of a heart attack brought on by years of heavy smoking and drinking, combined with his habit of eating like Henry the Eighth. I loved him dearly; I really did. He broke my heart, and I left him shortly before he died. Of course, I took half of everything." She laughed again, that same grim note. "I met Christopher while I was in the middle of my divorce proceedings, and he charmed me senseless. At first. Within a year, I wondered if he'd only married me for my money. I couldn't decide if that was ironic or just plain sad."

"But you still have a job," Niki noted.

Leda glanced at Grady, but it looked like he'd given up on trying to keep either one of them quiet.

"Yes, I like to work. It gets me out of the house. I help large businesses decide how to allocate their charity funds—and even though those charity funds are usually laughably small, and they exist mostly for show, the money does some good. One of these days, I might ditch the big financial group for the Bill and Melinda Gates Foundation, if they'll have me. I don't know."

Grady made some thinking noises as he stared down at his notebook. He looked up at Janette Copeland again. "All right, then you don't know for certain who the blackmailed employee was, but you think it might've been Kim Cowen. Do you know what he might've had on her—or anyone else?"

"Haven't the foggiest. I didn't touch the day-to-day operations, and I had nothing to do with hiring or firing. I didn't exactly pore over everybody's personnel files. Even if I did, you've had access to the same information. You're as likely to guess from her background as I am."

Leda wanted to know, "And you *definitely* don't know what the employee in question was blackmailed into doing?" The light was sizzling around her left eye again, like another ocular migraine might be brewing. She closed her lids tight for a second and rubbed at her temple.

"Honestly couldn't tell you. It was probably something gross, though. Christopher liked to set people up to take the fall for his own shortcomings or shady business dealings. God only knows how many people he torpedoed professionally, just to keep his own nose clean."

"Excuse me," Leda said, and stood up with a wobble.

"Are you all right?" Grady asked.

"Yeah, I just need some air. Some water. I need the ladies' room; there's air and water in there. Excuse me," she said again.

"I'll come with you," Niki offered.

The women left, and Leda staggered down the stairs with Niki hobbling along in her wake, trying to keep the both of them from falling. The bathroom was on the first floor, almost under the stairs. There were two unisex rooms. Leda flung herself into the one that wasn't occupied and almost shut the door in Niki's face.

"Sorry," she said, then moved out of the way and sat on the edge of the sink before she could fall over, facedown into the toilet.

"Don't worry about it, babe." Niki shut the door behind her and turned on the cold water faucet. She took a small stack of brown paper towels, soaked it, and patted Leda's forehead with it. "Tell me what happened up there. What'd you see?"

"At first I thought it was another stupid ocular migraine. But then I caught something else," she said. She was somewhat out of breath and didn't know why. The stairs weren't very steep or demanding, but she felt like she'd just run a couple of blocks to catch a bus.

"Care to share?"

"I saw Christopher, looking absolutely . . ." She fished for a word that would adequately convey the cruel disdain and amusement she'd seen for a split second. Barely a moment, but it'd shown her so much about the man. "*Triumphant*." She let out a long sigh and squeezed the wet paper towels—then threw them away. She hopped down off the sink and faced it, elbows leaning on the cold porcelain. With a twist of the faucet, she shifted the water from cold to hot and let the steam hit her face. "He found somebody he could manipulate into doing his dirty work. But he didn't know who he was dealing with, and it got him killed. I flashed on the killer. It *must* have been the killer," she repeated quietly. "I saw him pushing a car, rolling it into the water."

Niki wasn't following. "So . . . we need to look for a car in the water?"

She shook her head, then nodded, then shook her head again. "Nik, you're not hearing me. We already know about the car in the water. I think that whoever killed the Gilmans . . . it's the same person who killed Tod."

# 17.

The sun was starting to set, so it was getting dark inside Castaways in the shadow of Capitol Hill. Grady Merritt followed Leda and Niki inside, past Tiffany (who was doling out drinks to the happy-hour regulars), past Matt (who blew Niki a kiss), and past Ben's office. Ben wasn't in, and Leda seemed relieved about it.

"Ben's a sweetheart," she told him as she hustled past the cracked door. "But he has *opinions* about branding, and I just don't want to deal with it right now."

"Branding?" Grady asked, wholly confident that he was in for something ridiculous.

Niki snickered. "Psychic psongstress."

Oh boy. He'd been right on the money.

Leda said, "Stop it, Nik. It's bad, but he likes it, and it's *his* venue. He can call it whatever he wants." She stopped at an office door with a sign that read MATTHEW CLINE. The sign was written in marker on a Post-it note with its nonsticky end secured with a piece of tape. "Klairvoyant karaoke is a mouthful, and . . . and something about the letters fitting neatly onto flyers. I don't know."

Her best friend shook her head. "Yeah, but klairvoyant karaoke doesn't come with a lisp. You should push back."

"I don't care enough to."

"Yes, you do. It's eating you up."

"It isn't."

Grady followed them inside the small, cramped office. It was about the size of a good walk-in closet, with barely enough room for a desk, two chairs, and a big whiteboard. The board was turned around, facing the wall—until Leda shimmied around the desk and spent a minute and a half trying to flip it over without knocking anything off the walls.

When she'd finally accomplished her task, she announced with great gravitas: "This . . . is my murder board."

Her murder board was a hodgepodge of brightly colored index cards and novelty magnets. It needed only a few lines of string to make for a grand conspiracy theory.

Grady tried not to smile, because it seemed important to her. "That's quite a murder board you've got there."

Niki put her hands on her hips and cocked her head at it. "Every bit as good as something you'd find downtown at the station, eh?"

"Every bit," he agreed. Mostly they did use whiteboards, but with vivid dry-erase markers instead of index cards. "Looks like you've done some good work here. What have we got?" he asked, turning sideways to pass the desk and get a little closer. "Okay, I see how you're . . . how you're getting at that, yeah. You've got the two columns of . . ." He scanned them quickly. "Gilman details and details about your fiancé, each in their own distinct group. What's all this stuff over here?"

Leda followed his pointing finger. "Oh, those are just . . ." She swallowed. "Some things I found the other day. I didn't know where to put them, so I stuck them here."

Held up by one large round magnet with a picture of a hammer that read THIS IS NOT A DRILL, Grady saw a snipped-out bit of newsprint with an engagement announcement. On either side of it were stashed more bits and pieces of their life together. A receipt from a restaurant. A birthday card. A bookmark. "It's a lovely memorial. Except for all the stuff about murder."

"Yeah, I know. It's kind of morbid." She shrugged and hugged herself. "*Anyway.*"

"Yes, anyway," he said. "The only thing you're missing, from where I'm sitting . . . is anything much that . . . well, that connects the two cases."

Niki snorted. "I told you, you need cop string."

Leda sagged. "I don't *have* any cop string, and even if I did, he means figuratively. Nothing connects the cases except for my ridiculous inconsequential psychic vibes."

"So far," he added. "We're making progress, though. And you said on the way here, something about a more concrete connection to Tod's murder? I'd like to hear more about that." He backed away from the board and settled into the nearest chair. He folded one leg up and rested it atop his other thigh.

Leda half leaned, half sat on top of the desk. She balanced on one butt cheek. "Okay, I had a flash when we were out at the bar, and I saw the Gilman killer pushing Tod's car into the water."

"You're *sure* it was—"

But she was not having any interruptions. "I'm not *sure* of anything. Here's what I think is true, but I can't prove: I think Christopher Gilman was using the person who murdered Tod and Amanda to do his dirty work. Hell, for all I know, he might've been blackmailing him."

"Because he knew about the murders?" Grady asked, perplexed.

She picked up a pen from a mug shaped like a Star Wars porg, and she pointed it at him. "No, just the theft. At least at first. Christopher discovered some skimming, and he looked a little closer at the skimmer. Figured he might be useful to him."

"You should write that on an index card and add it to your murder board," Grady suggested. "There's plenty of room over there on the right. Start a new column. No, start two columns—one for unknown details, and one for things you know but can't prove."

"Good idea." She opened a drawer underneath her rear end and pulled out a pack of cards. "I'm running low on magnets, though."

Niki said, "There are more in Ben's office. He has a stash, but they're boring. Just round dots and stuff."

Leda frowned. "Why does he have round dot magnets?"

"They came with this whiteboard. It belongs to him, you know."

"Oh yeah. I forgot."

Niki squeezed past Grady. "I'll go get them, hang on." She returned a few seconds later with a handful of plain black dots.

"Aw, these *are* boring."

It was true, but Grady gave her some encouraging spin. "They're dignified and tasteful."

"What are you trying to say?" Leda asked, her frown unmoved. "My magnets aren't dignified or tasteful?"

Oops. He'd played that wrong. "No, no—nothing at all. These look stuffy and dull, compared to your previous efforts, but they'll have to suffice for now."

"That's better," she said, lightening the frown. "Yes, they'll do for now. Give 'em here."

Niki handed them over, and onto the board they went—along with new index cards with new information.

"Can I have a card?" Grady asked, hand outstretched and fingers wiggling. When one was provided, he pulled another pen out of the mug and started writing. "We suspect that Christopher was blackmailing an employee. We have a list of all murder-contemporary employees at the precinct, and they've all been checked out. That means we need to check again, because we missed someone."

Niki spoke up. "We know it was someone young enough that Gilman called him or her 'kid.'"

"Right," said Grady.

Leda said, "Somebody newer, maybe? Perhaps an underling or an intern, or—as his wife suspected—his assistant. Wait. I don't actually know how old she was."

"Midtwenties, if I recall," said Grady. "Now, Abbot Keyes said he suspected the wife, and Beckmeyer didn't suspect anybody," Grady said as he scribbled. "Suspicions don't add up to much if we can't find facts to support them."

"Fair enough," Leda said. "But we're narrowing the pool, and that's good."

Grady paused. "Only if Janette wasn't lying to protect herself. She's still in the suspect queue, herself. If she honestly thought that Kim was sleeping with her husband, it might've stung her pride—even if she hated the guy."

Niki asked, "Did she have an alibi?"

He shook his head. "Nope. She was home alone the evening of the murders." He tapped the pen on the card as he considered the possibilities. "And the cheap hotel where her husband died, in a distant part of town . . . that's the kind of place you'd take a lover, if you wanted to keep it quiet."

Leda interjected, "You said the room was paid for in cash, using his son's ID. It does sound like a sexy rendezvous—the kind you don't want your richly divorced wife to find out about. She'd already sued one ex for everything she could get."

"Over infidelity," Niki pointed out.

"Right—so she'd be especially sensitive to it. Maybe."

Grady very much wanted to join the enthusiasm, but he instinctively held back. "You're right, obviously. But something about the whole thing bugs me. A lovers' clandestine meeting in a mediocre hotel? If his wife found out, I don't think she would've believed it was Kevin's doing. She's too smart for that. Then again, it's always possible that Christopher was dumber than he seemed and thought he could get away with it exactly that easily."

Niki slumped into the other chair and scooted it back against the wall. "This is hard," she griped.

"Sure it's hard. If it wasn't hard, every idiot with a podcast would do it," Grady replied.

Leda let out a single syllable grunt that sounded like it was meant to be a laugh. "Every idiot with a podcast *does* do it. That's the problem, isn't it? Too many people who think they're experts, not enough actual experts?"

Grady went back to looking at his index card, and the chicken-scratch handwriting upon it. "That's *one* of the problems. But there are bigger ones. People lie. People forget. People have their own weird motives and suspicions that have nothing to do with reality—they imagine grudges and motives that don't exist. The difference between an amateur and a professional . . ." He heard footsteps banging down the short hall outside the office. "Is that the pros try hard not to do those things."

A series of fast knocks rapped upon the open door. "Hello there, darlings—oh!" A middle-aged Asian man stepped inside without waiting for an invitation. He wore a killer black suit and the brightest white sideburns that Grady had ever personally set eyes on. "Darlings, and . . . some random gent I've never seen before. Welcome to my bar, stranger. I hope these girls haven't looped you into their murder-board shenanigans."

"Grady Merritt, Seattle PD." He held out his hand for a shake.

"And if you want the truth, I'm afraid I've been enabling these shenanigans."

The newcomer accepted the handshake. "Ben Kane," he said. "Owner and general manager of Castaways. It's a pleasure." He clapped his hands together, as if to signal a change in conversation. "Well! Matt told me you were back here, and I've got all the flyers up for tonight. You've got half an hour until showtime, darling. Brush your hair, touch up your lipstick, do some vocal warm-ups . . . whatever makes you happy. You've already got a crowd."

Leda looked a little green around the gills. "A crowd?"

"Ten or twelve people? But they're definitely here to see you, my *psongstress*. A couple of them were actually holding the handbills I printed up."

Grady could almost hear the silent *p* that Leda hated so much. "Maybe I'll stick around for the show."

She shrugged awkwardly. "Oh, don't feel like you have to. I do these all the time. If you've got somewhere to be . . ."

"I do not!" Grady fibbed. "Half an hour, you say?"

Ben bobbed his head. "The flyers say six thirty, so you should definitely be onstage by seven. Hell, honey—I'll even buy the first round. Except for Leda. She always drinks for free. The rest of you plebs only get one drink apiece."

"Sounds more than fair to me. Excuse me for a second? I just need to make a phone call, and I'll go grab a spot at a table. Before they're all taken." Then Grady ducked out of the office into the hall and pulled out his phone to call Molly.

Her cell phone rang twice before she picked up. "Hey, Dad. Are you on your way home? Should I put a pizza in the oven?"

"Throw one in for yourself, would you? I'm going to be here another hour or two at least. But I'll be home before too late, don't worry."

"You're not out binge drinking are you? You gave me a very firm talk about binge drinking."

He chuckled. "Well, I *am* at a bar—but no. No binge drinking. One drink, because the first one's free."

"Why's the first one free?"

"Because I'm a guest of the entertainment, apparently."

"What?" she asked.

He leaned against the wall, grinning to himself. "The psychic travel agent does a karaoke show at this bar on Capitol Hill. I'll tell you about it when I get home. Wait." He shifted his phone to the other ear. "Aren't you still supposed to be at work? I don't hear any work sounds." When she didn't answer, he sighed. "You aren't at work, are you."

"I am . . . not at work." Before he could ask why, she said, "A pipe broke and flooded the seating area. It'll be a day or two before it's all cleaned up, so I won't be at work tomorrow, either. Get used to it, dude."

"Aw, man. Now I feel bad for leaving you alone tonight. I should come back."

Molly wasn't having it. "No, you should stay right there and have a little fun with your friends. I'm practically an adult—an adult with a PlayStation and Netflix, and absolutely no plans to have anybody over or do anything exciting in your absence."

He leaned his forehead against the wall. "If you swear to God."

"I swear to God that I have no plans to bring anybody over to the house, or order excessive amounts of delivery food, or anything like that. I *also* swear to God that I think you should totally stay there and enjoy yourself. When's the last time you left the house for something fun?"

"Not since . . ." He started to say "since you were a little kid," but in truth the answer was even worse. "Not since before you were born."

She laughed. "Okay, that can't *literally* be true. But it's pretty close. Stay there, Dad. Have fun."

"Okay. I'll see you when I get home."

They each hung up, and Grady put his phone in his pocket. Then he headed back into the main bar area, where he grabbed a little two-seater table by the wall and threw his jacket over one of the chairs before venturing over to the bar. There, a pretty green-haired black girl greeted him with, "Hey there, handsome. What are you having?"

"Uh . . ." He wasn't a big drinker, and she'd caught him off guard. "Whiskey sour?"

"Coming right up! You sitting at the table over there?" She cocked her head at his jacket, slung across the chair.

"Yeah, that's me."

"I saw you come in with Leda and Nik. I'll bring it over when it's made, or have Matt do it for me. Sit tight and enjoy the show."

"You've seen it before, I assume?"

"Oh yeah." She leaned forward on the bar, signaling to another patron that she'd be with him in a moment. "It's really cool; I'm not gonna lie. I don't know how she does it."

"She's psychic."

"Okay, I know *that*. I just find it kind of hard to imagine. How weird, right? Knowing things that nobody else knows, and most of the time, nobody believes you."

"I believe her. She saved my life."

"For real?" She cocked her head at him. "What'd she do?"

"She kept me off a plane that crashed." It occurred to Grady that the bartender was only the second person he'd told, after his daughter.

"Wow . . . that's . . . that's heavy. I love it, though. I'm glad you're still here, man." She stuck out her hand, and he shook it. "I'm really glad you're here."

Grady went and took his seat, and before long a good forty or fifty curious patrons had taken every stool at the bar and most of the tables.

A tall, thin man with fluffy dark hair and tattoos peeking out of his sleeves came onstage. The stage itself wasn't much bigger than a good-size dining room table, and the single microphone looked rickety and lonesome until he took it in his hands.

"Good evening, everyone!" he announced. "I'm Matt Cline, manager of this bar—and I want to welcome you here tonight." He paused for a smattering of applause. "I know you're all here to witness some klairvoyant karaoke, and"—a woman tapped his shoulder and handed him a flyer—"or . . . the psychic psongstress? Oh yeah, that's right. Goddammit, Ben. *Anyway*, tonight we have, for your listening pleasure . . . Leda Foley, a woman with many talents, not least of all her voice. She'll be up here in just a few minutes. Thanks for your patience." He set the mic back into the stand before he hopped down off the stage and disappeared behind it.

Grady settled into his seat and nursed his drink, pleased with himself for being out of the house, participating in an adult activity. The evening wasn't a work event, filled with cops doing cop socializing; it wasn't a family thing, with his former in-laws or stray members from his own relations passing through town. It wasn't about his daughter, or any high school event. He was free to be a grown-up, with a grown-up drink, in a grown-up establishment, after work with no obligations to haunt or distract him.

Then someone grabbed the empty chair across the table from him—and his daughter sat down. She smiled the smile of a teenager who has figured something out, made something happen, and now had surprised her father so thoroughly that he did not know what to say.

"You? What? Here?" He looked back at the door. "In a bar?"

"I told the guy at the door that I was with you. He asked who you were, and I told him you'd come here with the psychic singer, and you were working on a case together. I told him you were a cop, and you could arrest me if you had a problem with my presence."

"Oh God."

"The bouncer said it was okay for me to come inside, as long as I didn't try to sneak any drinks or smokes, and so long as I don't make any trouble. I will *not* try to sneak any drinks or smokes, okay? And I definitely won't make any trouble."

"*How?*"

Molly rolled her eyes. "I googled. It took about five seconds, Dad. Honestly. There are only so many psychic singers and dive bars on Capitol Hill. Your new friend is hot on Twitter."

"Did I tell you . . . did I even give you enough information for you to . . ."

"Yes," she told him firmly. A cop's daughter, through and through. He was proud, even. "Yes, you did. Now be quiet, would you? The show's about to start." She turned her chair to face the stage, crossed her legs, and pulled out her phone like she fully intended to live-tweet this whole damn thing.

He didn't know what to say, given that she was already inside a bar, and yes—the show was about to start. So he sighed, finished half his drink in a swallow, and settled in to watch.

# 18.

Leda Foley emerged from the bathroom with most of a Midori sour rinsed from her shirt. Ben had brought it to her—then spilled it when Niki had accidentally whacked him with her plastic boot. It had not been the world's most auspicious start to a stage performance.

But Leda was wearing gray and black, and the green shadow was scarcely visible. It might be a little more apparent under the spotlight, or then again, it might not. Either way, the show must go on, even if she did smell vaguely of honeydew.

Tonight, Grady was somewhere in the audience. The fact of it unsettled her more than she cared to admit. What if he saw her perform and decided he'd been wrong all along? He might decide that she was a fake, a crook, or worse.

Or, he might decide that she was a paranormal genius—and opt to sign her up as a formal consultant for the Seattle Police Department, just like that.

Could he do that?

Leda had no idea. But consultants for the SPD got paid, didn't they? Maybe she could drag this whole thing into a lucrative (or semi-lucrative?) side hustle. Maybe she'd just be happy to participate, and maybe even help solve Tod's murder.

Joining the investigation like this, teaming up with a detective and using these skills to solve problems . . . it might be enough. It might be time to open that terrible door, pick herself up, and move on with her life in this new, weird direction. It beat sitting alone in a dark storage room, crying into a box of a dead man's clothes. Even if it never happened—even if they never found who did it, and justice was never served at all—it could mark the end of mourning, or something like it.

Is this what she would replace it with? Crime fighting in her downtime?

Or was this too morbid, and too close, and still too soon? Leda wasn't sure. She wasn't even sure how to think about it, even though there were days that she thought of little else.

Well, it used to be months. She'd take whatever progress she could get.

She peeked out from behind the curtain and saw a bigger crowd than usual. Definitely the biggest so far, and yes, there was Grady. He was camped at a small two-seater bistro table beside the wall, stage left. He wasn't alone. Some woman was sitting with him now. Did he know her? Did he offer her the empty seat? Leda couldn't get a good look at her, as she was facing the other direction.

*Good for him*, she thought. She hoped he'd meet somebody foxy.

Niki put her face up next to Leda's so she could see through the crack. She grinned and said, "Get it, Grady."

The woman at the table tossed her hair and laughed.

Leda frowned. "Yeah, that's what I thought, too. But now that I'm really squinting at her, I think that's his daughter."

"What? I thought she was a kid."

"She's a teenager. And *that's* a teenager. Look at her jacket," Leda said, raising one finger to point it through the curtain. "Her shoes, her backpack."

"I carry a backpack all the time, and I'm a grown-ass woman."

"Yours doesn't have a steampunk Wonder Woman logo on it, and you haven't drawn on your Chucks with a Sharpie in a number of years. Correct me if I'm wrong."

Niki squinted a second look through the curtain crack. "Drat, I think you're right. That's gotta be a kid."

"Yup." She leaned back and let the curtains slip shut. "Maybe you need to have a word with Steve—he's the one checking IDs at the door, right?"

"Steve's a pushover. You know it, I know it. Homeless dudes know it. Even dogs know it."

Leda nodded as she dabbed her shirt one last time. "How many dogs is he up to now?"

"Six, I think. But you know what probably happened? She probably told him that her dad was a cop and she was joining him inside. Steve folds like a paper crane anytime anyone mentions anything about the cops."

"You might, too, if you were a black ex-con in this town. Or any town, I bet. Either way, who cares. She's here now." Leda gave up and tossed the paper towel into the nearest trash can. She pointed at her shirt. "Am I dry?"

"Dry enough. Too dry, even. Here, it's dangerous to go alone—take this." Niki handed her a drink.

"What is it?"

"Just drink it."

"It smells like bananas. Is this death by bananas? Again?" Leda asked, pointing a solid stink-eye at the glass of brownish liquid.

"It's death by bananas 2.0. Drink it. Get up there. Do your thing." Niki gave her a little shove.

Leda followed its momentum until she was standing onstage and people were clapping and the girl at Grady's table turned around and yes—she absolutely *had* to be his daughter. Grady gave her a little wave, and Leda waved back. Her stage smile was locked into place, and she did her best to forget that someone she actually knew—apart from the Castaways folks—was out there watching. It shouldn't have been weird. It didn't *have* to be weird. She was making it weird.

She cleared her throat and took the mic, and when the bar was fairly quiet, she covered the basics of what to expect. Her first offering came from a man in the middle of the seating area. He was white and heavyset, with a pair of caterpillar eyebrows and a silver soul patch. He gave her a cell phone case that was covered in glitter and pink flamingos.

She took it, held it to her chest for a few seconds, and picked up the thread quickly, almost easily. A young man. Not a son, not a lover. More like a mentee, she thought. A student, perhaps. Yes, student sounded right.

"All right, I've got it," she said—and handed the case back. She didn't think that the case had belonged to the young man, but it'd had some other significance for him. She didn't know what, and her powers of divination weren't strong enough to tell her anything else.

That was another useful result of all this practice: she was learning the limits of her abilities. Once she knew the limits, she could push them. It was all progress; even when she hit a brick wall, at least she learned where the wall was. Maybe, with time, she could take a sledgehammer to that wall. Or pick at it with a chisel and a hammer, for slower and steadier progress.

Each song was a hammer tap. Each happy audience member, a crack in the plaster.

To Matt she said, "We have to get into the way-back machine for this one. Give me, 'To Sir with Love.'" Soon the first bars were filling the room.

The man in the audience immediately burst into tears.

Leda was startled, but she kept going. By the time the song was over, the man was smiling broadly, accepting tissues, and talking softly to people nearby who were asking him if he was all right, and if the song was the one he wanted to hear, and if it'd meant anything to him. She knew the answers to all those things, not because she was psychic—but because she paid attention to details.

The brightness in his eyes were happy tears. The way his hands shook . . . that was relief, not fear. He nodded and chattered breathlessly, happily. Whatever she was telling him with the notes of the song, he understood it better than she did, and he was happy.

That's all she wanted.

The next offering came from a young Asian woman in a blue velvet dress, a denim jacket, and black combat boots.

*The dream of the nineties will never die*, Leda thought, but did not say out loud. The woman handed over a tiny key—the kind that goes to a locker, or a mailbox.

Leda took it, closed her fingers around it, and shut her eyes.

She saw feathers. Not like birds, but like a dancer's boa. Bright red and bright makeup. Bright mirrors with rounded light bulbs the size of her fist. It wasn't literally what was intended by the key, or so Leda didn't think. This hint was oblique, like they sometimes were. She didn't like those kinds of flashes, because she had the very strong feeling that they were as likely to be helpful as they were to be way off the mark.

"Okay, this is a tricky one . . . but I *think* I've got it." She gave the key back to the nearest audience member, who passed it back to the owner.

Leda was getting a music video. An older one, from a bit before her time. Another woman. That was nice. Leda had a bit of range, but she always had to adjust and struggle for a way-high soprano or a deep-voiced male singer.

"Matt, give me some Annie Lennox."

He opened the catalog and flipped the pages. "All right, which one?" Rationally, she knew he was only a few feet away, but his voice sounded small, soft, and very far-off when Leda was on the stage.

She hesitated. She was thinking of the video to "Why" but feeling like "Walking on Broken Glass" was closer to the mark. "Broken Glass. Give me that one, I think it's right."

A minute or so into the song, Leda saw the woman who'd requested it. She was standing with her arms folded, a soft, smug smile on her face and a faraway look in her eyes. Leda hoped that meant she understood and she was getting something useful from the performance—but it was hard to tell.

Now and again, she'd slip a glance down to Grady and his daughter. The girl was enthralled. Grady was intrigued.

The girl unzipped her backpack and started rummaging around in there, and for a minute Leda was on the verge of panic. What if the girl handed her something? What would she do? What if she saw something dark or terrible?

Thank God her father made her put it all away.

The show ran another ninety minutes, and then Leda was finished and so was her voice. She cut off the requests after a rousing rendition of "Shiny Happy People" that had the whole bar acting like merry first graders.

"Thank you so much, everyone—and good night!" she said, as

she worked the microphone into its holder and took her bows. Then she ducked back behind the curtain, leaned against the wall, and exhaled so hard she thought she'd turn herself inside out.

Ben was the first one to find her there. He grabbed her and hugged her and let her go. "That. Was. Amazing!" he gushed. "You really killed it, and I'm not just saying so because the bar receipts are probably going to be our highest all year, for a week-night!"

"It's okay, man. I know why you really love me—and it's not for my vocal stylings."

He beamed at her, and he put a friendly hand on her shoulder. "I'm entirely serious when I say that we should really work out some kind of contract. Even if I can't pay you much, I ought to pay you something."

"Or we can discuss how much I'd have to drink to keep you from feeling guilty."

"One way or another, you're getting compensation—but I'd rather it doesn't come at the expense of your liver. Want to talk about a percentage of receipts?"

"Actually, that sounds . . . pretty fair."

Just then, Niki slipped behind the curtain from the AV table where Matt was still packing up the equipment.

"That was a great set!" Niki hugged her hard and let her go in time for Grady to appear in the hallway—the teenage girl at his side. "Grady!" she called. "What's up with the jailbait?"

"Oh my God, please don't call her that."

Niki laughed and went to give him a friendly smack on the shoulder. "All right, I won't. What should I call her instead?"

The girl held out her hand and said, "I'm Molly."

"Niki," she replied. "And this is Leda."

"Dad's special travel agent," Molly said knowingly.

Leda said, "It's good to meet you, but I'm a little worried about anybody seeing you in the bar. How old are you?"

"Not old enough to even have a fake ID," she said with a smirk. "Or a driver's license," she said more pointedly to her father.

"Yeah, well. Insurance for teenagers is expensive and you're good at public transportation. Hey, speaking of which." Grady gave his watch a meaningful tap, and reminded them all that this was a school night. He concluded, "We can't be here too late."

They cheerfully went their separate ways. But not until Leda had secured a Post-it note promising 5 percent of bar receipts, open to negotiation, and assurances that tomorrow she and Grady would go interview Kim Cowen.

"If only Tod could see me now," she muttered as she wrapped her scarf tighter and headed to her car.

She'd like to think that he'd have been proud and excited for her. He would've brought fancy red roses to present to her at the end of the night, and she would've felt like a beauty queen, standing in the spotlight. He would have gone around the corner with her to the pizza place to decompress after all that public attention and performance. He would've driven home, so she could have another drink—liver be damned.

Or, then again.

If Tod had lived, and if they'd married, Leda might not have ever needed Castaways, the way she needed it now. Maybe this was her way of letting go of him, a piece at a time, and finding something new to . . . not to take his place, but to help spackle the hole he'd left in her life.

All the way home, she thought about how it felt strange but good—to be pushing for answers beyond the ones the cops had initially given her. The lack of closure had been such an empty ache in the center of her chest for so long, and her grief so insurmountable that it seemed like she'd never be able to take a deep breath without sobbing again.

But tonight she inhaled, pushing the air past the tightness, feeling around for the lump in her throat. It was there. The odds were fair that it always would be. But tonight it was smaller, and she did not sob, but smile.

# 19.

Kimberly Cowen worked downtown with an advertising firm, but she didn't want to meet at her own office. She hadn't held the job very long, and she wasn't interested in answering any questions about why cops might want a word with her regarding a murder case, thank you very much. However, she'd agreed to show up at the big library on Fourth Avenue.

"Meet me after work, upstairs near the local history archives, and we'll talk," she'd told Grady Merritt on the phone.

Leda found it all a little fishy, but Grady shrugged it off.

"People get weird when you tell them that you're in law enforcement and you want to talk. Everybody starts shuffling through their memories, trying to figure out if they've done anything wrong and wondering if they need a lawyer."

Leda shut the passenger door of Grady's car and leaned against it while he paid for parking. "But she already knows you, and she knows all about the case."

"She knows a *bit* about the case. She doesn't know more about it than we do, unless she's the one who murdered everybody." He started to walk uphill. "Come on, and be cool."

"I'm getting better about being cool."

"Are you?" Grady asked, his voice pitched a little too high.

Leda adjusted her purse, slinging it across her chest like a messenger bag. "Well, I'm working on it."

"That's more like it. Where's your shadow?"

"Niki? She had a doctor's appointment. It's just you and me."

They were about two blocks from the downtown library building, a flagship of King County's commitment to reading and education, and also a flagship of modern architecture, or that was Leda's guess. What other explanation could there be for a building that looked like someone had overinflated a glass Rubik's Cube? She'd been led to believe it was a vast improvement over the previous library at the same location, which in turn had been a vast improvement over the old house that had initially gotten the library party started—considering that the house had burned to the ground.

Leda Foley had never actually been inside this particular library. She'd been to the Columbia City branch, as well as the one in Fremont, and one in Rainier Beach—usually because she needed free Wi-Fi before it became ubiquitous around town. But this was the granddaddy of them all—eleven geometrically styled stories of pure, weapons-grade knowledge.

Inside, the library looked like the interior of a UFO, if the aliens were super into reading: lots of grays and vivid greens, electric yellows, and illuminated escalators that disappeared up into the ceiling or down through the floor.

Leda said "Wow" as she trailed along behind Grady.

"It's really something else, isn't it?" He led her to a narrow, mirrored escalator, and she climbed on behind him.

"It sure is. You know where we're going, right?"

"All the way to the top. Hope you don't have vertigo."

She stared at his back, on the steps ahead of her. "No, but what if I did?"

"Then you might want to wait this one out."

On the top level, the sky was the limit. The world above was glass and metal, and the whole city loomed around them, but when Leda stepped toward a window to look outside, yes, maybe she did feel a touch of vertigo. It was something about how the building jutted out over the street. She shook her head and fell back in line behind Grady, who was making a beeline for a common area with tables, chairs, outlets, and a number of people sitting around on laptops and wearing headphones.

"Over there," he said, pointing to a woman seated near the windows, at a small table surrounded by four comfy chairs. She was a young white woman with hair that had never been a natural shade of red on anyone, anywhere, in the history of hair. She was pretty and soft, with a bright blue tattoo of what looked like a bird on the back of her wrist.

As Grady and Leda approached, she closed a notebook. She rose to her feet. "Detective Merritt."

"Ms. Cowen." They shook hands, and Grady turned to Leda. "Kimberly Cowen, this is my associate Leda Foley. I mentioned her on the phone."

Kim smiled and extended her hand. "Nice to meet you."

"Likewise," Leda attempted to reply, but she choked a tiny bit on the second syllable. Her hand in the grip of the other woman's hand had sparked something. A moment of light. A promise. She blinked repeatedly, reclaimed her hand, and said, "Sorry, I don't mean to be strange. Just a touch of vertigo."

"Tell me about it. This place takes some getting used to, doesn't it?"

Grady dropped himself into the chair across from her, and Leda took the one to her right. "I love it here," he said. "I was so excited when it opened. I was still in school, and the old library was nothing to write home about. Mostly just shelves full of mysteries and romances with beat-up covers."

"No, it hadn't been anyone's priority in a while," Kim agreed. "This place is a palace in comparison."

"A sci-fi palace," Leda observed.

"Some of the neon accent lighting is a little much. But hey, someone picked it out, thought it was cool, and paid for it. Who am I to complain?" Kim asked with a shrug. She crossed her legs and leaned back in the overstuffed chair. She'd been there long enough to sprawl out; her end of the table was covered in folders, open books, a cell phone, and a tangled strand of earbuds that were tethered to a very old iPod Nano. The Nano's screen had shattered at some point and was being held in place with a strip of clear packing tape. "Now, what's going on with this case, Detective? It's been . . . what? More than a year."

"I know, I know. But I'm still here, and I'm still plugging away at it. We've gotten a few new leads, and—"

"Ooh, what kind?" Kim asked.

"Nothing I can really discuss at this time. However, I believe that you can help us, otherwise I wouldn't be here."

She settled more deeply into the chair. "Fair enough. What do you want to know?"

"Thank you, Ms. Cowen. We appreciate your cooperation. First of all, for the record, you were Christopher Gilman's assistant for how long?" He whipped out his little notebook and a thin ballpoint pen.

"About eight months," she said confidently, as if she'd been asked to calculate this particular detail more than once. "He hired me right out of grad school. It was maybe the worst job I ever had, though it helped me get some professional experience on my LinkedIn profile. Except for that, yeah. It was the worst."

Leda sat forward, elbows on the top of her thighs. "How so? If you don't mind me asking. Was he a creep? Did he try to sleep with you, in exchange for . . . for a good reference? Is that how it works these days?"

Kim laughed again. "Oh honey, no. He did not want to sleep with me—which is, I always assumed, why his wife let him hire me. In case you haven't noticed . . ." She sat forward and whispered the rest with an air of conspiratorial intent. "I'm a bit fat."

"No, no. You're not . . . don't be ridiculous. You're lovely!" Leda protested.

"Damn right I am—and lucky for me, my flavor of lovely was *not* Chris's preferred type. I know he burned through a couple of skinny girls before he brought me on board. I know that his wife eventually decided that she'd tolerate my existence in his orbit. I can do the math. Don't get me wrong, I'm pretty sure he tried to sleep with everyone else. But either his wife thought he wouldn't try to poke me, or she figured she outranked me from a social capital standpoint, so she didn't care."

Leda was surprised. "Good God, you've got a mercenary attitude about all this."

"Mercenary? I prefer to think of myself as practical. I know how the world works, and I'm prepared to operate within its parameters, at least until I can change them. But no, to come back around to your initial question: I wasn't shagging him, not in the office, not out of the office, not anywhere. If he was creeping on his wife, he did it on his own time—and he didn't do it with me. That's not why the gig sucked so hard."

Grady did not pause in his fast-paced scribbling. He didn't even look up when he asked, "Then why *did* it suck so hard?"

"Oh *God*," Kim said, with a stretch of the vowels that said she had a rant on deck—and she'd let it fly more than once, on more than one person. Over drinks, unless Leda missed her guess. "For starters, I was salaried at twenty-five grand a year. Do you know how far twenty-five grand a year goes here in Seattle? I'll tell ya: not very damn far."

Leda said, "Yikes," even though she was really, really hoping that she was going to make that much in the current year. Too much less, and she'd have to fold the travel agency and look into some other form of day job to support her singing and crime-solving hobbies. She didn't have a super-great track record with day jobs.

Her first "real job" had been answering phones at a streetlight outage hotline. She'd lasted four weeks before getting fired for experimenting with sex-phone-operator voices when she was bored. Then it'd been all of a single shift at a hospital laundry because she was desperate, but not desperate enough to get bags of sheets soaked with bodily fluids dumped on her head. It only happened once. The once was enough. After that, she'd taken a barista position at an indie coffee shop, but she'd somehow set the grinder on fire and melted half a plastic cabinet full of muffins. Next she'd tried petitioning with a clipboard and a lanyard, collecting signatures to protect Olympic National Park. She had no idea what the meth-head with the plastic shiv had wanted with the signed petitions, but she'd let him have them and run the other direction when he grabbed her boob and screamed in her face. After that, it was a series of receptionist and retail jobs—abandoned or evicted from—for an assortment of reasons.

She was still mad about being let go from the Clinique counter at Macy's. It wasn't *her* fault that a customer didn't mention a fierce allergy to talc.

If you'd asked Leda, after a couple of rounds of death by bananas, she would have freely admitted: Going back to a nine-to-five was essentially her deepest fear.

Kim was excited to have found a fresh audience, so she leaned forward and used her hands to talk when she said the rest. "Oh, I *know*. For a part-time gig, sure. For a freelance gig—something I could work while also working other gigs? Okay, maybe. But for a fifty- to sixty-hour-a-week full-time grind with no overtime and no benefits?"

Grady winced. "Ouch."

Kim shook her head and stared briefly at the ceiling, as if remembering all the times she'd openly prayed that someone would murder her boss. "And then he would call me—any time of day or night—with more work, more questions, more stuff he either couldn't—or wouldn't—do for himself. That man ate my life, and I'm glad he's dead. Is that what you want to hear?"

"God, no," said Leda. "Unless you killed him. Did you kill him?"

Grady groaned "Leda," and rubbed at his temple.

But Kim didn't seem especially offended. "No, I didn't kill him. I fantasized about it. A lot. Fantasizing is still free and legal, isn't it?" Her warm humor returned. "Honestly, if you find whoever did it—I'd probably start a GoFundMe to help pay for his legal bills."

The detective seized on the pronoun. "*His* legal bills? You think the killer was a man?"

Kim flopped her hand dismissively. "His, hers, whatever. Dude pronoun for the sake of statistical likelihood, though I wouldn't count out his wife. If anyone hated that guy as much as I did, it's probably her."

"We just talked to her," Leda admitted.

Grady shot her a harder look than usual. "Apart from marital hatred, why would you point at the wife?"

"Marital hatred is plenty of reason for plenty of people to kill plenty of spouses," Kim pointed out. "Plenty of them get off scot-free, too."

Another flash. Leda blinked one long, slow blink, then sniffed and rubbed at her nose as if she needed to sneeze. It was the phrase *scot-free* that had tickled the back of her head.

"Especially the ones with money."

Leda considered this. "Money?"

"If she didn't do it," Kim continued, "I wouldn't be surprised to hear that she'd paid someone to do it."

Grady's look grew dimmer and darker. Leda knew she was spilling information, but she couldn't stop herself. How did anyone ever get any information, unless they were willing to give some away first?

Kim answered the question anyway. "Come to think of it, no. I don't think she'd have done it for money. I mean, poor Kevin got caught up in it, didn't he? That couldn't have been deliberate. Everybody liked *him*."

Grady kept his eyes locked briefly on Leda's, as if he could stop her from opening her mouth through sheer force of will. "That's what everyone says." He looked back at Kim. "You liked Kevin, too?"

"Sure, I did. I always figured he got wise to his dad's skimming campaign, and someone just . . . I don't know. Lumped him in with the real bad guy. Kill 'em all, and let God sort 'em out. You know what I mean."

The word *skimming* jumped out at Leda. It wasn't the first time she was hearing it.

Maybe Grady noticed it, too. He paused. "You said as much a year ago, when all of this was fresh. You think Christopher was taking money from the company?"

"Yeah, he wasn't as rich as he liked to pretend. Most of the money belonged to his wife, and the company was his own pet project. He probably didn't even think of it as stealing, since it all belonged to him anyway. In his head, you know. But the guy was absolutely a criminal, from head to toe."

Grady made a *hmm* noise. "People find all kinds of ways to justify their behavior. Do you think he was up to anything more complex than light theft?"

Kim stared into space for a few seconds. "Maybe something to do with insider trading? Or . . . God, he really hated that Beckmeyer guy. I hope he didn't have anything to do with him."

"Richard?" Leda blurted.

"Yeah, that was his name. Richard Beckmeyer. Always seemed like a cool enough fellow to me, but he rubbed Christopher the wrong way. Christopher wanted to burn that dude to the ground."

"Why did he hate Richard so much?" Leda pushed.

"Richard was close to the money, courtesy of his wife's investments—and Chris didn't trust him. I was always kind of waiting for the day that Chris would tell me to go TP Richard's house or whatever. It all started when Richard turned up that stupid account in the Cayman Islands."

Grady looked up from his notes. "What account?"

"Oh, it was linked to the company's bank account—but it was in the name of Ringo Gilman."

Leda was the one who asked. "Who's Ringo?" Another son? A distant relative?"

"A dog," Kim said. "Chris's childhood dog, who he still had a picture of. That stupid picture, of that stupid dog . . . it was the one thing he had in his whole life that ever . . . I don't know. Humanized him, I guess. Made me feel a little sorry for him— this adult man, with money and a wife and a great son and his own company . . . he still didn't have anyone close to him. No one had ever taken the place of some dog he'd had when he was a kid."

"Did he ever get another dog?" Grady asked.

"Not that I know of. Janette was allergic, I think. Or she said she was. Maybe she hated dogs. She struck me as the kind of woman who'd throw a fit if she found one sitting on her couch. She was always so . . . fussy."

Grady sat back and left his notepad on his knee, his pen held loosely in his hand. "Dogs aren't for everyone."

"Yeah," Kim agreed. "But she was the kind of lady . . . I think she'd go out of her way to kick one. I never liked her."

"Even though you both hated her husband?" Leda asked.

"All right, we had that in common—but there was something about her . . . it's hard to explain. She basically refused to talk to me, even when I needed her help with something business-related. After Chris was gone, there was so much paperwork to be done, untangling this company from all the others it had contracts with, or owed money to. There were so many things I needed signed—by her, since he was dead. And it's like she'd just totally checked out. She wasn't depressed or upset, she was free—and she acted like it. All she ever wanted was to get away from that guy, and I don't blame her. I wanted away from him, too, but I didn't kill him . . . and I always thought that maybe she *did*."

A hunch was pinging hard in the back of Leda's head, prompted by Kim's mention of other companies. She knew she was likely to earn an eyeball-scolding from Grady, but she couldn't stop herself, so she didn't. "Ms. Cowen, are you familiar with another digital content company called Probable Outcomes? They folded a year or two before Digital Scaffolding got a good toehold in the market."

"Oh yeah, I knew about Probable Outcomes. As soon as they closed, we had a dozen of their former people applying for jobs with us. We kind of ran them out of business. Well, that's overstating it," she backtracked. "We were their biggest competition, and this town wasn't big enough for the both of us. They went under, and we survived."

Leda gasped, "Oh my God!"

She frowned. "I'm sorry, what?"

"No, no." The psychic flapped her hands. "Please, I'm sorry, don't let me interrupt." But she was absolutely vibrating. There it was! The connection she'd been looking for, between the two cases! Why wasn't Grady excited, too? He must not have seen it on her murder board, or else he'd forgotten. Well, it was a busy murder board. He could be forgiven for blanking on a single detail.

The detective tried to drag the conversation back around to where he wanted it. "So that company failed, and yours survived. For another year or two, at least."

Kim smiled a warm, happy smile—as if the thought gave her genuine pleasure. "Yup, for another year or two. Now they're both defunct, and honestly, the world is probably a better place. The services those companies provided were taken over by bigger consulting firms, and the world kept on turning, didn't it?"

"Not for Christopher or Kevin," Grady said carefully, watching her face as he spoke.

"Well, no. Not for them."

He fidgeted with his notebook. "Do you remember, off the top of your head, any employees from Probable Outcomes who came on board at Digital Scaffolding?"

"There were three or four, I think. I'm sorry. I don't remember the particulars, it's been so long, and I went out of my way to forget everything that had anything to do with that place. God, it's like I had PTSD coming out of there."

"Was there anyone named Scott?" Leda asked fast, while Grady was still scribbling.

Both Kim and Grady looked at her like they weren't sure where she was going with this. That was okay. Leda wasn't sure, either.

"Nobody springs to mind, but like I said, it's been a minute," Kim said. "The old records might tell you, but I don't know what became of them. So much of that stuff was shredded or otherwise disposed of. If anything's in storage anywhere, you'd have to ask

Janette, I guess. She's the one who closed the company. She'd have to keep something around for the sake of the IRS; they make you keep records going back seven years, I think. Maybe I'm wrong."

"You've seen those records, right?" Leda asked.

"Some of them, but not all of them. Like I said, you need either Janette or . . . or one of the accounting people, maybe? Richard or his wife? I honestly don't know where you'd go, or who you'd talk to, if you wanted to know more about the personnel makeup of a company that's been out of business for almost a year."

"That's fair," Grady told her. "We can do some digging around elsewhere."

"Hey, thanks for staying on the case. I'd still like to know what happened to those two. At least, I'd like to know what happened to Kevin. I don't honestly care what happened to Chris."

Leda said, "Ouch. Tough, but fair."

"I liked Kevin. He was so kind and thoughtful. I was working my way up to asking him out. He was only a couple of years older than me." She sighed, and it was a sigh that said she had already mourned the lost opportunity but still considered the possibilities quite fondly. "And to think, I'm the one who sent him to that hotel that day. I didn't mean to. I didn't know he'd never come back."

Grady leaned forward. "You did?"

"Yeah." She nodded. "He was looking for his dad. It was on Chris's calendar. I didn't know it was a secret. Plus, I would've told Kevin my social security number if he'd asked me for it."

Leda's face scrunched up in confusion. "Wait, he put a secret meeting on a calendar?"

Kim nodded more enthusiastically than the question seemed to warrant. "Oh yeah. He couldn't remember anything, unless it was written down somewhere, on something. The really shady stuff went onto his Google calendar."

"But you had access to it?" Grady asked.

"Right. The man was not a genius." She shrugged and shook her head. "I'm just sorry that he wasn't smart enough, or kind enough, or . . . or . . . aware enough to keep his own son out of it. That's the thing that sticks with me more than anything. I wish Kevin hadn't gotten caught up in it."

# 20.

"She didn't do it." Leda told Grady excitedly on the way back to the car.

"Why do you think she's innocent? And what was with your little moment back there, with the questions about those other companies? Did you flash on something?"

Leda grinned widely and leaned back to steady herself against the incline, as they staggered together down the hill. "Not a flash exactly—more like a hunch. But now we know what the connection is between Tod's murder and the Gilman murders!"

"Wait, we do?"

Smugly, she declared, "Probable Outcomes."

He snapped his fingers. "Yes! *That's* why the company name sounded familiar. You had it somewhere on your murder board." He was getting excited now, too. "I feel stupid for forgetting it."

"It's okay! It's a crowded murder board, and there's no way you could remember everything on there. And I *know* that Kim Cowen didn't do it because she was head-over-heels in love with Kevin Gilman. Did you see the look in her eyes every time she said his name?"

"I did notice that, yes. But true love isn't much cover for a murder motive. Claiming to have been in love with a victim is kind of a classic excuse."

"Is it?" Leda asked.

"Yes." He stopped to wait for a light to let him cross. Leda stopped beside him. "Just because she had the hots for one of the victims, that doesn't mean she didn't kill them. If we're operating from the theory that Kevin was merely caught up in the violence, then it could've been anyone—even someone who was not-so-quietly in love with him. She could've killed Christopher and then panicked when Kevin caught her in the act."

The crosswalk light gave the all clear. Leda stepped onto the street first, letting Grady trail along behind her for once. "That's true, but that's not what happened. My psychic senses are tingling." She glanced back at him, making sure he was keeping up.

"Are they tingling about somebody named Scott? And if not, what was *that* about?"

"Yes. There's definitely a Scott involved."

When they got to the car, Grady unlocked it from the driver's side and Leda let herself into the passenger seat. "You think Scott's our killer?" he asked.

"No clue. Or rather, it's not a very good clue, but it's the one I've got. Now what happens next? Who do we talk to now? Did any random Scotts turn up in your investigation?"

He was quiet until they'd pulled into traffic. They'd almost made it to the interstate on-ramp when he said, "None spring readily to mind. I can get into the corporate records in storage at the precinct; some of that stuff was seized as evidence at the time, and our mystery Scott might turn up there."

"What about the IRS?"

"That was just a guess. The IRS won't give us the paperwork without a lot of hoop-jumping. No, Janette is more likely to have that stuff . . . and she probably doesn't. The odds are better than zero that it's all been shredded except for the tax-related financials and whatever we have downtown, and I don't know if that'll be enough to tell us anything. We've already gone over all of it with a fine-tooth comb—and at one point we used a *real* forensic accountant," he added. "We already knew about the accounts in the Cayman Islands, and we already knew that someone was helping themselves to the corporate coffers. It might be new information to you, but we knew most of this already. I mean, we-the-police. Not we-you-and-me. I hate to say it, but this was not the world's most productive interview."

"Except for Scott," Leda persisted.

"If you say so. It's a common male name, both first and last. But it hasn't appeared anywhere that I can think of, anywhere connected to this case—*or* to the case of your late fiancé," he added before she could chime in. "If it was, you would've said so by now."

Leda folded her arms and sulked.

Exasperated, he added, "I'm not saying it's nothing. I'm just saying that I don't know what to do with it. What if I found you some more stuff to touch? Do you think that would help?"

Leda was in a full-on funk when she said, "No."

Grady's phone rang. He glanced down and said, "Oh shit. Hey, do me a favor, would you? Pretend you're not here."

"Why? Who is it?"

He pointed to the dashboard, where she saw the words *SPD DISPATCH* scrolling along the radio display. "It's work. This is Bluetooth. Please don't make a sound, because I don't want to make any explanations right now. I'm asking you as a friend and colleague and a person who doesn't want to lose his job because he has a kid and a dog to feed. Okay?"

"Okay, okay. I'll zip it."

He pressed a button on the steering wheel. "Detective Merritt speaking."

A woman's voice came through his car's speakers. "Grady, I know you're not on duty right now, but your presence has been requested at a crime scene."

"I'm sorry, come again?" he asked.

The dispatcher cleared her throat. "There's been a break-in at the Beckmeyer residence, and Richard has asked for you, specifically. That's all I know. Do you need the address?"

"Holy shit. No, I've got it," he said, jerking his car toward the nearest exit. "Tell him I'll be there in twenty minutes. Is everyone all right?"

"His wife took a knock on the head, and it sounds like maybe there was a fire—but I don't think there are any serious injuries."

"Thanks, Lucy," he said to her. "I appreciate you."

"Even when no one else does, Merritt. Go save the day."

He pressed another button, and the radio came back on. "Richard's house is on the way back to your part of town. Can you behave yourself at a fresh crime scene, where crime is still being actively investigated?"

If anything, the idea perked Leda right back up again. "I'm looking forward to doing so, yes. Do you think it's related to our case?" she asked, eagerly clutching her purse. She dived down into it, in search of her cell phone. When she found it, she whipped it out.

"I don't know yet, but maybe Richard does. I can't imagine why else he'd ask for me." He glanced over at Leda, who had unlocked her phone and started texting. "What . . . what are you doing? Are you texting Niki?"

"No. Yes. Okay, of *course* I am. But she texted me, first."

"Do *not* summon her to this crime scene," Grady commanded.

"I wasn't going to. I forget the address anyway. I'm just keeping her in the loop."

"Why does she need to be in the loop. Why." He did not so much ask as complain.

Leda kept on typing and didn't look up. "She's my best friend, and I tell her everything. Don't you have a best friend?"

"Not exactly."

"But you've had one in the past, yes? And you understand the impulse to share absolutely everything, absolutely all the time?"

Grady shook his head slowly, then stopped to read some road signs and adjust his course. He turned a hard left that took him over the interstate and into the edges of fancy-pants suburbia. "Guy best friends and girl best friends must be different. Or maybe you two are just..." He zipped through a yellow light. "Creepily codependent."

"We are comfortable in our codependency, if that's what it is." Leda texted another line or two and waited while a bubble with ellipses appeared to show that Niki was responding.

"Whatever makes you happy."

"Now you're talking." The bubble made a *zoosh* noise as it filled with text in Leda's phone. "Ooh, she's at the aquarium with Matt."

"In a plastic boot?" he asked.

"He was threatening to get her one of those scooter things. Maybe he did, I don't know. I just hope the silver fox is all right."

Grady pulled out into an intersection and waited to make a left. "It sounds like he's fine. We'll be there in a minute, and you can ask him yourself. Wait." He stopped himself almost immediately. "Don't do that. Don't ask him anything. Actually, don't talk at all, unless someone talks to you first. If that happens, say as little as possible."

"I'm not a child, you know."

"This will be different." He squeezed the steering wheel. "This is an active crime scene. If I even *think* you're about to get underfoot, you will be banished to the car."

"I get it, I get it. I'll stay quiet."

He muttered, "I don't believe you, and I know I'm going to regret this."

Ten minutes later, they pulled up to the tasteful, posh craftsman home—which was now crawling with uniformed police officers. The cops were joined by a fire truck, which took up most of the parking area, so Grady parked his car on the street almost two blocks away. It was the best he could do.

"All right, come on," he said, leaving the car and slamming its door.

"Right behind you." Leda hustled to catch up. The detective's legs were longer than hers, and he was striding with a purpose.

Quietly, and over his shoulder, he told her, "Stay close to me."

Up the sidewalk they went, past uniformed cops and a firefighter or two. They were rolling their hoses and milling around the truck, talking into radios and generally packing up. Whatever fire emergency had occurred was under control now.

The cop at the front door gave Grady a head nod and Leda a perplexed look.

She stood up straight and followed behind him like she belonged there and wasn't merely along for the ride. The cop didn't stop her. Neither did the other two who lingered in the parlor, or the one in the living room—where Richard Beckmeyer and his wife sat side by side on the couch. Richard rose to his feet when he saw Grady.

"Detective! Thank you so much for coming, and hello again, Ms. Foley." He shook their hands warmly and gestured down at his wife. "This is my wife, Sheila. She was home when the break-in occurred, and as you can see, the maniac tried to kill her!"

"He *didn't* try to kill me," she protested. Sheila was seated on the couch, her head and forearm bandaged, and a bruise on the side of her face—near her left eye. "Or I don't know, maybe he did. I wasn't exactly bright-eyed and bushy-tailed when he tried to set fire to the office. I suppose the house could've burned down around me."

Grady said, "Manslaughter, not murder. The results would be the same for you, though. I'm glad you're all right, ma'am."

"Thank you dear, I'll survive just fine. I think I'll have a black eye tomorrow..." She patted at the bruise. "But all in all, it could've been much worse." She was a pretty woman, well into her sixties, with a silver bob that had taken a beating from the afternoon's invasion. Even so, she sat with poise and spoke calmly, like someone accustomed to being listened to.

Leda sat down beside her in a show of solidarity, and Grady took the chair opposite them. Richard sat down, too, and Grady pulled out his ever-present notebook.

"Mrs. Beckmeyer, I'm sure you've already given a statement— maybe several times over—but can you tell me what happened? There was a break-in, I understand."

She nodded firmly, then clutched the side of her head as if she wished she hadn't. "Richard was at the grocery store, and I was home alone. Out back, in the yard," she specified. "It's a nice enough day—and dry enough, too—so I was tidying the garden, getting ready to close it all down for the season. There's not much to pick, not anymore. Mostly just the squash."

Richard nodded, a tired look in his eyes. "There's been a *lot* of squash."

"I'll plant less next year. This year, I was trying something new," Sheila said—mostly to Leda, since Leda was sitting so close and listening so quietly. "But I was out back, tending the garden, and I heard the sound of glass breaking. It was somewhere in the house. At first I thought it might be the neighbor's cat again."

Her husband said, "Princess Pookie?"

"Well, why not? He's gotten inside our house three times in the last month. He likes your office, that's what it is. He likes to sleep on your chair."

Leda asked, "Princess Pookie is a boy?"

Sheila grinned. "As we all learned, when he knocked up Mr. Wiggles last year. Now they're both fixed, but our neighbor lets dear Pookie come and go . . . so he comes. And he goes. Anyway, he's never broken anything before—he just sneaks in through the nearest open window and makes himself at home. I don't mean to complain. I've become quite fond of him, honestly."

Grady waved his pen in a little motion that said he'd like to get back on track. "So you thought it was a cat, and it wasn't a cat."

"Correct," Sheila said confidently. "I knew Richard wasn't home, and I didn't expect him back. You have no *idea* how long he can dicker around in a Whole Foods, and he'd only just left the house. So my first thought was the cat. I didn't want him to cut his little feet or anything, so I put down my gardening and headed inside."

"With the spade. You forgot to put down your spade," Richard reminded her.

"That's right," she added. "I was holding my spade. I came in through the back door, over there." She gestured. "And I saw a person dart across the hallway, toward my office."

Grady got ready to write. "A person. Can you be more specific?"

"I only saw them for an instant, and from the back. I think it was a white person, wearing dark clothes. Either a hat, or dark hair. But I wouldn't even swear that it was a man, or a woman. It was someone a little bigger than me, I think? Let's say it was a young man, for the sake of argument."

"And right-handed," Leda guessed.

Sheila said, "I'm sorry, come again?"

"The bruising . . . it's all on the left side of your face and head. Isn't it?"

"Oh, I see why you'd think that, yes."

Grady noted, "Unless they hit her from behind."

"He came at me from the side," she clarified. "He was hiding around the door when I poked my head in. All I saw was a flash of something dark—his arm, I think? I don't know—and then I saw stars." Her voice went thoughtful as she reached for any lingering extra detail that she'd missed so far. "I swung at him, out of pure reflex, just before I fell. I hit him with the spade, on the shoulder or neck. I don't know if I hurt him or not. I didn't see any blood."

Grady was looking down the hall. He could see it over his shoulder. "Your office, that's the second door on the left, correct?"

"Yes, and Richard's is the one across the hall, on the other side."

Grady's head bobbed as he scrawled in his book. "Then what?"

"Then I was on the floor for a few seconds, maybe? The person stepped over me at some point. I was dazed, but not entirely out of it—and I was afraid to move or open my eyes. I just heard shoes very close to my head. I don't know how much time passed exactly, but after a bit, I smelled smoke. I stayed there for a few seconds, wondering if I was right—wondering if I was having a stroke. You're supposed to smell burnt toast, isn't that right?"

The detective shook his head. "I have no idea."

"After I smelled smoke, I heard fire. That faint crackling noise, very nearby. That got me up and moving, I tell you what. I got to my feet, and I started walking."

Leda craned her neck. Down the corridor's walls, she saw dirt-smeared handprints. Sheila had struggled to hold herself upright. A flash threatened to ping in Leda's head, but it was too distant, too faint. It wouldn't tell her anything.

"The fire was in Richard's office, and the fire extinguisher was in the kitchen—so I closed the office door thinking . . . thinking that would contain it? I'm not sure. It seemed like a good idea at the time. But I went to the kitchen, got the extinguisher, and opened the door again. The flames were all over his desk, his filing cabinets. I think someone threw lighter fluid all over them, that's what it seemed like."

A passing uniformed officer paused on her way through the living room and said, "You can still smell it in there. The intruder *definitely* used an accelerant. They just didn't do a very good job of it." Then she walked away.

Grady pointed his pen at her. "Good to know. I'll follow up, once the report is finished. Please, continue, Mrs. Beckmeyer."

"Well, I emptied the fire extinguisher, and it helped—but didn't finish the fire off. Finally, I came to my senses and grabbed my phone to call nine-one-one. I was still on the phone with the dispatcher when the fire truck appeared. Apparently a neighbor saw the smoke and called before I did. I'm very grateful. They were so prompt. They absolutely saved the house."

*And maybe her, too*, Leda thought. The sirens chased him off before he could do her any further harm. That's what the flash was saying. A fire burning in the office. A woman lying on the floor, half in the hallway. Mostly unconscious but moaning softly. A figure ransacking the rest of the house, hunting for something. Abruptly, Leda asked, "Do you think the burglar stuck around, or did he take off right away?"

"I honestly couldn't say. I opened the door for the firefighters, so they didn't have to smash their way inside. I staggered out onto the porch and . . . you know what? Now that I think about it," Sheila said, squeezing Leda's hand. "I was sitting on the porch swing, stunned and trying to stay out of the way—and I heard something moving through the shrubbery over there." She pointed past the front door and off to the right. "At the time I thought it sounded too big to be the cat. I think it was the intruder, sneaking away from the scene. You should tell somebody," she said to Grady. "I didn't think of it until just now—when she said something. Yes, there was still someone outside, right up until the truck came . . ." Her voice trailed away, and she gazed toward the porch and past it.

Leda worked to keep herself from looking too smug.

Grady jotted more notes. "I'll grab the crime scene folks when they're finished with the office. We can look for footprints, take fingerprints, and see if the creep got careless and left anything behind. Thank you, Ms. Foley," he said, with a note that told her he hoped he'd heard the last from her until they could debrief later, in the car.

She gave him a look back, and she hoped that it adequately conveyed her commitment to doing what she was told, at least for the next few minutes.

But then Richard said something that gave her pause.

"I'm just glad the damage wasn't any worse. There's nothing too precious in my office—just old files. If the intruder took anything, I couldn't tell you what it is. We've already checked the jewelry, the safe, and . . . and what else is there that's worth any money in the house?" He looked to his wife. "Maybe the baby grand piano? But it seems to be unscathed. We got off easy. Of course, the burglar might do the same, and get off scot-free himself. I realize that these crimes aren't always solved quickly, or at all."

Leda jumped like she'd been shocked. "I'm sorry, a piano?" Then she mumbled, "Scot-free."

Grady froze. This wasn't the way it usually went, and he was clearly concerned—for the case, for the victims, and maybe even for Leda. "Ms. Foley, are you all right?"

"Scot-free," she said again. "And the piano."

"Those are . . . two different sets of words, Ms. Foley," he said carefully. "Do they have something in common?"

"I'm sorry, excuse me." She left the couch and went outside to the porch. She sat down in the swing and wished for a paper bag to breathe into—but lacking one, she timed each breath slowly, to the push of her foot and to the sway of the swing, until she could get her head right again.

Grady emerged a few minutes later. He sat beside her and asked quietly, "Are you okay? Seriously."

"Seriously, yes. There's something, though. A connection I'm not seeing. My . . ." She stopped herself from saying "psychic powers" just in time to keep a couple of firefighters from hearing. "My Spider-Sense is tingling like a mofo. It feels like I'm forgetting something, but that's not what it is. I'm *missing* something."

"I believe you. And I trust you, mostly. But let's get out from underfoot here. I've talked to the crime scene lead, and she's going to check the side of the house for prints."

"He was wearing gloves," she told him.

"He? Definitely a he?"

She hesitated. "No, not *definitely* a he. But my *gut* says it's a he. I'm going to keep calling him a he," she said with finality. "He's the killer, Grady. I've never been so sure of anything else, not in my whole life. He came here to . . . to . . . destroy evidence."

"Of what?" Grady asked.

She saw columns of numbers, tables of information, manila folders being opened and discarded. "Businessy stuff. I don't know for sure, but he was going through the filing cabinets, drawers, everything, looking for anything that would point back to him." Another flash, weaker this time. "He wasn't even sure he would find anything. Something happened recently, something that made him worry that there might be something left, something to point a finger at him . . . for . . . for murdering everybody."

"Everybody?"

"The Gilmans," she said. "Christopher the dick, and Kevin the beloved. And Amanda Crombie. And . . ." She took a deep breath. "Tod."

# 21.

Three days later, Leda's phone went off at an ungodly hour.

The first text message read: Leda, get up. She didn't hear the buzz that announced it. She heard the second one, though. That time the text read: Leda, NOW. It came from Grady. Grady was texting her. In the middle of the night. He'd called her, but the volume was turned down on her ringer. It wasn't really a ringing tone, anyway. It was still the chorus of chipmunks singing "Chandelier," and who the hell could sleep through *that* but not a couple of text messages?

It was 4:51 in the morning. Still dark outside. Not even a hint of pink on the horizon.

She sat up in bed, wiped her eyes, and jumped when a third text landed. I'm coming to get you. Be dressed.

"Dressed in what? Get me for what?" she asked the phone.

The phone didn't answer. She unlocked it and composed a new text. All she could manage was: What?

Twenty minutes. Have pants on.

And that was the full extent of the information she was working with.

Bleary-eyed, she rolled out of bed.

Five minutes later she was wearing jeans, socks, and a unicorn sweater that read MAJESTIC AF. Or should she choose something more professional? Was this a professional call? For professional business?

"It sure as hell isn't a personal visit. Not at this hour," she grumbled to herself. She went to the bathroom to slap her contacts into her eyes. She brushed her teeth and hair, wondering all the way what was going on.

By 5:00 a.m. Leda had thrown her hair into a ponytail, swabbed some cherry ChapStick onto her lips, and was about as presentable as she was going to get. She wasn't as awake as she would like to be, but she was out of coffee and she couldn't think of any place where she might get some at that hour.

Grady's car pulled up to the little bungalow just as Leda was washing down a granola bar with a swig of milk directly from the carton. His headlights were bright through the front window, and she could hear the car idling on the street. He tapped the horn twice.

Leda cringed. Most of her neighbors weren't up at that hour, except for that one weirdo who was probably jogging already.

"I'm coming, I'm coming," she said, as if he could hear her. He honked again, right as she was finding her purse and checking it for her keys.

The keys weren't there.

Where were her keys?

On the coffee table, in a bowl. Got 'em.

She threw her feet into the boots she'd left beside the door the night before, and—still hopping to get her right foot settled—she left the house and locked the door.

Grady was parked with his right two wheels on the sidewalk, in accordance with local custom. He'd almost hit a fire hydrant.

Leda opened the passenger door and threw her purse inside. She followed it, grousing all the way. "Somebody ought to give you a ticket for that."

"For what?"

"For the . . . you're real close to . . . there's a . . ." She couldn't rally the words she needed, so she flapped her hand toward the hydrant, even though he probably couldn't see it from where he was sitting behind the wheel.

He said flatly, "Janette Gilman is dead."

"Oh my God," she blurted. Her seat belt wasn't even buckled when he threw the car back into gear. It jumped off the curb and pulled back into the street, narrowly avoiding a tree, a mailbox, and one of those rent-a-bikes that people routinely left all over the damn place.

A squealing, scraping noise suggested that maybe he hadn't missed the bike after all, but whatever was snagged in the bumper, Grady shook it. "She was working late," he continued. "The building was locked, but somebody climbed a fire escape and broke a window to get in."

Murder was better than caffeine. "Another broken window! We have another murder!" Leda nearly leaped out of her seat.

"Don't get ahead of yourself. She fell down some stairs and broke her neck. There's always the possibility that this was an accident."

"It's also possible that her death has nothing to do with our cases. I mean, technically it's possible. But if you thought that's what happened, you wouldn't be here, and I wouldn't be out of bed before the sun comes up."

"Correct." He squeezed the steering wheel, his knuckles tight and pale.

"Can we stop for coffee?"

"Not yet. We can grab some when we're done. For now, you're on your way to an active criminal investigation again, and you'll stay there by the grace of whoever's working the scene. I know this sounds weird and strange and probably awful, too, but I want you to see this woman's body. I want you to touch it, if you can."

"Oh my God," Leda said again.

Grady shot her a fast look, then looked at the road again. A stoplight ahead was turning yellow. He drew up to a halt, even though he probably could've gunned the engine and made it through. He dropped his head down onto the steering wheel and let his forehead rest there. "Oh God, our first conversation . . . it's the only thing you made me promise, that I wouldn't show you any dead bodies."

"I mean . . . yeah. We've had this talk."

"I'm so sorry, I just got caught up in the whole thing, and when my partner, Sam, called me an hour ago and said this was going down, I didn't even think. I just ran with it. I had this wild hare up my ass, this crazy thought . . . like, if I could get *you* there. If I could get *you* to see, and touch, and . . . and *flash*, or whatever it is you do. With a fresh body? If anything's ever going to give you a hit, surely . . ." He trailed off. "Surely this would be it, right?"

They sat there, silent in the dark car, parked at the now-red light. There were no other cars at that moment, though a flicker of headlights behind them suggested a few were coming. Morning rush hour wouldn't start for another hour.

Leda said, "I've never actually seen a dead body, except at a funeral. I guess . . . I guess it's fine. I think I told you, I didn't see Tod's. His mother identified him, and they closed the casket. And it's not like I knew Janette. I only met her the once, so, no big deal. Yeah, I can do this," she concluded. "Let's go. Come on, the light's green."

He looked up and saw that she was right, and he was about to get honked at by the cars that were coming up behind him. "Only if you're *sure*."

She was not sure. "I'm sure. I can do this."

As if to soothe himself, Grady said, "There's always a chance that you won't get close enough to the body to make anything happen, anyway. This isn't exactly standard procedure, and odds are better than fair that we won't get away with it. Either way, when we get there, stick close to me. Err on the side of too quiet, instead of too friendly. If anyone asks, you're a consultant I've been working with, on a case related to Ms. Copeland's dead husband. Do *not* volunteer which dead husband. Don't do it."

"Got it."

"If you ever change your mind, at any time, all you have to do is say so—and I'll have you out of there so fast, it'll make your head spin. I realize now that I am a terrible person for asking you to do this. I am truly the worst man who ever lived, and just say the word—I'll run you home and we'll pretend like this never happened."

But things were happening anyway. Tod's murderer was within her grasp, she could *feel* it. Even if that feeling was more "strong desire" than "intellectual certainty." If she turned back now, she might never get another chance.

"No," she told him. "I don't want to go back home. I want to go catch this creep." In fact, she desperately wanted to go home. But she more desperately wanted the person who killed Tod.

"You mean it?" he asked nervously.

"I mean it. Let's go."

Before long, they were on the interstate, and from there it only took another thirty minutes to reach Janette Copeland's office building. It was crawling with cops and cop-affiliated personnel. An ambulance sat at the ready with its rear doors opened, its interior empty.

Leda saw it at the same time Grady did. She said, "They haven't removed her body yet."

"No, but it looks like they're about to." He discreetly crooked his index finger at two guys in uniforms with an empty gurney between them. The gurney's wheels weren't cooperating, or else the steep, damp, busted-up Seattle sidewalk wasn't cooperating. Either way, their progress was reassuringly slow. "Let's head inside," he added. "Hurry, before they pick her up."

The Murtree, Hanglesworth, and Smith Financial Services offices occupied the bottom three floors of a smallish high-rise at the edge of the downtown core. Leda noted that she was within walking distance of Castaways, if she felt truly motivated and didn't mind hoofing it directly, steeply uphill for a few blocks.

Not that she had any intention of doing so. It was early, she was confused, and she was trying to orient herself in the downtown tangle.

Obediently, she followed Grady, sticking to his shadow almost closely enough to be inconvenient—but he didn't fuss at her, and nobody stopped her. Several cops gave Grady a head bob of recognition, and Leda a scrunched face of confusion; but together they made it into the lobby without any trouble.

Inside, the building looked exactly like Leda had expected. It matched the mirrored-glass-and-steel exterior, with lots of shiny surfaces and hard, flat right angles that gave the place a modern, expensive feel—if a rather unfriendly one. Not so much as a foyer rug or a fluffy potted fern softened the place.

The sun was still only just thinking about coming up, so the lights within the building were blinding. Leda wouldn't have said no to a pair of sunglasses, but maybe she was only tired. And a smidge hungover.

But only a smidge—which was admirable, considering Ben's "free drinks for singers" policy. A mild case of morning cottonmouth was evidence that she was a responsible adult.

She squinted around and saw crime tape, some of it still in

rolls, lying on counters. A puffy-faced night guard in a polyester uniform gave earnest details to two official-looking women with serious faces. All the elevators in a bank along the wall were open, paused that way, and Leda didn't know why; but there was no one to ask except for Grady, and he was on a mission—leading her through the scene with a swift, formal pace that said he totally had permission to be there.

And so did anybody who was with him.

Two sets of escalators were stopped, same as the elevators. One was marked out of order, which was silly, since that only meant stairs, but Leda kept that thought to herself. Contrary to her personal nature, she kept all her thoughts to herself, all the while resisting the urge to take the back of Grady's jacket by the hem—purely to make sure she didn't lose him like a kid in a busy mall.

They were most of the way through the lobby when someone stopped Grady with a quizzical "Merritt? What are *you* doing here?" She was a tall, slender woman with yellow hair that was long enough to put up in a clip. She looked tired and hastily dressed in street clothes—Leda thought she must be another detective—but she was carrying a cup of coffee that was big enough to drown a cat.

He muttered something under his breath. Leda thought it probably had four letters and wouldn't be welcome on a Tuesday-evening procedural on CBS. But he turned around with a too-early-in-the-morning version of a bright, happy-to-see-you smile. "Hey, Carter. Sam called about an hour ago. His wife was awake with the baby, and she heard about this on the police scanner."

"That's the weirdest 'up with a baby' background noise I ever heard of."

"Tell me about it. But it's not my kid, so I don't care if they traumatize him before he learns to walk."

Carter asked, "Does this have something to do with a case of yours?"

"Yeah, the Gilmans. This guy and his son got shot at a hotel on the other end of town. Janette Copeland was the ex-wife and stepmother of the pair, respectively. I only just talked to her the other day, and Sam knew about it. I know this isn't my scene, and I hope you don't mind." Then he said quickly, "But if you do, I can skedaddle. Won't hurt my feelings if you send us packing."

The other officer looked him up and down, then she looked at Leda. She opened her mouth like she was about to ask who exactly this random woman was, then she shut it again like she'd changed her mind. "I trust you to stay out from underfoot. Is this the consultant I heard you've been running around with?"

As if he'd only just noticed Leda standing there, halfway hidden behind him and trying very hard to look like she was casually lingering and not at all hiding, Grady said, "Her? Oh, yes. This is Leda Foley. Leda, this is Lieutenant Allison Carter."

"It's a pleasure," said Leda, doing a little bow. She hoped it read *polite and professional, if a tad distant* and not *too afraid to extend a hand for a shake.*

"Likewise, I'm sure. Anyway, stay close to this guy," Carter told her. "He knows how to behave."

"I absolutely plan to do so, yes. Don't worry. You won't hear a peep out of me, and I won't touch a thing!"

Before Leda could go on, Grady stepped in. "So the body's . . . where? Upstairs?" he asked.

"Up the escalator and around the corner. There's a secondary mezzanine up there. It opens to the floors above. She went down the escalator headfirst, over the glass rail along the side. You know, the one that's designed to prevent that sort of thing."

"Did it break?" Grady asked.

"No, and although she might have simply been way off-balance and fallen, it's more likely that either she hauled herself over it in an attempt to escape—or else someone picked her up and threw her."

"Not an accident, then."

Carter shook her head. "Nobody thinks it was. The guard over there—" She cocked her head at the guy; he was dabbing his forehead with a handkerchief. "He heard people fighting upstairs, and then there was a strange tumbling noise like something rolling or falling, and then a crash. He's pretty shaken up. Called it in right away."

"Did he chase whoever else was in the building?"

"He says he never saw anyone else, but he did hear footsteps when he found Janette. The fall wasn't really that far, you'll see it yourself when you get up there. She landed wrong. Humans are so damn fragile; that's all it took." Carter mimed a yank of her head, and a cracking noise. "But if this is tied to some old case of yours, I'd *really* like to hear about it," she told Grady, giving him a look that was sharp enough to blow a tire.

"Absolutely. Yes, ma'am. We can sit down in your office later today."

"Later today is good for me, thanks. And be quick about this. Whatever you're doing here, do it and get out before anybody else asks questions."

"Will do." Grady gave her a floppy salute and turned away. He put one hand on the small of Leda's back to guide her, and he used the gesture to say softly into her ear, "Carter's all right, and she'll look the other way, but she's careful. If we overstay our welcome, she'll toss us out."

"Gotcha."

He ushered her toward the escalator and then took the lead climbing position. Leda was hot on his tail, sticking close and staying quiet. Up the escalator to the next level they went, and on that next level, the building opened up. A wide, oval-shaped mez-zanine overlooked the further descent of the escalators below—as well as several grouped seating areas for informal meetings or hasty lunches, a number of tastefully potted plants and small trees, a customer service/information desk with room for three employees behind it (though no one was there at the time), three sets of elevator doors, two sleek metal trash cans, several officers, two forensics investigators . . . and the body of Janette Copeland, lying beneath a sheet beside the escalator landing.

Leda said, "Oh, wow."

The sheet did not cover everything. A few fingers poked out from one end, flawless manicure intact. One foot also protruded, exposing stocking-covered toes. Where was the shoe? Then Leda saw it a few feet away, an evidence marker placed beside it.

Grady whispered, "Are you ready to do this?"

She stared at the sheet and whatever was underneath it. There wasn't any blood, or Leda didn't see any. Was that normal? Shouldn't there have been blood? Janette hadn't fallen more than twenty or thirty feet, but that was far enough, wasn't it? Was it better or worse that there wasn't any blood—that this only looked like a lady napping beneath a sheet in a large office building?

Better, Leda decided. Or not worse. Worse would have been seeing the face of a woman who'd bought her a pitcher of sangria earlier that week.

"It's okay, I've got this. I'm ready."

# 22.

Grady Merritt watched Leda carefully, ready to pull the plug on this little experiment at a moment's notice despite his frazzled frame of mind. He felt like garbage, and it wasn't just the hour or the lack of coffee; it was the way he'd leaped without looking when he'd called the travel agent, then texted her, and then dragged her out of the house before the sun was up—all for the privilege of poking a dead body in case it gave her a flash of insightful horror that he could use to help solve the case. She was a civilian who had no experience with this kind of thing, and she'd never even set eyes on a dead body that wasn't in a funeral home— by her own admission. When he laid it all out like that in his head, he felt even worse.

He deserved nothing less than for Leda to turn on her heels and walk away, blocking his number as she went.

But he *really* hoped she wouldn't.

While Grady kept watch, using his body to block her from the view of others when he could, Leda slowly approached the sheet and circled. The forensics folks stayed out of her way. They might have thought she was a blood-spatter expert, or a consulting physician who specialized in violent demises—anything was possible. Different experts and consultants came and went from the police department all the time.

Dammit, he should've given her gloves. Dammit, he should have thought of a story before they'd arrived. He wouldn't lie to Carter, but he'd lie to most of these other people if he needed to.

But it was so early, and this was so far removed from standard procedure. He hadn't thought of anything, and it made him angry—because he usually thought of everything. It was his *job* to think of everything.

Leda crouched down beside the exposed hand with the tasteful nude polish on the nails.

His throat was dry.

Leda's knees wobbled as she leaned forward and touched the dead woman's fingertips with the back of her own hand. She jerked back quickly and almost fell—but caught herself. Steadying herself, she tried again, and this time, she let the touch linger. She didn't close her eyes or touch her temple with her free hand, like the psychics on TV, but she did stare thoughtfully into space.

No performative woo-woo stuff with that one—just pure, random, minimally predictable and marginally helpful talent.

He'd take it. It was all he could get.

Then she rose to her feet and clapped her hands together. "All right," she said. "I've seen enough."

He all but leaped to her side. What did that mean? Had she seen anything useful, or nothing at all? He couldn't ask her yet. Not with so many people around. "Are you good? Everything okay? Are you ready to go?"

She only answered that last one. "I'm ready to go."

Grady ushered her back the way they'd come, out of the mezzanine area, down the stationary escalator, past the guys from the medical examiner's office who'd finally gotten their gurney situation sorted out, and back down the street to his car. Neither one of them spoke until the doors were shut and the engine was running.

With his hands on the wheel, and Leda's hands rubbing together in front of the heating vents, he stared through the windshield and asked, "I hope that wasn't too bad."

"It . . . wasn't that bad. I mean, it was *bad*—she's dead, and I've never touched a dead person before. But we're all going to be dead eventually, right? I don't think I'd be upset if people touched me when I'm dead, so I figured she wouldn't care if I gave her a little tap. That's what I told myself, and it worked."

He looked at her, with his eyebrows wrinkled in a frown. "That's what you were worried about? Offending the dead woman?"

"Kind of? It's like I told you a long time ago, I don't see ghosts or talk to dead people, but sometimes I get a sense of them, hanging about. I have enough crappy luck as it is; I don't need to run around peeving any phantoms. For all I know, the dead are petty."

He laughed, even though it felt rude. "No, I get it. It's bad karma. But did you learn anything, or was this a bust?"

She nodded and slid down in her seat, pulling up her knees until they were resting on the dash. "It was disjointed, yeah. At first it almost knocked me over, it was so vivid, but then I got a handle on it. Janette was getting ready to leave. She took her coat off the back of her office chair." Leda stopped rubbing her hands together in order to mime the act. "She locked up behind herself and left. She was down at the bottom landing of the mezzanine when she realized she'd forgotten something. I don't know what, but I think it was her purse. You'll have to ask if they found it."

"I'll do that."

"The escalator was out—as you saw—so she had to hike up that real tall one to get back to the office. Or . . . or she chose to? Unless the elevators weren't working, either. I thought they were stopped because of the investigation, but maybe they turn them off at night."

"That's not typical, but you never know. Good to check."

"My point is, she used the escalator stairs. It took her a minute to get back up there, and when she did, someone was in her office. The door was jimmied, and someone was moving around in there. That's where it gets fuzzy. It might be because . . . look, I'm not saying I talk to ghosts."

"As you've made quite clear."

"But what if some bit of her essence was hanging around, helping me? Feeding me information? For the first time, honestly, it felt like I was getting directions from somebody else."

"You think you were talking to a ghost."

"No," she said. "But I think there's a chance that a ghost was talking to *me*. And the last thing she really remembered clearly was how annoyed she was with herself, when she realized she'd left her purse behind. Yeah, I'm pretty sure that's what it was," she said, more to herself than to Grady. "She surprised the guy in her office. They fought, and he pushed past her. I think he just wanted to get away, but she followed him. She grabbed him," she said, miming that, too.

"You're sure it was a man, not a woman?"

"He was wearing a ski mask, but yes."

Grady grunted, amused. "A ski mask? That's so . . . 1985, isn't it?"

"Fashion is slow to catch on in the criminal world, or something."

"Can you tell me anything about him?" he asked. "Tall, short, fat, thin?"

She shook her head. "He's a dark-colored streak, moving jerkily around. Trying to get away. He wrestled free . . . he made a run for the escalator, and she caught him there. They struggled, and that's it. That's all I see."

"Hm." Grady wasn't exactly disappointed, but he wished she had something more concrete to offer. "You don't think this was a premeditated murder."

"No, it was more like manslaughter. For all the good it does Janette."

"It did Sheila Beckmeyer some good, since hers was only attempted. If the guy intended to kill her outright, he probably would have." He was starting to get a picture of the perpetrator. Not a physical picture, but the guy's type. "We're dealing with a guy who's bad at murder and not very committed to it. His first killing might have been an accident. But once you've killed one person . . . in for a penny, in for a pound, as they say."

It was Leda's turn to frown. "I don't get it."

"Our perp is bad at murder," he told her. "That's the point. He's backtracking, trying to clean up any evidence he might've left behind connecting him to the Gilman murders, or any other murders he may have committed. But he's willing to defend himself with violence if he needs to."

"You're making him sound like a serial killer."

He shook his head. "No, he's not a serial killer. He's just a regular killer, caught in a loop of his own devising. He's killing now to cover his tracks—even though he's obviously making himself a bigger target. But something triggered him. Something tipped him off, and he feels cornered. He's swinging at shadows."

For a few seconds, neither one of them said what they both were surely thinking.

Leda was staring up at the rearview mirror, pretending she was looking for an opening in traffic to pull into. She wasn't making eye contact, and it was just as well. "*We* did it. We tipped him off," she said.

"Nobody knows that for certain." Grady put the car into gear and took the next opening, sliding back into the downtown, early-morning-rush traffic so he had something else to pretend to pay attention to also.

"It'd been more than a year since he'd hurt anybody, and then we showed up. We started asking questions, talking to the old witnesses . . ."

"Could be a coincidence."

She said, "It isn't, though."

"Here's the thing, okay?" He hit a stoplight, so he had a few seconds to tell her the most important part, before they were back on the road again. He turned in his seat so he could face her. "Even if it's not a coincidence, that's not on you. It's not on me, either. The bad things that happened to Sheila Beckmeyer and Janette Gilman are not your fault."

"They kind of are . . . ?"

"No. They are absolutely not. Whoever this guy is, all the blame is squarely on *his* shoulders, not yours. Not mine. He's the one out there, wreaking havoc. You and me . . . we're just trying to rein him in." Grady sat back again and glared through the windshield like he could force the light to change with the power of his mind.

It worked. The light changed. He turned his attention to driving again, just in time to not run over a jogger who darted into the crosswalk against the light. He slammed the brakes and swore, then pulled out into the intersection.

Leda put her knees back up on the dashboard and settled in, looking tired and unhappy. "Then we really need to get moving. Who knows how many more people he plans to attack."

"I don't think he *planned* to attack any of them. He's a murderous free radical, that's all. He's bouncing from victim to victim, from scene to scene . . ." Grady lost track of his train of thought. "Hey, you want some coffee? It's . . ." He checked the dash. "Almost seven. Coffee places are open by now. Can I buy you a cup?"

"Sure, I guess."

"Got any ideas? Anything in Columbia City?" he pushed, wanting to distract her from the thought that she had had a hand in getting people hurt.

"Yeah, I've got a place."

Half an hour later, they were free of morning traffic and wending through the south-end neighborhoods that would take them back to Leda's home turf. They pulled up to the curb near the travel agency office and walked around the corner to a small, bustling establishment that was more of a corridor than a shop. People stood in a tight line that doubled back on itself and almost out the door.

"At least it isn't raining," Leda said as she took up a position at the end.

"Small blessings. This place is pretty popular, huh?"

"They do a waffle bar, for breakfast people who want more than a bagel or Danish."

He said, "Ooh!" because that sounded great, actually.

But Leda didn't look hungry. She looked wrung out.

So he said, "Maybe I'll try that next time I'm out here."

When they reached the counter, Leda left to grab the last table while Grady ordered. He joined her shortly, with two tall cups of black coffee in tow. Without a word, Leda reached into the sweetener tub and grabbed every yellow packet present. She tore them all with one rip and dumped the contents into her cup.

He sipped his coffee straight, the way God intended.

When Leda had stirred everything to her liking and downed about half the resulting brew, she finally said, "I needed this. The coffee I mean. Not the guilt of having contributed to the misfortune of others."

"I told you—"

She cut him off there. "I know. Rationally, I know you're right. But it's hard not to feel some culpability here."

"I understand, but there's only one thing that'll make you feel better about that."

"Oh yeah? What?"

He said, "You help me catch the bad guy and hold him accountable. Once we catch him, he can't hurt anybody else. Accidentally, or on purpose."

"I'm doing what I can. I touched the dead lady and everything!" She took another long swig of her coffee, even though it had to be hot. She grimaced and wiped her nose on the sleeve of her sweater. The sun was finally up, but the light was watery and gray, and Leda clearly had no intention of rising or shining. "That's weak, man. That's really weak. Even if we *do* catch the guy and send him to jail for life, it won't do Janette Gilman any good."

"No, but it'll save whoever's next on his list. Look, that's the nature of this business—there's a billion variables, and you're never going to see the whole picture because you're not God, and you have to get okay with that. You can't let it get in the way of doing your job."

"*My* job is to book travel for people who don't know how to make phone calls or compare fares online," she snapped. "If I'd stuck to that job, Janette would still be here. She'd be getting ready for work, or rolling into the office right about now. She wouldn't be rolling into the morgue."

He sighed down into his coffee, and steam blew back into his face. "That's true, and there's nothing we can do about it. Just like there was nothing we could do about losing your fiancé, and nothing Janette could do about losing Christopher or Kevin. The world is full of things we can't control. All we can do is keep trying, keep working. Keep investigating until we finally dig down to the truth."

She snorted softly. "You called this a business. Is that what it really is? A business?"

"It's a figure of speech, that's all."

"If you say so."

He wanted to throw up his hands, but he only lifted his cup. "I don't know what you want. I don't know what to tell you. I appreciate your help—and it *is* help. I know it's not easy for you, and I know I've asked a lot. You're free to bail at any time, and you always have been. If you need to cut loose now, I understand. What else can I say?"

"I'm not trying to cut loose," she said, but her body language said she was thinking about it. She was hunkered over the table, her head hanging low over her coffee, her hands fidgeting with the paper sleeve that kept her fingers from burning.

"Maybe we should take a break from this. It seems like maybe you need some time."

"Or maybe I'm just not a morning person, did you ever think of that?"

He knew good and well that it wasn't so simple, but she obviously wanted an excuse, so he shrugged. "Sure, okay. I'm not a morning guy, either."

"Good. We're both sad dirtbags before noon. So who are we talking to next?" she asked. "Who's still alive, and uninjured?"

"Me and you," he said, a little too quickly, and a little too flippantly. He caught himself before she could finish fashioning a frown that was sure to be positively *withering*. "And Kim, though I might touch base with her, considering. Maybe she'll want a police detail at her house."

"That would be nice. You think she'll be the next target?"

"No idea. But there's me, you, Kim, and the employees from Probable Outcomes who came on board at Digital Scaffolding. There were several of them, I forget how many exactly."

"You said they all alibied out."

"They did, but alibis are only as good as the investigation at the time—and this is the only hard, tangible connection between the death of your fiancé and the Gilmans. That should be our next angle, if you're still on board."

She relaxed her stance and stared past her obscenely sweet coffee instead of down into its depths. "Okay. That's a good idea. I got distracted by the Beckmeyer break-in, and then this whole thing with Janette—may she rest in peace." She looked up at him and nodded. "Don't worry, man. I'm still in. The caffeine is working, and I'm starting to wake up. Let's get back to work."

"Whoa there. You've got to give me a day or two, okay? Hell, give yourself a day or two." It wouldn't take him more than twenty minutes to pull the names together, and maybe another half hour to track down current contact information for all of them. But he had a feeling that he'd pushed too hard, too far, and that Leda needed some breathing room—whether she'd admit it or not.

"A day or two? Time is of the essence! This guy is really getting around."

"Yes, a day or two, and that's all, I swear. Things take as long as they take, okay? So let's say Thursday. That'll give me a couple of days to round up the suspects and arrange at least one meeting."

"It feels like starting over at square one," she complained.

"Nuh-uh," he said. "We've found a promising connection between your case and mine, and now we just have to massage it until a good suspect falls out. This is police work, Leda. Sometimes it's tedious and time-consuming. But if you do it right, and you do it long enough, you can usually find your way to an answer."

"You've got a lot of faith in the process, don't you?"

"I do." He nodded. "Furthermore, I have a lot of faith in *you*. But we can only go so fast here. We don't want to screw up the case for prosecutors down the road." He didn't want to screw up Leda, either. She wouldn't want to hear that part, and if he said it out loud, she'd argue with him.

She took a deep breath that was half coffee steam, sneezed, and wiped her nose again. "All right, I trust you." She glanced down at the Fitbit she seemed to use as a watch. "Shouldn't you be heading into the office yourself, right about now?"

"Sooner rather than later, yeah." He gathered up the napkins, empty sweetener packets, and plastic stirrers they'd used between them and stood up to bus the table. "And tomorrow afternoon, I'll give you a call and let you know what's up. I'll try to arrange something for Thursday."

Leda lifted her half-empty cup and toasted him with it. "Right on. I'd better . . ." She looked around, like she was seeking some direction to escape. Any direction. "I'd better throw on some makeup and get to work myself."

# 23.

Leda did not swing by the office on the way home. She didn't have the energy, despite the sixteen ounces of coffee she'd dumped down her throat. She felt exactly like she ought to, considering she'd been dragged out of bed far too early, then hauled to a crime scene—where she'd subsequently fondled a corpse in hopes of a psychic episode. If you asked her, the episode in question had been one of her worst and least helpful. Contrary to Grady's insistence, she didn't feel like any of it had meant a damn thing. It was all stuff he could've guessed, and stuff that would come out in a careful police investigation anyway.

That was the worst part.

It'd hit her hard, once they'd made it back to the car and she'd given him the short version of what she'd seen. It'd been brutal and weird, and largely meaningless. What did they know, before she came along? They knew that someone had murdered Janette after a struggle. What did they know, after she'd done her thing? That someone had manslaughtered Janette after a struggle.

All she'd done was narrow the gender down to "a dude, definitely," and they were already leaning that way in the first place. It was the weakest of all possible clues.

Truly, she was the most inconsequential of psychics. A Cassandra doomed to know gnarly details about the truth—but only if they're no good to anybody, anywhere, at all. Ever.

Except for the one time she kept a cop off a plane.

She felt sorry for herself while she hunted for the eyeliner she wanted, and she marinated in self-pity as she smoothed her hair into a ponytail. She wallowed in woe as she hunted for a better shirt and some different boots, since the first pair she'd worn that day were wet from the early-morning outing in the damp Seattle dawn. Upon noticing that her socks didn't match, she removed her boots and found a set that went together. No one would see them, but *she* would know, and it would drive her crazy if she didn't fix it.

All in all, she'd rather go back to bed than do anything else.

But now it was after 8:00 a.m., and the rest of the world was up and running. She should at least show up at her office and check her emails. After all, *technically* she had a job. Technically, she was a small-business owner.

Dragging her feet all the way, she walked into the office. It still wasn't raining, and she'd thought the fresh air might perk her up.

She'd thought wrong. She kind of wanted to die.

Instead, she unlocked her office and sat down at her desk. She powered up the computer and, lo and behold, she had emails! From people who wanted to go places! Encouraged by happy adrenaline, she sat up straighter and began typing professional-sounding words that might persuade folks to hire her. Within an hour, she definitely had one new client—and probably a second client, too.

Well, after a morning like the one she'd had, there was nowhere to go but up.

Right?

A third email landed. Her Google and Facebook ads must be working! It wasn't enough to float the business, but it was a good sign. She needed a good sign. As she sent off the requested information and double-checked her email signature, she honestly felt like maybe the day would brighten up after all. If she could hit some perfect threshold of happy customers, word of mouth would pick up, and that would help grow the business. Things were coming up roses all over.

By lunchtime, Leda was thinking about taking a break. Maybe she'd knock off, head home, and take that nap after all. Honestly, she deserved that break.

Also, maybe she deserved sushi.

She hadn't heard from Niki since the night before, so she shot her a text asking if she was free for lunch. It'd been like, eighteen hours. There was so much to catch up on! Niki was probably just lounging around her apartment anyway; and if she agreed to drive all the way out to the south end for sushi at their favorite place . . . then she could probably be persuaded to goof off until the evening, when they could head over to Castaways together.

Niki didn't bother to text back. She called instead. "Hey, I was just thinking about you."

"Of course you were. I'm awesome."

"You sound . . . tired," she observed carefully.

Leda sighed. "Only because you know me so well. It's been a hell of a morning already—I'll tell you all about it when I see you. Will I see you for lunch? Can you come down here and keep me company? I'll buy you sushi. You like sushi."

"Not as much as you do, and you know I love you—but I've got to skip it."

"What?"

Niki said, "Another doctor's appointment. I'm sitting in the waiting room right now."

"Oh God, get off the phone. Don't be the guy who talks in a quiet room full of sick people who just want to be left in peace. Everyone hates that guy."

"Yeah, but I'm the only guy here, so I don't care. I might be getting my boot off. At the very least, I'm getting a lighter one."

"Already?" Leda asked.

"It's been weeks. 'Already' can't come soon enough. I'm ready to have some mobility back. But hey, while I've got you here," she said. "Are you coming to Castaways tonight?"

"I'm pretty wiped out, but I'm thinking about it. Why? Did Ben want to print up posters?"

"Oh, he will, sure. But that's not why I'm asking. Ben wants to start doing *theme nights*. Since you can't do a show on command every night of the week."

"Theme nights?" Leda asked. "Like . . . tiki night? Goth night? Furry night?"

"Those sound amazing, yes. I'll write down those ideas for him. He'll be thrilled. Tiffany will whip up some themed drinks, employees will dress up, and patrons will be encouraged to do likewise."

"How?"

Niki said, "Not sure yet, but Tiffany had a good idea. Like, we get Steve to hand out tickets to people in costumes—and they get two bucks off a drink after happy hour. Something like that."

"I like it. But what does this have to do with me? Do you want to do a couple's costume and Matt says no? You know I'll dress up with you, baby. Any day of the week."

"It's like you read my mind. Say, hypothetically, that Ben's first theme night is 1950s kitsch . . ."

Leda screeched, "Lucy and Ethel!"

Niki cackled. "Damn right! Do you know where those costumes are? Where did you put them?"

Leda hesitated, her glee snagging on the memory of where she'd last seen the dresses and wigs. "They're in the storage unit downtown."

Her friend was quiet for a few seconds. "The Ricky and Fred costumes are there, too, I guess."

"Yeah, it's all mixed up with Tod's stuff. It's okay, though. It's time. Those costumes are too damn cool to be stuffed in a box over mere grief, don't you think?" Leda tried to sound more light-hearted than she felt. "You and me, we're going to *kill it* at the first ever Castaways theme night. I'll bring the Fred and Ricky costumes, too. In case Matt wants to be Ricky again."

More silence, then Niki said, "I'm not sure what to say right here, you know what I mean? Nobody ever wore the Fred costume, so it's not like it was really Tod's. But it *feels* like it was. The only person I can think of, is maybe Grady—but that's not the kind of working relationship you two have, I don't think."

"Correct."

"Right. So. Me and you will be Lucy and Ethel. I'll give Matt the Ricky costume, and you can just . . . hang on to the Fred costume, or whatever makes you happy. Maybe you'll find your Fred someday, and we'll have a big *I Love Lucy* party, and it'll be a whole new chapter for you."

"Maybe."

"Leda? Hon? You okay? I'm sorry—I didn't mean to turn this into something weird. I'm really sorry."

"No, it's okay. Not your fault, and I'd be happy to bust out the Lucy and Ethel garb. I was going to knock off soon anyway, so I'll run by the storage unit this afternoon and dig up all that stuff. I'll bring it with me, and see you tonight."

"Are you sure it's okay?"

"You heard me, I'm good. I'll come around at the tail end of happy hour. Tell Ben I'm in, and he can call me whatever he wants on the posters."

"He already does." Niki paused. She held the phone against some nearby part of her body while she listened to someone say something. She came back and said, "All right, but I have to go now. The doc's calling me back to the exam room. Take care of yourself, please? And if you decide you don't want to do this, that's fine. I promise, nobody will be mad about it."

"I'll be there tonight, costumes in hand. Go get your boot off, so we can dance."

They hung up, and Leda sat alone at her desk, staring at her computer monitor and not seeing any new messages—good, bad, or otherwise.

She powered it down and collected herself. She took a deep breath and grabbed her purse. Food, that's what she needed. Food and then storage unit and costumes and Castaways. She slung the bag over her shoulder and rose to her feet. This was fine. Everything was fine. She hadn't had literally the worst morning in the history of mornings, and tonight there would be free booze. She could do this.

She *could* do this.

First, she went back home and got her car. She didn't need Jason for sushi, because the sushi bar was around the corner from her office—but if Niki wasn't coming along, too, sushi was somehow less appealing. Nah, she'd go pick up a burrito she could bring along for the ride. Something to distract her while she went plowing through a small locked room full of heartache.

She found a Chipotle on the way, got a burrito the size of a newborn, and took it (along with a large, caffeine-loaded soda) to go.

Back to the old Tully's roasting facility she went, wending through the industrial end of the city to get there—because it was easier than hopping on the interstate, where it'd take twenty minutes to go two exits. Might as well use the twenty minutes to see the sights, honk in support of some protestors, give five bucks to a dude holding a sign at a stoplight, and not get run off the road by midday commuters running late or just plain running.

Under the streets was a forest of concrete with a canopy of asphalt high overhead. Leda found a place to park, and it should have felt perilous—it was right underneath an on-ramp—but instead it felt lucky, because it was only half a block away from her destination *and* it was in a two-hour free-parking zone. It was like she'd found a unicorn and left her car on top of it.

If she'd been more awake and less depressed, she might have been in a good mood. She always liked to think of her parking luck as a daily omen, and this was a good one.

But no.

She was grumpy and antsy, and a little bit shaky from too much caffeine and not enough food or sleep and maybe a weird psychic hangover from the dead lady in the bright building. But she'd fix the food part once she got to the unit.

Inside the big old building with cars whizzing past it, she went to the storage unit she'd been keeping since before Tod had died.

She'd first rented it a month after they'd gotten engaged. They'd planned to combine households—and even though those households belonged to a couple of single, job-hopping, broke-ass millennials, there'd still been so much *stuff* that would have to go someplace. It was supposed to be a temporary measure until they could get their own place, but then Tod had died, and they'd never moved in together. Then she'd moved into the bungalow with somehow less room than her old apartment, and even more of her things got crammed into the dark little place. Now it was a labyrinth of boxes, bags, and loose furniture piled like King Tut's tomb up in there.

Tod's parents had taken most of his things, but she'd kept a few, and plenty of her own possessions had reminded her of him. The rest was a mausoleum of things that she didn't always want to touch but couldn't bear to part with.

Too many little flashes, sparkling through her brain like TV static and fireworks. Little memories, playing out again and again. It had nothing to do with psychic powers and everything to do with nostalgia.

She flipped on the light and shut the door behind herself. One of her mother's old dining room chairs was pushed against the wall. She sat down in it and pulled a full, flat box of books over to use as a table, and she started on the burrito in earnest.

A burrito was exactly the right thing to eat alone, in a small storage unit that was more dark than bright, even with a light bulb swaying overhead. Nobody wants anybody to see them wrestling a burrito. It's not dignified. It's slivers of onion and scraps of carnitas falling on the floor, and never quite enough napkins.

"Son of a *bitch*," she complained aloud, her hands covered in runny salsa and sour cream drippings. But there was a box in the unit that had cleaning supplies and trash bags. She'd left it behind after cleaning out her old apartment. It was still hanging out around there someplace, she just knew it.

Before long she found an old plastic bucket with the useful cleaning contents—including half a roll of paper towels.

"Sweet," Leda proclaimed.

While she was over there, she looked around—burrito in hand, still spilling its innards past the foil wrapping and onto the floor. "Gonna have to get that before I go," she reminded herself. Rats could be an issue down in the south end, between the sound and

Lake Washington. If she helped encourage a rat problem for the storage facility, they'd kick her out. It was written into the agreement she'd signed when they gave her the keys.

Near her there were boxes of books she hadn't read in decades but couldn't imagine getting rid of. Over there, the summer clothes she'd worn on spring break to Daytona Beach three years in a row. In that corner, a box of sandals that she didn't get a lot of call for—except for a month or two in the dead of summer.

And over there, she spied a box with club clothes and late-night dancing gear that she hadn't made use of in ages. The costumes were probably in that one.

But she resisted opening it right away. She had food. She didn't want to get food all over the costumes. That's what she told herself as she wandered the small space, reading labels and trying to tamp down all the memories of hopes and plans that hadn't gone anywhere.

After half the burrito was down the hatch, she was no longer hungry. She swabbed up the lost lettuce, the fugitive bits of pico de gallo, and the smattering of stray cheese shreds, and stuffed it all into the paper take-out bag. Then she tossed the rest of the burrito after it, brushed her hands off on her pants, and decided it was time to dive in.

Sitting cross-legged on the floor, she reached into the box where the costumes were most likely to be and started shoving things around.

Fishnet gloves, nah. Crinolines? Yes, probably. She pulled those out and set them beside her. Hooker boots? Lucille Ball would *never*. Dear God, the early 2000s had really been a hell of a time for patent leather and lace, like some kind of late-Gothic-revival period.

More gloves, fingerless this time. She'd had them since college, when she'd bought them for an eighties-themed social event.

She'd worn a banana clip in her hair, too much hair spray, and a bunch of jelly bracelets on top of an outfit Madonna might have tried in 1984. Then again, she might not have. It was kind of a mess from top to bottom, and Leda laughed to remember it. She'd tried to play a piano in those fingerless gloves, but the bows on the back were so big that they flopped over her wrists, and they kept jamming in the keys.

In the keys.

On the piano.

Something flickered in the back of her head.

The keys, her fingers running across them, picking out "Chopsticks" and getting hung up on every other note. She'd been using another name back then. No. She'd never used another name. Yes, and she'd gotten off scot-free. No, that wasn't it. What was she thinking of?

Electricity sparked between her ears, pinging off her memories, her clues, and her abilities. It was like a circus in there, so bright and loud and sudden that she could hardly see. She rubbed at her eyes, and it only made the light show worse.

"Ugh," she groaned. Another ocular migraine. Probably it was her own damn fault, brought about by too much caffeine. She'd read somewhere that caffeine could do that. Or was caffeine supposed to be good for migraines? She didn't know anymore.

Leda dropped her head until it was hanging over her lap, and she rubbed firmly at her temples.

That night in the student assembly hall, playing with the piano keys—even though music was blaring from the speakers on either side of the large television in the gathering area. The TV had been showing some anime or another, with the volume off and the captions on. She didn't remember what it was called, or what it was about. She'd been playing the piano, a few notes at a time. Two fingers. *Tappity-tap.*

She'd gotten away with it, scot-free. No one had complained. No one had caught her. No one had seen what she'd done.

No, there was no Scott. Nothing was free. Not the piano. Not the keys.

No, that's not what her brain was trying to tell her at all. The message wasn't coming from her own brain. It was coming from the killer's.

She clutched the sides of her head, fingers tangling in her hair. "What is this?" she asked nobody and nothing. "I don't understand." She fell over, curled up in a fetal position. She held her hands over her eyes. Her heart raced. Her vision flashed, again and again and again.

Suddenly, yes. The connections. The electricity. Right before she passed out cold on the floor of the storage unit. She finally understood who Scott was, and where he fit into the puzzle of who had killed Amanda Crombie, and the Gilmans, and Ms. Copeland, and Tod, too.

# 24.

When Leda Foley woke up, her half-eaten burrito was cold in the bag, but there weren't any rats yet.

She was winning already.

She dragged herself upright and scrambled around on the floor until she'd collected her thoughts. Nothing like that had ever happened to her before. Nothing so strong and hard, nothing so concrete and fast. It'd knocked her right out.

The side of her head was cold from the concrete she'd left it on, and her right arm was asleep. Her mouth was so sticky and gross that she finished drinking the soda she'd brought—even though it was mostly melted ice by that point. It didn't make her feel any better, but it didn't make her feel any worse, either.

And she felt pretty damn good.

Wait, was that right? She wadded up the paper cup and stuffed it into her bag of burrito detritus. Was it *good*, knowing the answer to a murderous riddle? Or did it turn her stomach?

Maybe a little of both. She scrambled to her feet, collected her trash, grabbed the whole box that held the costumes—she saw the curly red Lucy wig, and she knew she'd found them—and then picked up her purse. She wobbled, straightened up, and corrected herself. "A *lot* of both."

The door slammed behind her as she fled.

She staggered to her car, and once she was seated with the engine running and the heater warming, she pulled her phone out of her purse. She called up Grady's contact info and smashed it with her index finger until it dialed him.

"Leda, I didn't expect to hear from you so soon. Is everything okay?"

He hadn't gotten the last syllable all the way out when she blurted, "I know who killed the Gilmans!"

He was stunned for a beat. "I'm sorry, what?"

"The murderer is a guy named Scott Keyes, but he changed his name to Abbot about a couple of years ago. Before that, I bet you he had some other family name. He's changed it a couple of times," she said with more confidence than she felt. "Something tells me there's a strong family resemblance in the Keyes clan."

Grady asked, "What does that have to do with anything?"

"His alibi. He said he was at his stepbrother's funeral. You said he turned up in photos. I bet you a dollar it wasn't him. He's a lying liar who lies, and a murderer, too. You need to go arrest him, like, right now."

"You know better than that."

"Okay, then get *ready* to arrest him!"

"Come on, Leda. You know good and well that's not how it works. Wait, hang on," he said quietly. Leda got the distinct impression that he was in a room full of people, and he was trying not to sound too crazy in front of them. In the background, she heard murmurs, phones ringing, and a general patter of conversation. Then, a few seconds later, he was up to full volume. "I was in a meeting, sorry. Now I'm out. What do you mean it was Keyes? What's this business about a Scott?"

"Scott Keyes is Abbot Keyes. He changed his name. He's the one who did it, Grady. He murdered all the people!"

"Do you have any proof, or is this just a psychic flash telling you this?"

"Can't it be both?" she asked desperately. She threw her car into gear and hit the road.

"No!" he told her, a dash of exasperation shining through his voice. "Psychic feelings don't count for jack squat in the legal system! Can you prove it? If you're that certain, then you need to . . . to . . . find a way to make everyone else certain. Help me help *you*, as they say."

Her thoughts raced through her head, and her car raced through a four-way stop. "Meet me at Castaways. I need my murder board. I don't know if I can *prove* it to you, but I can definitely *show* it to you. *Please* go pick him up."

He sighed, and she could practically hear him squeezing that little spot between his eyebrows with frustration. "I *can't* go pick him up, because I don't have any evidence that he's done anything wrong. But I'll call in a favor or two and see if I can get eyes on him."

"What does that mean?" She cut somebody off on the way to the interstate on-ramp. The other driver flipped her off and honked, but she barely noticed and didn't even flip them off in return.

"It *means* I'll see if I can get someone to track him down so that we *can* bring him in, if it turns out that you can give me probable cause. I'm sorry, but you have to give me more than your personal paranormal confidence."

"I understand, I do. I get it," she said. "Just meet me at the bar, that's where I'm headed right now. I can show you. I can lay it all out, and you'll see. I'll make you believe me."

Before he could reply, she hung up on him and threw her phone back into her purse.

Both hands now on the wheel, she gunned it for Cap Hill.

Thirty minutes later, she finally found a parking spot within two blocks of Castaways, around the corner from a popular indie bookstore and a defunct KFC. It was a tiny private lot between two buildings, in a space that might have better served the city as an alley, but it was almost rush hour and she'd have to take whatever she could get—even at ten bucks an hour.

Maybe she could get Ben to pay for it, if she did a few songs.

But first.

First, she had a murderer to unmask.

She clicked the door-lock button and kicked the door shut. Where was she again? She checked the nearest street sign and oriented herself, made a mental note of where she was leaving Jason the Accord, and darted toward Castaways—just as it started to rain in earnest.

Behold, the first real downpour of fall, signaling the absolute end of summer. No more final gasps of warm air, no more pretty, dry days. In another couple of weeks, the time would change and it'd start getting dark around three or four o'clock, and Seattle would return to its uniform normal: gray, chilly, and damp . . . for the next six months at least.

Leda welcomed it.

But for half a second, she *did* wish she had an umbrella. Locals didn't typically carry them, because a good, hard rain didn't happen that often—mostly it was just a dull drizzle, and a hoodie would suffice to protect her hair. But she wasn't wearing a hoodie, her travel umbrella was unhelpfully stashed in her car's glove box, and she was already halfway between the lot and the bar when this fact occurred to her.

It didn't matter. She could be soaking wet and still spell out a case for arresting Abbot Keyes.

Leda ran the rest of the way, her hair slapping her face and her feet getting wet. Puddles and rain soaked up her boots past her jeans to her knees, but she ignored it. She shoved the door open and brushed past Steve, who was still collating the two-dollar drink discount tickets that Ben had printed off at the nearest Kinko's.

"Hey, Steve!" she said over her shoulder.

"Leda, how you doing?"

"Fantastic!" she shouted without looking back.

Tiffany laughed from somewhere behind the bar, but Leda didn't pause. She skidded to a halt outside Matt's office, where Matt was actually located—just this once.

He looked up, startled. "Oh . . . hello? Is everything okay?"

Leda pointed at him, and then the corkboard behind him. "I need that!" she announced.

"Now?"

"Now!" She vaulted over his desk. "We have to catch a killer!"

He pivoted in his squeaky rolling chair. "*Right* now?"

She grabbed her index cards from his top-right drawer and a marker from his mug full of writing implements. "*Right now!*"

"Well, hell. Let me get out of the way." He pushed his chair back as far as he could so she could turn the board around without braining him.

"I'm sorry. I'm really sorry. I didn't know you'd be here . . ." She started scribbling on cards and laying them out on his desk, where seconds before he'd been entering employee hours into his laptop.

Matt closed the laptop and tucked it under his arm. "What happened? Do you know who did it?"

"I do!" she declared, equally triumphant and frantic. She had to get it all down while it was fresh in her head. She finally had the solution, she knew what had happened, and it all made sense. Tod's killer was practically within her grasp. All she had to do was stick the landing.

She reached back into the drawer to retrieve a ziplock baggie full of magnets and pulled out a few of the boring dots. She picked them apart from one another and started slapping cards onto the board—adjusting their location and annotating them as she went. "I was in the storage unit with all of Tod's old stuff, and I was eating this burrito . . . and . . . and I got a migraine, but it all came together."

"All hail migraines. And burritos, I guess."

She accidentally knocked off the marker's cap, then picked it up and stuffed it into her mouth to hold it while she kept writing. "Yes. Burritos. Food of the gods, right there," she murmured. "Tod used to love burritos, did you know that?"

"I um . . . I did not. Hey, did you call Grady?"

She nodded, the cap bobbing on her lip. "He's on his way over. He'll be here any minute." She'd be ready for him. She'd be ready for *justice*.

Ben stuck his face around the corner. "What's going on?"

Matt said, "Murder!"

The general manager bounced with glee. "Oh, goodie! Have we solved the case?" He sidled into the tiny office that barely fit one man and one desk and one magnetic board. With the addition of the velvet-clad elder-Goth boss, it felt like an elevator car at the downtown convention center.

Matt retreated until he was sitting on a three-drawer file cabinet against the wall, awkwardly crossing and uncrossing his legs—

trying to figure out where to put them. He settled on the corner of the desk, while Ben rested on the farthest corner of the same. Leda hugged the board and tried not to mess up her progress. She smeared two brightly colored cards onto the floor with an inadvertent swipe of her arm, collected them, and stuck them back where they belonged.

Niki came skidding into the room. She drew up short when she realized how little space was left, so she accepted the tiny square foot she found immediately in front of the desk. "What's going on? What are we doing? Why is everyone in here?"

Leda paused and pointed the marker at her. "I've figured out who the murderer is, and now I'm mapping it out on the board so I can show Grady, and he can go arrest the bastard who killed Tod. Matt was in here already, Ben came in to see what the commotion was about, and now you're here . . . so I think you're all caught up."

Tiffany poked her head around the doorjamb. "Catches who up, with what? Oh, hey, party in Matt's office . . ." She slipped inside to squeeze herself beside Niki. "What are we talking about?"

"Murder!" Niki and Matt shouted.

Ben laughed. "I was going to say 'psychic mumbo jumbo,' but I didn't want to offend my star attraction."

"Psychic mumbo jumbo, yeah," Leda said, taking no offense. "That's kind of what happened, actually. I think I've figured out how it works!"

"How what works?" Grady asked. He shuffled inside a few inches—next to Tiffany, who nudged Niki so far to the right that she opted just to sit in Matt's lap atop the file cabinet. It creaked and teetered beneath their weight but held steady.

Leda grinned like a maniac. "There you are! So glad you could join us."

"I got here as fast as I could. Um, is there someplace we could do this . . . somewhere with more floor space?"

Ben suggested, "We could move the murder board to the stage, if you like."

Silence fell. Leda looked at the board. Matt and Niki exchanged a shrug. Tiffany said, "I'll make drinks for the big reveal! There's nobody in here yet, so I'll just tell Steve to keep people out for a few minutes."

Ben clapped his hands. "Let's do it! I'll grab my laser pointer."

Leda felt a weird twist in her stomach, like this wasn't how she'd expected it to go. A big reveal? A man was dead. Two men. No, three. Fine, a lot of people were dead. But Tod was the one who mattered the most to her. She almost protested; it felt a little public and flashy. But then again, it was a hell of an occasion. It wasn't her friends' fault that they hadn't known and loved her fiancé the same way she had.

She forced herself to brighten her face into a performer's smile. "You have a laser pointer?"

"Yes," Ben said. "And you may use it, upon this momentous occasion!"

With that, he squished himself past Grady and around Tiffany, and vanished down the hall in the direction of his own office. The bartender followed, heading back to the bar. Matt used his feet to push his rolly chair into the small space the shift opened up, and Niki hopped off his lap.

"I'll help with the board," she offered. "You guys go take a seat. We've got this."

Grady said, "Take a seat?" like he was none too sure about this.

Matt gave him a friendly slap on the shoulder and said, "Yeah, man. Front-row seats. Come on, I'll get us set up."

"This is nuts," Grady said as he followed him out. "This is *not* how we conduct police business."

But relocating the murder board only took a couple of minutes, and they only lost a few index cards and a handful of magnets in the hallway as Niki and Leda maneuvered it toward the bar and stage area. Once there, they found that either Ben or Matt had added a pair of chairs to stand in for an easel.

The women set down the board, and Leda went back to the corridor to collect all the bits she'd lost along the way. While she arranged, adjusted, and added a few notes to the cards, everyone else took up seats at two of the small tables down front. Tiffany brought out a flight of multicolored drinks that looked vaguely like fancy party favors. She passed them out, keeping one for herself.

"Everybody ready?" Leda asked, since she was as ready as she was ever going to be. Then she frowned past the lights on the floor and said, "Wait, where's Ben?"

"Right here!" he called from the front door, where he was locking up. "I put a sign up saying we'll be open in twenty minutes. Oh, this is so *exciting*!"

"How about that laser pointer?" Leda reminded him.

He pulled it out of his pocket and tossed it to her, underhand. "Catch!"

Leda ducked, and the pointer hit the board, then bounced off the stage and into Matt's drink. He fished it out and handed it up to the psychic psongstress, who wiped it dry on her pants. With a press of the button, she had a handy red dot. She waved it at the ceiling, and then got the hang of swiping it around. With a great flourish, as if she were directing an orchestra, she made the dot dance across the shiny whiteboard, the brightly colored index cards, the novelty magnets, and the chairs that held them all.

"Ooh," Ben purred. "This is going to be *fun*."

*If not fun*, Leda thought, *then decidedly satisfying*. She took a deep breath. Straightened her back. Tossed her hair; exhaled by blowing a big raspberry.

And started talking.

# 25.

Leda Foley lifted her borrowed laser pointer like Lady Liberty's torch. "Ladies, gentlemen, and the otherwise affiliated . . . I suppose you're all wondering why I've gathered you here today."

This opening line received a smattering of enthusiastic applause from Tiffany and Niki but groans from Grady and Matt. Ben gave her the rolly hands gesture for *Keep going*. She kept going.

"I'm here to reveal the identity of a murderer!"

Grady called from the front row of the audience: "You already told me who it was."

She pointed the laser right at his forehead. "Yes. I did. I told you, and you said it wasn't enough that I merely *knew* who did it. You said I have to *prove* who did it."

"Well, who was it?" asked Niki. "Don't leave the rest of us hanging!"

Leda aimed the pointer at her best friend's cleavage. "I will. But first, a brief explanation of what I've learned about my psychic abilities throughout the course of this case."

Now everybody groaned. Ben booed and cupped his hands over his mouth when he called, "Cut to the chase!"

"Everybody calm your tits!" Leda commanded. "I'm *getting* there, but the answer won't make any sense unless I explain how I *got* there, okay? And Grady's the only one who knows the whole story, so I'll have to set the scene for the rest of you."

Before anyone could argue, she quickly said, "For most of my life, this whole clairvoyant thing has been really hit-and-miss. I spent a lot of time making incorrect predictions based on my psychic flashes, or that's what I thought. What was *actually* happening was that I was drawing the *wrong* conclusions from the *right* information. I was bad at sorting out the signal from the noise. Singing here at Castaways has helped a lot with that, so thank you, Ben—and Matt, and everybody else who's been making that possible over the last few months."

Tiffany led the tiny crowd in another small fit of applause.

When it died down, Leda said, "Even so, I've been generating a lot of useless hits for poor Grady over there when it comes to the case of the murdered Gilmans. I was pinging hard on things like the name *Scott*, and a piano at the Beckmeyers' place. I had no idea what any of it meant, but I knew it was important. My point is, I knew I was right, but I didn't know what I was right *about*. I was thinking about it all wrong—trying to tie each little piece of info to some specific theory, when in fact, I needed to take all the small weird things as a whole and look at them *that* way. It's like I've been playing a game of Password with myself."

Niki frowned. "I don't get it. I *want* to get it, but I don't."

"Let me try this from another angle." Leda turned her attention to the murder board. "Let me walk you through what really happened, starting with Tod Sandoval and Amanda Crombie."

"You can do that?" asked Matt.

She steeled herself, assuming her best teacher pose. "Well, I'm going to try. Some of this is stuff I know from psychic visions, some of this is stuff I figured out from the clues at hand. Some of this, I'm pulling directly out of my ass. Let the record reflect that I never said otherwise." She stabbed her laser pointer at the left-hand column of index cards. "Now, here goes: Tod and Amanda didn't meet until a few minutes right before they died, we know that much. We also know that they met at a gas station a little east of town. Here's what I think happened next . . . cobbled together via psychic flashes and good ol' intuition. And I know, I know. Some of this is speculation, but I'm asking you all to play along, okay? Hear me out: Tod had just filled up his car when he heard someone calling for help in a loud whisper—it was Amanda, hanging out just outside the service station lights. She didn't want to be seen, because she knew she was being followed. She'd been run off the road nearby and attacked by a strange man—but she'd escaped, and now she was hiding and trying to get help."

Matt was on a question-asking roll. He raised his hand and didn't wait for Leda to call on him. "Why wouldn't she take a chance, sprint inside, and ask the desk person to call the cops?"

Leda pointed the laser at his sternum. "I don't have the faintest idea."

"Actually, *I* do," Grady said. "She'd lost her glasses. She was really, really nearsighted, and she couldn't be sure that the assailant wasn't right behind her or looking for her around the gas station. She couldn't even be sure that she wouldn't accidentally ask him for help."

"Good to know. At any rate, she picked Tod. She asked him for help, and of course, he tried to help. He was Tod. He always tried to help." Leda's voice hitched, but she was on a roll and she couldn't stop now. She swallowed and kept going. "He offered her a ride, but they didn't get very far. He ran off the road and crashed into the guardrail near the lake, and maybe he was stunned—maybe he thought he'd blown a tire and got out to check."

Tiffany raised her hand. "Why did he run off the road?"

"I can't say for certain, but I can guess: The killer saw Amanda get into Tod's car, so he followed them. He'd already run Amanda off the road, and he figured he could do it again. He could've flashed his high beams . . ." Her voice wobbled. The high beams. The brilliant white light behind her eyes.

"It *wasn't* just an ocular migraine," she marveled aloud. "It was the high beams." Several hands went up, but she waved them all away. "Never mind. One way or another, Tod and Amanda were both out of the car. Tod tried to be a hero, and it didn't go well for him. Amanda didn't get very far on foot without her glasses. When they were both dead, the killer stuffed Tod into the car and pushed it into the water."

Grady's hand shot up. "Why did he leave Amanda's body in the culvert? Why not stick her into the car, too?"

"I have no idea," said Leda. "I never touched or saw anything of Amanda's, and I don't have that connection to her experience. But if you forced me to guess, it was probably just because it was easier. If he shot Tod near the car, all he had to do was stuff Tod *into* the car—and get rid of two birds with one stone. If Amanda made it far enough away that it'd be hard to haul her back, then he might as well stash her someplace close at hand."

The detective nodded. "You have a point. He could've tipped her in almost anywhere. But we still don't know why she was the target in the first place."

Leda waved her laser around one of Amanda's index cards. "She was an accountant. She found evidence of embezzlement."

"Another connection between the two cases," Grady observed.

"Amanda caught someone skimming from Probable Outcomes, just like our Gilman killer was caught doing the same."

"Correct. It turns out that stealing money is like any other crime: If you've gotten away with it once, you can do it again. And the same goes for murder. After Tod and Amanda, our villain just kept on thieving. Which brings us over here, to"—she waved her pointer at the right-hand column—"Christopher and Kevin Gilman. And Janette Copeland," she added—indicating one of her freshly written cards. "All murdered by the same dude. I'm not even sure he killed Tod on purpose, but once he'd knocked off one person . . . taking out a few more didn't seem like such a stretch to him."

Leda took a step back and stood to the side of board. "Now, let us consider the Gilmans. Christopher may have been a real dick, but he wasn't stupid—and when one of his newer employees began stealing from Digital Scaffolding, he took notice . . . but he didn't blow the whistle."

Tiffany, who had not been privy to the whole case thus far, raised her hand and asked: "Why not?"

Leda said, "Allow me to refer you to this card." She pointed at one that read, in its entirety, *Christopher Gilman: dick.* "Chris was a jerk and an opportunist. He realized that he had dirt on the thief. With this information, he could use this dirt to manipulate the thief into doing even worse, grosser things than skimming a little cash. Things like . . ." She swirled the red dot around a card that read *Richard Beckmeyer: frame-up victim.*

Matt said, "What?"

Grady filled him in. "Christopher Gilman wanted to get rid of Beckmeyer and his wife, the angel investor, so he tried to blackmail the thief into smearing Beckmeyer into oblivion—or at least out of the company. But it didn't work."

Niki asked, "Why not?"

Leda took the reins on that one. "Because our thief was *also* a murderer. Christopher thought he was just some pencil-pushing millennial schmuck, but no! This was a man who'd killed other people to cover his own ass once before—and he was prepared to do it again. It was probably easier this time. Why, you ask? Well, for one thing, his first victims were just plain unlucky. Tod was in the wrong place at the wrong time. Amanda had the misfortune of being the woman who figured out that a thief was sitting in the next cubicle over. But Christopher Gilman? Everybody hated that dude. More than a couple of people suggested that they were glad he was gone, not least of all his now-dead widow."

Matt said, "Ouch," and crossed his arms, settling into the chair with the grin of a man who's stumbled across a truly excellent reality TV show.

Their hostess with the laser pointer agreed. "Ouch *indeed*. But if he wanted people to remember him more fondly after his death, he shouldn't have been such a douchebag when he was alive. Now, I don't know how much dirty business the thief actually per- formed for Chris Gilman, but eventually, our guy had enough of being manipulated. He lured Chris out to the hotel with . . . with God knows what. A promise of money or information? Perhaps."

"But what about Kevin?" asked Grady.

Leda indicated the nearest card with Kevin's name on it. "Kevin knew his father was hot garbage, and he'd become suspicious. That's where Kim Cowen comes in." She used the laser to high- light the woman's bright orange card. "Kim was Christopher's assistant. She was the one who handled the nitty-gritty of his day- to-day life, and she had a big-ass crush on Kevin. Kevin suspected that his dad was up to some shady shenanigans, and on that fateful day, he asked Kim where to find him."

Niki said, "Oh no . . ." and covered her mouth with her hands. Through her fingers, she said, "She must blame herself."

Leda nodded. "She absolutely does, even though she knows it wasn't her fault." She cast a glance at Tod's column of cards and tried not to think about all the ways she'd twisted the events surrounding his death until she was to blame for it, in a thousand different ways. "Sometimes you can know something and still . . . *not* know it."

But this wasn't about her. It was about Keyes.

Once more, she swallowed hard and raised the pointer. She'd come this far. Time to bring it home. "Kim told Kevin that his dad was taking a private meeting out in Shoreline, and Kevin decided to crash it. I think he meant to confront his father, maybe even threaten him, I don't know. I never got a good read on him, or his intentions. The important part is that he found his dad. Somewhat inconveniently, Christopher was in the process of being murdered, and since Kevin got an eyeful of it . . . Kevin got murdered, too. Meanwhile, the thief escaped to murder another day."

Ben asked, "Shouldn't we be calling this guy a murderer, not a thief?"

"Good point. Going forward, he's Mr. Murder. You like that better?"

"I *do*," Ben said happily.

Leda held the laser pointer like a gavel and pretended to bang it. "Then it's duly entered into the record. Mr. Murder went back to his regular life, pretending that he hadn't murdered anybody or stolen anything. And it worked! For a while, at least. Then some cop who didn't blow up in a plane crash came sniffing around with a travel agent who was pretending to be a police consultant."

Grady's hand shot up. "Technically, you weren't pretending. Technically, you *were* consulting—and you did a good job. You gave me fresh information to work from."

Leda aimed the laser back at Grady, very briefly. "Thank you. I appreciate the vote of confidence."

Niki waved her arms, trying to hustle the reveal along. "Leda . . . *then* what happened?"

"*Then* Mr. Murder got scared." Leda aimed the laser at Niki, and let it linger. "Mr. Murder got scared, because we brought an extra consultant when we interviewed him, and Grady introduced her as a forensic accountant."

"Oh my God." Niki put her hands back over her mouth and drew her feet up onto the chair. It was only then that Leda noticed she was wearing a much smaller boot on her injured foot.

"It was bull, obviously. But Mr. Murder bought it. By sheer, stupid coincidence, he was afraid he'd been found out yet again, and he started to panic."

"You mean, it was . . ."

Triumphantly, Leda declared, "Yes! It was Abbot Keyes! The guy you met in the coffee shop at the UW bookstore."

"The Victorian orphan?"

"The very same," Leda said with a big smile and a hearty nod. "His real name is Scott Keyes, or it used to be. He legally changed it a month or two before he got hired at Digital Scaffolding. It's funny, I couldn't figure out how or why I was pinging so hard on the piano keys, and on the name Scott . . . but there you go. He tweaked it just enough to adjust for internet searches on his name and work history, but not so far that he could be accused of trying to reboot his identity. Maybe he was tired of the Francis Scott Key jokes."

Matt cackled, then asked, "Wait . . . would people seriously make those jokes?"

Leda shrugged. "*I* would. But we all know I'm a weirdo. Anyway, after we left him, he spiraled and got careless. He knew we'd be running down the list of people from Digital Scaffolding who might've had access to accounts, and he was afraid he was about to get hoisted by his own sloppy petard. That's why he ran around town, making efforts to clean up after himself—and only making things worse in the process.

"He started with Richard Beckmeyer. Richard was the last guy Chris Gilman had a problem with. He hadn't worked at the company long, but he and his wife had access to the financials, and they might've kept backup records. Apparently they hadn't, or at least Keyes couldn't find them in time to make off with them. But he had to look, so he broke in and nearly killed Sheila Beckmeyer in the process."

Tiffany asked, "Wait. How many people has this guy accidentally killed, or almost killed?"

Leda paused and did the math out loud. "Accidentally? I don't know about Tod, but maybe Tod—plus Kevin Gilman. They're both definitely dead, and so is Janette Gilman. She was an accident, too. Kind of. Then there was Sheila, and she survived."

"This guy's a freaking hazard," the bartender muttered.

"A danger to himself and others, yes," Leda agreed. "After Sheila narrowly survived his burglary and attempted arson, he moved on to Janette Gilman, thinking she might be holding on to the paperwork, or taxes, or anything at all that might peripherally implicate him in wrongdoing. He tried to ransack her office when she wasn't there, but she doubled back and caught him—and it all went south. Literally. She fell off a very tall and broken escalator, and that was the end of Ms. Gilman. I mean, Ms. Copeland."

She added, "She hated her dead husband so much that she went back to her maiden name as soon as he was gone."

Matt said, "Wow," and looked like he'd very much like a bowl of popcorn for this show. "And she still died, and it was still his fault. Man, this guy sounds like a real winner."

Leda was confused. "The dead boss, or the killer?"

"Both of them," he said with a serious head nod of disapproval.

"Totally correct." She adjusted her grip on the laser pointer and directed it back at her murder board. "Now, you may be asking yourself, 'Self, why did no one make the connection between the murder of a woman at Probable Outcomes and two murders at Digital Scaffolding—even though Digital Scaffolding hired several people who'd formerly worked at Probable Outcomes?'"

Niki demanded to know, "Yeah, why not?"

Grady held up his hand. Without waiting to be called on, he said, "The murders occurred a couple of years apart, for one thing—and for another, we didn't know that Keyes used to work at Probable Outcomes. He left that off his résumé, and since he'd changed his name, he wouldn't have turned up in any cross-reference searches between the two. But the fact is, until Leda joined the conversation, we didn't realize that we needed to look for a connection between the two cases, or the two companies."

Leda said, "Yes. What that nice man just said. That's why. Since Keyes had zero connection to Tod, that complicated any searches the police might've made for someone with a motive to kill him. No one knew whether Tod or Amanda was the original intended target. Now we do! Now we can go collect Keyes, throw him in jail, and maybe give him the chair!"

Grady cleared his throat, loudly and pointedly. "We don't have the death penalty in Washington anymore. And when we did, it was either lethal injection or a noose."

Leda let the laser pointer droop. With a frown, she asked, "Noose?"

"Yeah, the state used to let you choose."

"People could choose . . . hanging?" she squeaked.

"Well, it didn't happen very often."

Leda couldn't decide if she was relieved or disappointed. Probably disappointed. "Then he can just rot in prison for the rest of his life."

"*If* we can spin all this speculation into evidence. You've definitely given me enough to bring him in for questioning, but don't get ahead of yourself. There's still a lot of work to be done before we can lock him up and throw away the key."

Deep down she'd known this particular roadblock was coming, but it left her deflated all the same. "But you believe me, don't you?" If he believed her, then there was still a way forward. "Don't you?"

Everyone looked at Grady. Grady kept his eyes on Leda. "I *do* believe you, but I'm just one cop. You need more cops, a judge, and probably a lawyer or two to believe you, too. I think we can make it happen, though—I really do."

"You do?"

"Yeah, and that's why I sent a couple of uniformed officers to swing by the university and keep an eye on him before I drove out here."

Niki turned to him. "How do you know he's at the school?"

"I made a phone call to an administrator and got his class schedule. Right about now, he's in a programming class that runs until seven o'clock." Grady took out his phone and checked the screen. "Oh, hey, excuse me a minute." He rose to his feet, then paused to address Leda. "I don't mean to sneak out before the end of the show, but ..."

She waved encouragement at him. "No, don't be ridiculous—go! Go make sure he's in custody! I'm done here anyway, I guess." She checked the board, ran her eyes down all the index cards, and then nodded to herself. "Yep. That's pretty much everything. I have solved a murder!"

More applause, led by Ben and Tiffany together. Everyone who wasn't already standing rose to their feet, and Leda took a little bow.

"Thank you, thank you," she said, keeping one eye on Grady as he discreetly walked away and began poking at his phone's screen.

"I'll um . . . I'll put this stuff away now, so you can open the doors. You ought to be open by now anyway. People will get restless."

"That was magnificent! Just magnificent!" Ben's clapping finally died down, but the big, beaming smile on his face did not. "Oh!" he barked, "Leda! Wait—did you bring those costumes? Niki said you would have them with you."

She ceased her efforts to lift the murder board off the chairs without knocking anything loose, and let it sit back on top of the chairs. "They're in my car. Do you want them right now?"

"I *did* put rockabilly down as tonight's theme! It's already on the flyers."

She rolled her eyes and grinned at him anyway. "I'm not sure how 'rockabilly' Lucy and Ethel are, but I guess they'll do."

He gestured like he was wearing a dress with fluffy crinolines. "But the skirts, yes? You have the tiny waists, and the big slips, and the curly-hair wigs?"

"Yeah, yeah. All that and then some. It'll be fine. Let me just put this away. . . ."

Matt said, "Don't worry about it—I'll take care of it. You go get the dresses, and you can change in my office before we let the crowds inside."

"Great, thank you. I really appreciate it," Leda told him as she hopped down off the stage. "Give me five minutes, and I'll be right back."

But before she could make a run for Jason, Niki tugged her elbow to get her attention. "Hey, are you . . . is this . . . is everything . . . okay? That was pretty intense. Good," she added, "but intense. If you want to take a minute before getting back to real life, nobody will hold it against you."

Leda hesitated. "I love you for asking. . . ." She looked back at the stage, being swiftly disassembled from crime-solving and reassembled for karaoke.

Niki followed her gaze and said out loud what Leda had only been thinking. "Well, they don't know you like I do. They didn't know Tod."

She nodded, slowly and then more firmly. "I appreciate it. I appreciate you. But I appreciate them, too—and as far as they're concerned, the show must go on."

"Are you sure?"

"I'm sure." She squeezed Niki in a fast, intense hug and turned her loose. "Now get in there and get ready to rock and roll. I'll be back in a minute."

Riding high on adrenaline and busily running away from some uncomfortably mixed feelings, she ducked into Matt's office. She'd left her purse in there, and she'd need her car keys. She seized them in her fist and flinched. A halo of light flashed around her left eye.

"I know, I know," she told it. "The headlights. I get it. Knock it off, already." She grabbed a travel umbrella that had been sitting on Matt's desk for a week or more and added that to her arsenal. This was fine. Everything was going to be great.

But the light kept flashing, white and cold, as she took the keys and ran out the back door, into the rainy night.

# 26.

Grady didn't like the messages that had popped up on his phone while he'd been listening to Leda's extemporaneous murder presentation. He dialed Lieutenant Carter, since she was the one he'd trusted with his oddball request.

She answered immediately. "We've got a problem."

"What kind of problem? Did your guys find Keyes?"

"No, they did not. He wasn't in class, and he's not at home, either. I've put out a BOLO on his car, but I don't know how much good that'll do us. Did you learn anything useful, or was this a wild-goose chase from the start?" she asked.

"Definitely not a wild-goose chase. Since last we spoke, I've learned that the guy changed his name. We're looking for a Scott Abbot Keyes. He dropped the Scott, so nobody noticed that he used to work for a company called Probable Outcomes."

"Okay, why is that important?"

"Because he's made a habit of stealing money, then killing to cover it up." Grady went into a brief outline of what had happened to Tod and Amanda. "I realize it's circumstantial—but a mountain of circumstantial evidence has to amount to something eventually, right?"

"You know better than that, Detective. Your psychic consultant is rubbing off on you."

He stayed silent for a beat. Then he asked, "Who told you?"

"I thought she looked familiar, so I looked her up and realized I'd seen her on those flyers around the hill. Don't take this the wrong way, but I *do* hope you're not using up our scant police resources on a psychic travel agent." Then she clarified, "In her capacity as either a psychic, or a travel agent. I'm sure she's lovely, but we have protocols in place for a reason."

"No, no. It's not like that. She's got a real gift, and I'm not saying that lightly. I would've never known about the connection between the murders without her; I haven't paid her in anything but coffee. Actually, I owed her a check—out of my own pocket. She's working for cheap, because she wants answers even more badly than I do. Her fiancé was one of the first victims."

"Ah." It was Carter's turn to think about her response. "You understand, any defense attorney who finds out we've arrested a guy on the suggestion of a clairvoyant . . ."

"You don't have to say it. I'm way ahead of you, and I've been very, very careful to keep her on the periphery—and make sure I can independently verify anything she tells me. I'm not conducting a case based on hunches or crystal balls."

"That's good to hear, but you and I both know you brought that woman to an active crime scene. At least twice."

So she knew about their visit to the Beckmeyers' residence, too. Grady cleared his throat. "I couldn't very well bring her into the station to talk to Richard or Sheila, now could I?"

"Grady."

He sighed. "I know, I know. But she's not going to compromise anything—I won't let her. Anyway, right now I'm more worried about Keyes coming after her or her friend, the forensic accountant."

"What? You hired a forensic accountant, or you got the state to send somebody in?"

"Not a real one. It's a long story. But the guy thinks we have more dirt on him than we do, and he's running around town, trying to clean up any loose ends."

"You're afraid the psychic is a loose end?" Carter asked.

"She's the only one left, unless he thinks our fake accountant knows something. There's always the chance he might go after her, too."

"Does the fake accountant know anything that can incriminate this guy?"

"Of course not. She's a bartender who works at Smith Tower. It was just a story I used on the fly." Rather than explain any further, he added, "We need to get him in for questioning. He's going to keep hurting people until we do. Listen, I can come down there and—"

"Detective, I *promise*. We're working on it. If this guy turns up—you'll be the first to know."

His eyes swept the swiftly filling room. "That's what I'm afraid of."

"What does that mean?"

"That I'm here with the psychic and the bartender both, and I'm not saying they're sitting ducks, but you can see it from here."

The lieutenant said, "Maybe you should stay put."

"Yeah, I think I'm gonna." With that, he thanked her and let her go. He tucked his phone into his pocket.

Tiffany saw him put the phone away and made him an offer. "Can I get you a drink?"

"No, thanks, I don't need the booze."

"Are you sure? You're wound up pretty tight tonight. I'm surprised you're not more excited about this whole thing! Leda solved a murder, dude!"

"We don't know that for a fact just yet."

"Oh, come *on.*" She set a highball glass full of ice in front of him and pulled out her soda gun. As she filled the glass with Coke, she told him, "You can just admit that it was amazing. Have you caught the guy?"

"No, we're still looking for him. I'm sure we'll have him soon."

"You don't sound very sure of that."

"I don't?"

She slipped him a coaster and a straw. Then she leaned forward, lowering her voice. "No, you don't. Is something wrong? You can tell me. You can tell bartenders anything. We're like priests."

He grunted a laugh. "Nothing's wrong," he fibbed. "I'm just impatient."

"You're a terrible liar."

"Oh, come on."

She found a maraschino cherry, reached across the bar, and dropped it into his glass. "What's really eating you?" She leaned forward on her elbows and gave him her widest-eyed look of *Talk to me* earnestness.

He surrendered and took the beverage, leaning against the bar while he considered sipping it—but kept forgetting to. "Keyes should've been in class, and he wasn't. The guy's a flake, and we knew that much already, but he seemed to really be trying to pull himself together. Even if he's given up on getting his life in gear, he wasn't at home, his car's in the wind, and there's no telling where he's gone or what he's up to."

"You think he's up to shenanigans?"

"I'm confident of it. And here's the thing, right? He's exactly the sort of guy who blends into the background. Average-looking fellow, on the short and thin side, but ordinary-looking enough. He changed his name a little bit and virtually disappeared. That's all it took, just like that." He snapped his fingers for emphasis.

"You think he'll vanish again?"

"Well, he already suspects that we're on to him. Jesus, the forensic accountant thing." Before Tiffany could ask, he said, "It was just a joke. I was talking with Leda and Niki about what to say, and they were making up cover stories ... and somebody suggested we call Niki a forensic accountant, since that sounds official and police-related. So when we all sat down, that's how I introduced her. It was a quick, stupid lie. Completely off-the-cuff. But it's the thing that spooked him. It's the thing that sent him running to the Beckmeyers' place, and then to Janette."

Grady and Tiffany might have talked more, but the doors were open, and people were pouring in, and Grady no longer had an official bartender/priest dedicated to his own personal problems. He took his Coke, saluted her with it, and retreated from the bar.

Grady held his phone down on his palm faceup, so he could stare at it—*willing* it to produce good news. As if he, too, were developing mental powers, a text alert from Lieutenant Carter appeared.

He seized the phone.

Found suspect's car. Officers on the scene saw items from Janette Copeland's office in the back seat. Getting a warrant for his apartment.

Immediately, he texted back. No sign of him? Where's the car?

No, but the car will be headed for impound. Found it near Pike and 12th.

His stomach sank. He knew it. The son of a bitch was headed *here*.

He picked up a flyer that had fallen to the floor. It was bright pink with a picture of Leda behind the microphone along with showtimes, some silly advertising copy with too many exclamation points, and the address for Castaways—no more than four blocks away from the corner of Pike and Twelfth.

It couldn't be a coincidence.

He scanned the room. He spotted Niki first and pushed through the crowd to reach her, ducking around the tables and chairs and squeezing in behind the table full of sound equipment at the base of the stage, where Niki and Matt were getting ready for the show to come.

"Hey, have you seen Leda?"

Niki and Matt looked at each other. Niki said, "No, but Ben said something about her going to get the costumes out of her car. She said she'd had trouble finding a spot to park, and there was no place free out back. She might've settled for one of the pay lots."

"Any idea which one?" Grady asked, trying to keep the desperation out of his voice.

"Not a clue. She'll be back soon, man," Matt said with a reassuring smile.

Niki asked, "Why? Is something wrong?"

Grady looked over his shoulder, trying to catalog the whole room and everyone in it—but it was too dark, too crowded, with too much motion. "Niki, you remember what Mr. Murder looks like, right?"

"Sure. Why do you— Oh my God."

"No, no. Stay cool," he said. "But keep your eyes open." Then he tapped his phone in his pocket to make sure he still had it. His gun and badge were back in his car.

Just before he dipped back into the crowd, he said, "Don't go anywhere, don't do anything, and don't say anything to freak anybody out. I'll be right back."

He didn't know if he meant it.

# 27.

Leda let the back door slam behind her as she ran out into the early night. The tiny travel umbrella was rarely used, and when she popped it open she was greeted with a cloud of dust that turned to mud as soon as the rain hit it. It dripped down her sleeves as she fled the alley.

She paused beneath an awning just outside the back alley. A gutter sent a pool of roof water down onto the sidewalk, and she used this to rinse the umbrella before holding it over her head again. That was better, yes. Now all she had to do was remember where she'd parked.

Oh yeah, the lot near the bookstore.

She looked back toward Castaways and saw a young couple laughing and splashing through the rain, dressed like Elvis and Elvira. It was still a little early for Halloween—so they must be headed to the bar to see Leda's show. Which she was not at. Because she had left her outfit in the car. Like a dumbass.

She walked leaning forward, keeping the umbrella low over her head and staring down at the sidewalk to avoid puddles and trash and other people's feet. The hill was hopping, even though it was a weeknight and it was barely seven o'clock. The community college had let out most of its classes, people were heading out to dinner, and it was late enough to drink without feeling awkward about it. Before long, Castaways would be *packed*.

It only made her more anxious. She was increasingly comfortable performing in front of others—even a lot of others—but she hated to keep people waiting.

She stepped off the curb and found herself ankle-deep in a cold, dark puddle. With a shriek she hopped out. A car was turning her way, so she darted into a small jaywalking infraction that no one would notice.

Wait. Was she going the right direction?

Leda paused.

She'd gotten turned around. She looked around, searching for a sign that might tell her something useful. Instead, she saw Abbot Keyes. Scott Keyes. Whoever the hell he was.

Mr. Murder.

He was standing on the far street corner, doing the same thing she was—seeking landmarks with which to orient himself. He held a bright pink piece of paper that was disintegrating into the consistency of a damp washcloth. Ben's latest flyer.

"Oh my God," she breathed. He was looking for Castaways. He was looking for *her*.

But he hadn't seen her yet.

She swiveled on one soaked foot and began a casual, not-at-all-frantic stroll back toward the bar so she could warn her friends. That's what she should do, right? She hadn't brought her phone; she'd taken only her keys.

Keys. Keyes. Abbot Scott Keyes, or Scott Abbot Keyes? She couldn't remember.

The light behind her eye was an ice pick through her skull. She smashed her hands to her face, as if she could rub the brightness and pain away.

She went from a saunter to a stagger, then back to a saunter again. Had to act cool. Had to be just another normal black-wearing Seattleite on the hill, wandering toward a drink or some other distraction. If she kept her face down, no one would notice her.

As badly as she wanted to, she didn't look back. She wouldn't let herself—not until she reached the nearest corner and ducked past it. She pressed herself against a cold stone wall and lowered the umbrella. She peeked around the side of the building to see if he was still there, or if he'd followed her.

He was gone.

No.

There he was—walking toward the bar. He was closer than she was. Even if she made a run for it, she probably wouldn't beat him. But she *had* to warn her friends. Could she come back in through the rear door? Only if it wasn't locked. She tried to remember if she'd heard it latch when it'd swung behind her, but she couldn't. It probably had. It always did.

Her heart vibrated between her ribs.

She needed to get a message to Grady. Maybe some random person would let her use their cell phone? She'd left hers in her purse, back at the bar. If she couldn't beat Keyes to the bar, maybe she could call somebody and tell them he was coming.

Her eyes darted left to right, and suddenly the street felt very empty—when only a moment before it had felt so crowded. She was off the main drag, tucked away beneath an overhang that kept her mostly dry. Her black umbrella wouldn't draw any attention, unless she started going up to folks and asking for help.

She thought of Amanda Crombie, blind and afraid, lurking at the edges of a gas station island and praying that the killer wouldn't see her.

Was she thinking of Amanda, or feeling her?

The vivid white light rendered her left eye useless, and the halo of the migraine was creeping toward her right eye. "No, no, no . . ." She rubbed them, for all the good it did. She blinked hard, forced herself to concentrate, and saw no one in immediate hailing distance except for a couple of homeless guys and a pair of teenage girls with vape pens that probably weren't holding nicotine cartridges.

Teenage girls would have phones, right?

"Hey . . . hey, you girls," she hissed from the shadows, like some kind of trench-coat-wearing creeper. "Hey, girls. Over here."

Only one of them noticed, and she was not impressed. "Ew, leave us alone."

"I need help! Can I use your phone?"

The other teen looked up to see who her friend was talking to. "What? No. Get away from us."

Desperate, Leda said, "If I don't, will you call the police? You can call the police on me, if you want! I can rob you, if that helps!"

But the girls hurried off without dialing 911, getting as far away from Leda as they could get, as fast as they could possibly go in their very heeled boots and very tight skirts.

Leda swore and hugged herself, knocking the umbrella on the wall beside her. "Screw it," she declared. She had bigger problems than wet hair under a wig. She peeked around the corner again and still saw no sign of Keyes. Was he already inside Castaways? She didn't dare go inside to find out. What if he started shooting? He had a real track record for accidentally killing bystanders, and she didn't want the body count rising any higher. She dropped the umbrella in the nearest overflowing trash can, got her bearings, and started to run toward the big bookstore near the ball field. She'd parked across the street from it, she remembered that much.

In her trunk she kept a small hatchet-like device she called her "Nazi Knocker," in case of skinheads. It was an ax, a prybar, and another couple of things she couldn't remember right that second, all in one. Small enough to hide in a coat, hearty enough to bash in a brain. It was a weapon, and she wanted a weapon.

She was flailing, and she knew it. But her head hurt, and her eyes weren't working right, and there was a murderer looking for her, in her safe place, where her friends were. Desperate and disoriented, she struggled to focus.

A weapon. She had one in her car.

She took off running, splashing down the sidewalk with one eye on fire and the other one fighting to keep her going in a straight line. The migraine had tried to tell her, hadn't it? It had warned her, as best it could. This one was tied to her psychic senses, she understood that now. This one had never been a mere clue; it'd always been a warning, and she'd ignored it, and look at her now: wet, terrified, fleeing a murderer.

Leda skidded to a stop at a big intersection with too many lanes converging in too little space and too few stop signs. No stoplights. Cars honking, arguing among themselves over who had the right of way. The light in her left eye was wobbly fireworks, but her right eye was clear enough to see a window of opportunity between two bumpers. She turned sideways and squeezed between them, avoiding a Jeep as it tore through the intersection.

Safe on the other sidewalk, she kept moving. The bookstore was only half a block away. Her car was practically right in front of it.

Wait. The bookstore would have a phone. She drew up to a stop.

Yes, a phone was a better idea than a weapon. She could call Grady. He knew what Keyes looked like, and he could just arrest him if he saw him skulking around Castaways, acting all innocent.

Everything within easy reach was either a closed business or a locked first-floor landing for a condo building. She tried one door for good measure. It was locked. Should she press a bunch of buttons and see if someone would buzz her in? No, she discarded the idea.

The bookstore was a sure bet, and it was *right over there.*

In a matter of moments, she was sliding off the sidewalk and up the stairs to the Elliott Bay Book Company. The old wood floors creaked a symphony as she slipped across them, her wet boots and wet clothes creating her own personal obstacle course as she flung herself onto the front counter.

"You have to help me!" she gasped.

The woman behind the counter gasped, too. "Are you all right?"

"No! I need a phone! Do you have a phone? Please, I need to call nine-one-one!" Leda couldn't remember Grady's phone number, but she could remember that one just fine.

Alarmed, the bookseller pushed a landline phone across the counter. "Here, use it. Do what you have to. Do we need to evacuate? What's wrong?"

Leda seized the receiver and started mashing buttons. "No, but my stalker"—for lack of a better word—"is right there, out on the streets, and he's looking for me, I think, and the police are looking for—" She stopped herself, because a guy had answered the call.

"Nine-one-one, where is your emergency?"

She almost said it was in the bookstore but caught herself in time. "The Castaways bar on Capitol Hill—or it will be, soon!"

"I'm sorry? What is the nature of this emergency?"

Through the window behind the bookseller, she saw a flash of dark hair and a dark jacket—both soaked, but both recognizable even in profile. He wasn't at Castaways. He was following her instead. He must've seen her after all, and she had to make a decision.

Oh God. She didn't have time for this. "The police are looking for a man named Abbot Keyes in connection with a series of high-profile murders," she said as quickly as she could. "He's following me around Cap Hill right now, and he'll probably end up in the Castaways bar—because that's where he thinks I am! Please, call Detective Grady Merritt and tell him what I've told you!"

Leda slammed the receiver down and shoved the phone back to the wide-eyed woman behind the counter. "Is there a back way out of here?"

At a loss for words, she merely pointed.

"Thanks!" Leda said.

She tore through the stacks, dodging between quiet readers with paper cups full of steaming coffee or chai. The front door opened and the bell jingled, but by then Leda was gone. She wove between genres, dashed past the café, and found the back door where the emergency exit was located.

It had an alert bar across it, one that read (in bright red letters) that an alarm would sound. Leda was 100 percent fine with that idea, so she flung her body against the bar and pushed with all her weight.

The door was on a delay, but after a few seconds it gave way. A screeching alarm rang out. The café workers covered their ears, and people started shouting, wondering what was happening. From the front of the store, the bookseller who'd given Leda the phone hollered, "Someone's already called the police!"

Leda was free in another dark, wet alley.

One foot sloshing, one foot merely soaked to the toes, she stumbled again. In the lights of the store, the light behind her eyes hadn't seemed so bright. She'd almost forgotten about it. But now, back in this bleak, dank place that smelled like rotting food and urine, it was too bright again.

Leda stumbled, collected herself, and stopped at the edge of the alley beside a dumpster—wondering which street she was looking at. She'd never been out the back way at Elliott Bay, and she was disoriented.

Which way was Castaways? Where people were surely wondering where the hell she was.

Right now, all she could do was keep herself alive while hoping and praying that Grady had gotten her message and that police would flood the hill with their navy-blue SUVs and flashing lights, and Abbot Keyes would get caught up in the ensuing dragnet.

It wasn't so much a plan as a wish.

Against her back, she felt something hard and cool. Next to her ear, a low and shaky voice. "Got you."

She froze and immediately wished that she'd done anything else. Kicked, screamed, fought. Flailed or hollered or shoved. But she didn't do any of that. She didn't even check to make sure that it was a gun pressing against her ribs. She just stood there, him behind her—as close as a boyfriend, his face tucked down low near her neck. He wasn't much taller than she was. Probably barely outweighed her, too. But he had a gun, and he'd killed before.

Leda could barely breathe. Her mind sprinted from option to option, hunting for an escape hatch in this terrible, wet, dark, sudden trap. But there weren't any options. Certainly not any *good* ones. Where was she? Her head swiveled around, seeking landmarks to orient herself. She recognized a steampunk-themed hair salon and triangulated her position using that, a lesbian bar, and a hot dog kiosk.

Okay. The bookstore was one block to her left. Castaways was one block to her right.

On the bright side . . .

*Was* there a bright side?

There had to be a bright side.

Okay, well . . . Abbot Keyes was *not* at Castaways, shooting up the place in search of Leda or Niki or Grady. He might not even know the others were there. Leda was the one he wanted, and if he got to hurt her, he'd probably call it a day from a murder standpoint. Silently, she prayed to anybody who might be listening: *Get Grady. Please let him have gotten the phone call. Please let him find us. Please.*

*Please. Please.*

*Please?*

# 28.

"Move," said Abbot Keyes, nudging her away from the shelter of the awning.

She didn't fight him, and she sounded mostly calm when she asked, "Where are we going?"

"I don't know yet. I'll . . . I'll figure it out, when we get back to my car."

Keyes sounded even less calm than Leda felt—which was not reassuring considering that the man tended to murder in a panic. She had to fight her nature and stay calm. She believed from the bottom of her heart that if she started screaming, he'd shoot. He didn't even have to threaten to do it. It was written in his tense posture and in his anxious voice, in the press of the metal on the back of her thin jacket.

He was cornered, and he had little to lose.

He pushed her up the hill, away from both the bar and the

bookstore. She dragged her feet and stumbled. "Is this the same gun you used to kill Tod and Amanda?"

"What? Who? Oh. Jesus, no. I threw that one into the sound. I never really meant to hurt anybody," he said as he urged her into the crosswalk.

"I find that hard to believe."

"Yeah, I get that." He stayed right up against her, hiding the gun and his intentions, but he didn't sound confident. Probably, he never sounded confident. Probably, he was better at murdering people than he was at anything else he'd ever tried, and he was still behaving like he was pretty sure he'd muck it up.

"This is stupid," Leda tried to tell him. Maybe she could keep him talking long enough for the police to show up. It beat just walking meekly along with him. "Let's go back to the bar and talk this through, okay? Or you could just ditch me and make a run for it. That's always an option. I'd even say nice things about you. Just tell me *what happened*." She was impressed with herself. It almost sounded like a demand. It hardly sounded like begging at all.

"What do you care?"

She stopped, and he ran into her. The gun hit her spine, hard. She winced but held her ground. "Tod was my fiancé. You didn't know?" She looked over her shoulder but only saw the side of his neck and the fabric of the hoodie he was wearing pulled up over his head. "You didn't even google me, or anything?"

"I didn't think about it," he said grouchily. "Come on, keep moving." But as they started walking, he muttered into her ear. "He wasn't supposed to be there. It wasn't supposed to happen. I was only trying to talk to Amanda. I was going to offer to . . . to split it with her, but she maced me and things . . . things got out of hand."

"That happens to you a lot, doesn't it?"

"Shut up. This is your fault."

She laughed. It was a brittle laugh, but she meant it. Things were only funny when they were true, right?

Then her frantic amusement soured. The more she thought about it, and the farther she walked with his gun shoved against her coat, the madder she got. Who the hell was this guy, that he got to take out his frustrations on everybody else? All God's children have problems, but he gets to be a murderer? An indiscriminate murderer, even. He didn't even *mean* to kill half the people he bumped off. Somehow that made it worse.

Yes, he was the literal definition of "worse than useless," and she was going to be his next victim. It didn't just anger her; it embarrassed her.

She stopped walking. He pushed, but she balked. She was not going to simply waltz off to her doom with this maniac. She *refused*.

"You're only delaying the inevitable," he groused into her hair as he shoved her forward. "If you'd rather, I could just shoot you right here, then shoot my way out of the neighborhood, and kill anybody else who gets in the way."

She thought about it, as she dug her heels into the sidewalk. "You won't, though. That's too large-scale for you. You're clumsy and reckless, but you're not stupid. You'd rather blend in and vanish. That's more your brand."

"I don't want to blend in!" he almost shouted.

"Why not?" she almost shouted back. "It's the only thing you're really good at!"

Leda looked around on the street and saw a young couple walking a small dog, an older homeless man with a cardboard sign, a dozen black-clad folks in a flock headed toward the Goth bar a few streets away, and a drag queen checking her makeup in a storefront window's glass.

Abbot Keyes shoved her around a corner—then changed his mind and grabbed her shoulder and pulled her back. He swore under his breath and jammed the gun harder against her. He hadn't been fast enough to keep her from seeing it, though: the police were out in force, swarming a small pay lot between two large apartment buildings.

Leda hadn't seen Grady, not in the split-second glimpse she'd caught. Her eyes were mostly clear now, the ocular migraine having cleared out by surprise or by force, and the police were right there, across the street. She was so close to safety she could *feel* it.

Abbot Keyes held her tightly around the waist with his left hand and stabbed the gun into her side with his right. She could feel that, too. He kept knocking the muzzle against the lower edge of her rib cage, roughly and repeatedly.

"Were you going to just . . . put me in your car and drive me someplace to kill me? That's just so . . . so stupid!" She was practically yelling. People were starting to look.

Keyes brought his mouth down close to her ear and said, "*Stop screaming.*"

But she'd spent too much time not screaming already. Staying quiet hadn't gotten her anywhere, and one way or another, time was running out. For her. For him. For everyone, eventually. She wrestled in his grip, a little bit at first, and then with all her body weight. "Let go of me!" she demanded. "Let go of me!"

Behind them, a woman gasped. "That man has a gun!"

The woman's voice startled her in the best possible way. It meant that Leda wasn't alone anymore. Someone else saw what was happening. Maybe Abbot would panic, and maybe he would shoot, but he was going to do that anyway, wasn't he? Might as well go down screaming.

"Yes!" Leda cried out, against orders. "He has a gun! Everybody get down! Run! The police are right over there—somebody get the police! Help! Somebody help me!" Maybe he'd kill her, maybe he'd hurt her, and maybe he'd hurt other people, too. But he'd run out of bullets eventually. And how many other people would he go on to hurt, if she just let him get away?

No.

The street was watching. One guy took up the cause and started yelling, then everyone else joined him. Everyone saw Abbot. Everyone knew what he was. It was too much for a man who had always blended in.

Distracted, he relaxed his grip. It was all Leda needed to swivel in his grasp.

She wrenched herself free and face-planted into a bakery window—which did not break, and she made a mental note to thank God later, because she didn't have time right then and there.

For a count of three or four seconds, she and Keyes stared at each other across the space of a sidewalk square. He was confused and rattled and surrounded by people, and he couldn't possibly shoot them all—maybe he couldn't even shoot his way out of the neighborhood, how many bullets did a gun like that hold, anyway? He was good at blending in. If he played his cards right, he could walk away. But playing his cards right was never his strong suit, was it? He hadn't even thought to hide the gun. Its tip poked out from under his jacket sleeve.

"You know what?" she asked him, as she balled her hand into a fist. "You've taken *enough* away from me." Before she could think it through, before she had a moment to get extra terrified, and before he saw it coming—she swung for his face and caught it, hard enough that the crack she heard might have come from his nose, or her fingers. She didn't know and didn't care.

He staggered backward, the gun hanging at the end of his arm like a ball he'd forgotten to throw.

She lunged forward to hit him again, but he backed away just in time. She waited just a hair too long to wind up and kick him square in the balls; by the time she'd swung her leg back, he'd turned around and started running.

Leda took a deep, ragged breath and backed up against the window, watching him flee the scene. "Somebody stop him!" she shouted as loud as she could. "Where are the police? Get the police! That guy has a gun!"

At the end of the block, the drag queen she'd passed earlier casually stuck out a high-heeled boot and caught Abbot's foot on the fly. He took wing and soared for a few feet before crashing down at the curb, collecting himself and making another go at escape.

Over his shoulder he glanced and saw two uniformed cops charging in his direction. He squeaked and took off for the nearest alley.

Somebody would run him down. Somebody would bring him to justice, Leda *had* to believe it—otherwise this whole adventure had been for nothing, and that simply wasn't an option.

Somebody was Grady Merritt.

He leaped from between two cars and tackled Abbot Keyes to the ground. Keyes struggled, and then he didn't.

The rain poured out of the sky, and down the hill, collecting used needles, dirty napkins, plastic utensils, cocktail straws, half-eaten slices of pizza, a few dead rats, more than a little urine, some broken windshield glass, a splash or two of vomit, and a strand of plastic beads . . . and it washed them all the way down to the sound—past Scott Abbot Keyes, who was unconscious and face-down in the gutter by the curb.

Grady cuffed him, rolled him over, and pulled him back onto the sidewalk before Abbot could aspirate enough of Seattle's liquid detritus to hurt him. Grady slapped Abbot's cheeks a couple of times until the younger man blinked rapidly, uncertainly, and damply. "Come on, asshole. Wake up. I need to read you your rights."

# 29.

Two days after Abbot Keyes nearly drowned in a gutter on Capitol Hill while being arrested on multiple counts of murder, Leda unlocked the door to her office in Columbia City. She opened the door and froze. Niki was already in there, asleep on the love seat. Her hair was a mess, her mouth was open, and a thin stream of dried drool was crusted on her chin.

"Nik?"

Niki shot awake and jerked upright, flailing until she rolled right off the short couch and onto the floor.

"What . . . are you doing here?" Leda asked.

From the floor, Niki replied, "I was very, very drunk, and I accidentally told the Uber guy to take me here. I couldn't remember the address, but I remembered it was next door to the sushi place. I . . . there was . . . I had . . ."

"You have a key."

"Right. I have a key, so. I let myself in to . . . to . . ."

Leda sighed. "To sleep it off?"

"I don't think I had a plan, to be honest. I just needed to lie down." Niki pulled herself back up, whapping her (now much smaller) boot cast against the edge of Leda's desk. "Ow. Anyway, you look . . . alert."

"I didn't have that much to drink last night."

"You didn't?" Niki gave her a stink-eye glare that said she didn't believe her. "It was *your* party."

"No, it wasn't. It was my makeup concert, since I bailed the other night." She dropped her purse on the desk. "I was home in bed by midnight. Besides, it's . . ." She sat down behind her desk and fished her phone out of her purse. "After nine o'clock. It's not exactly the crack of dawn over here."

"Yeah, but you still deserved to sleep in."

"I couldn't." Leda had awakened shortly after the sun came up, and she'd never made it back to sleep. She was tired but restless, so she figured she might as well get some work done.

"Are you having, like, PTSD? Is it something like that? Do you need some weed and a good cry?"

Leda opened her laptop and pressed a button to turn it on. "Probably at some point, but not right now. Thanks for the offer, though. It's been a hell of a week, right? I mean, not *just* the thing where I almost got murdered, but everything else, too. It's been three days of cops and journalists, and I just need a quiet, nothing-gonna-happen day where I can pretend that my life is normal."

"Your life has never been normal."

"But wouldn't it be nice if it was?"

Niki shrugged. "I don't know. Sounds boring to me."

"I could use a little boring right now."

Her friend relented. She settled upright in the love seat, leaning back and crossing her legs. "Fair enough. How did *The Stranger* interview about all the murdering go?"

"It went fine. It was weird, and I sounded like a maniac, I'm sure. But the interviewer was nice, and I got in a plug for the travel agency, so maybe we'll see a little bump in business. Murder is great advertising. Maybe? We kind of got off in the weeds for a bit. I told them how I met Grady and everything."

"Oh boy. When will the piece go live?"

"It went live online last night; those *Stranger* guys work fast. Now the *Seattle Times* wants to do a piece on me, too, but I don't know, man. I've had enough publicity this week for the rest of my life."

Solemnly, Niki said, "Publicity leads to work, and work leads to money."

"It also leads to bizarro emails from dudes who want to know if I'm single. As it turns out." With a cringe, Leda opened her email and waited for the internet to deliver whatever fresh hell was new on deck.

"Has that actually happened yet?"

"I've gotten three of them so far, and one was really freaking creepy. The guy's obviously been to my shows at Castaways. His email started out with three paragraphs about what I was wearing, where I was sitting when I wasn't on the stage, and what drinks Tiffany had made for me in my downtime . . . but then wrapped up by saying that he didn't want to come say hello because, and I quote, 'That would be weird.'"

Niki laughed. "Seattle dudes are the worst."

"Maybe some dudes are terrible everywhere, just like some ladies are. Oh my God," she said suddenly, shifting gears. "I have a *lot* of emails."

"Clients? Skeevy dudes? Long-lost relatives who've passed away and left you their fortunes?"

"No emails from dead relatives, no, but . . . hang on." Leda opened one and skimmed it, then skimmed the next one. "But hey, if all twenty-four of these emails are from people wanting travel arrangements—and I think they might be, except for the spam—then holy moly, I might be able to make rent and feed myself for a few weeks!"

"Hot damn!"

Leda skimmed more emails as fast as she could. "It's almost, like, if you keep a cop from getting on a plane that's going to blow up, people want to trust you with their travel plans! Oh God, oh no . . ."

"Oh no?" Niki asked.

"Oh no!" Leda repeated. "What if I book these people for their vacations, and one of them dies? On a plane, or in a rental car, or in a hotel fire . . . oh man, there are a *billion* ways a traveler can die on a trip. What if I send someone to Florida, and they get eaten by alligators? What if I send someone to Aspen, and they die in an avalanche?"

"You can turn literally any good thing into a Greek tragedy, I swear to God."

"But I'm not wrong! Look," Leda insisted, turning the laptop around so Niki could see the screen. "Most of these people are afraid to fly. This guy, right here . . ." She tapped the touch screen to load the email. "This guy is terrified of boats, but his wife wants to take a cruise. He thinks that if I book it, I'll keep him from any ship that's going to sink! I don't know if I can take this kind of pressure!"

"Leda, babe. Your job is to make sure that their flight details are correct, their layovers are doable, and their rental cars are waiting for them at their destinations. You aren't God. You can't guarantee that anybody will go anywhere and come back in one piece."

"But these people don't know that!" She whipped the laptop back around and scowled at her screen.

"Who cares? The only thing that needs to be true is that

you'll make their arrangements correctly and support them if they run into difficulties. It's not like your website offers them a money-back guarantee if they die en route."

"I don't have the money for a website."

"Sounds like you will after this."

Leda mumbled, "Yeah, maybe. Speaking of, Grady finally paid me. I told him he didn't have to, but he insisted on honoring our original agreement, and he paid me out of his own pocket for helping him with the Gilman case." She sighed and closed the laptop with a soft click. "Nik, I don't know if I'm ready for this."

"For greatness?"

"For the worst tragedy of my life and the second-worst day of my life to become the seeds of that greatness. I'll never get away from Tod dying, or from the feel of Abbot Keyes's gun at my side."

Niki rolled her eyes. "Nobody ever *really* puts the past behind them, no matter what anyone says. Yes, bad things happened to you—really bad things. But you survived them! Now that chapter's closed, and you can . . . well, you don't have to forget any of it. You don't have to pretend it never happened. But you've got the whole rest of your life to live, so how are you gonna live it? As a psychic psongstress? A travel agent? I vote for some combination of the two."

"You think you get a vote?"

"I damn well *better.*"

Leda laughed. "Yeah, okay. You get a vote. And since I don't have any better ideas . . ." She might have said more, but a knock at the door stopped her. She and Niki looked back and forth at each other. Niki mouthed, "Grady?" but Leda shrugged. "Come in," she said, with what she hoped was an appropriate measure of confidence and professionalism.

The door opened.

A silver-haired, heavyset, black-clad white woman let herself into the office. She left one hand on the doorknob while she gazed around the little space, taking in the posters, the desk, the love seat, and the two younger women. "Hello," she said. Her hand slipped from the knob, and she drew the door shut behind her. "My name is Avalon Harris, and I'm looking for *you*, I believe. Leda Foley?"

Leda rose to her feet. Something about this woman called for decorum, and she wasn't sure what it was, exactly. Avalon Harris wasn't very tall, and she looked tastefully like a grandmotherly version of the kids who hung around the Goth bar on Capitol Hill. Black head to toe; silver jewelry; sleek, short hair that looked like spun starlight. Leda held her hand across the desk to beckon her inside.

"Yes, that's me—hello, and it's a pleasure to meet you. Please, come in and have a seat."

Ms. Harris took her hand and shook it, then took one of the two office chairs that faced the desk. There was precious little room, but she sidled into it neatly, and then crossed her feet at the ankles. "Thank you so much."

"This is my associate, Niki Nelson," Leda added, hoping it made Niki sound less like "random hungover person who accidentally slept in my office" and more like "coworker or perhaps employee."

Niki waved. "Hello!"

Leda said, "What can I do for you? Are you interested in one of our travel packages?"

Avalon Harris folded her hands in her lap. "Well, I'm not going anywhere anytime soon, so, no—that's not it. I've actually come to see you about your other specialty."

Niki said, "You must have read the article in *The Stranger*."

"What? No. I learned of your existence through the flyers on Cap Hill, about the shows you've been performing at the Castaways bar. I'd been meaning to attend one, but last night I was called away at the last minute—and I'm afraid that I missed your show."

Leda closed her laptop and pushed it aside. "Oh, I'll do another one soon."

"I'm glad to hear that," she said with a small smile. "By all reports, you're terribly talented. My ex-husband went to one of your shows and reported that you were absolutely the real deal."

"You have an ex-husband? Who calls you and gives you hot entertainment tips?" Niki asked.

Leda flashed her a look that said she was being rude, but that'd never stopped Niki before and wouldn't stop her now.

If Avalon Harris minded, she didn't show it. "Oh, yes. Edgar is a dear. We remain close friends. He reached out to me after your show because we have something in common, you and I."

"We do?"

"Indeed. Not so much the psychic-touch angle, though I do have a bit of that. Mine's not terribly strong, I'll confess. I'm a much better medium, though that's somewhat unreliable, too." She waved her hand as if to dismiss the whole business as a gamble. "That said, I have a great deal of experience and a significant amount of education on the subject."

"Are you . . . do you . . . ?" Leda wasn't sure how to formulate her question. "Do you want to work together? Is that why you're here?"

"No, not particularly. I stopped consulting for the cops on a formal basis decades ago, but I understand you've recently been approved as a consultant for the Seattle Police Department."

"How . . . how did you know that? Wow, you really are psychic!"

She laughed. "Darling, I can read. Your publicist has amended the recent flyers to include the distinction. I suppose it lends you an air of authority."

"Oh God. Ben . . ." Leda mumbled. "Okay, yes, but right now

it's just a verbal agreement—there's no paperwork. That'll take a while, or that's what they tell me. And they'll only call me in if they're totally stuck and they think they can use me. The consultant offer isn't a promise of anything. It just makes me more official and less . . ."

"Less sneaky?" Avalon asked with a gleam in her eye. "You and Detective Merritt did so much work behind the scenes, off-the-books, semiofficially . . . it must be nice to know that they'll give you a pass, going forward. From what I've heard, they'd be fools to let you get away."

"Aw, shucks."

"No, I'm serious. You have a great deal of raw talent, and I'm here on the off chance that you'd like to learn to wield it a little . . . better? More precisely, let's say. I can't turn you into an all-knowing, crime-solving machine, but I think that you could probably use some armor."

"Armor?" Leda asked.

She nodded. "Shields, perhaps. If you like that analogy better. Here's the thing," she said, leaning forward and tangling her fingers loosely together. "I've seen people like you before. I've known and loved them, and I've lost a few of them."

Leda swallowed. "Lost them? Like, you misplaced them??"

"One died by misadventure, and one died . . . through more personal means," she said carefully, and Leda wondered if she meant suicide or drugs, but she did not ask. "Another went absolutely mad and never came back. It doesn't happen to everyone with a gift like ours, but it happens too often, I'd say. So I am here, today, sitting in your office, offering myself up as a friendly ear. Or, if you're interested, as a teacher."

"Oh. Um . . ." Leda looked to Niki, who shrugged. "That sounds lovely, if I'm honest. I've never really met anyone else who could do anything like this, much less had any friends or teachers who knew what it was like. But I don't have any money or anything, if that's—"

Avalon cut her off there. "No, don't be ridiculous. I have plenty of my own."

"I'm sorry, I didn't mean to offend . . ."

"It's all right." She took a deep breath, as if she felt the need to compose herself. "You're well within your rights to be suspicious, and now that you've got a modicum of fame, you can expect all sorts of weirdos and charlatans to creep out of the woodwork, but I'm not one of them. And I didn't make my money from telling fortunes or consulting with grieving families, either."

There it was. Leda got it now. Avalon Harris had been accused of this in the past, and it was a touchy subject. She didn't need clairvoyant abilities to read the woman's face. "I apologize, I was just thinking you were offering classes or something."

It wasn't the perfect thing to say, but it was close enough. The woman softened. "No, nothing like that. I'm only here to offer you my company. And my card." She reached into a small, shiny leather purse with a silver chain and retrieved a business card. "Here, I want you to have this."

Leda took the card. It read quite simply *Avalon Harris, Psychic Medium and Adviser*. Then an email and phone number.

"If you'd like to get coffee sometime, or if you simply want to bend an ear that understands precisely what you're up against, when a case is bloody and hard . . . I'm here."

"In Columbia City?" Niki asked.

"On Bainbridge Island, actually—but it's a short ferry ride, and I'm semiretired. My days are flexible, and I'm interested in paying it forward, you could say. I lost my own mentor a few years ago; my God, the woman was nearly a hundred when she passed, but she was such a giant of the field. And also . . ." She hesitated, but then said, "I lost my son last year. He wasn't murdered, and there's no question about what happened. I'm not seeking any answers. I'm just hoping to help someone else who might find their life filled with . . . unusual difficulties like ours."

With this, she rose to her feet and gave both Leda and Niki a short bow.

"Thank you for your time," said Avalon Harris, who then collected her purse and left the way she'd come in.

When the door had closed, and the women were alone again, Niki exhaled like she'd been holding a whole balloon's worth of air in her chest. "Wow. That was weird."

"Only weird, though. Kind of exciting, for sure! There are other people out there who . . . who do what I do and are probably better at it than me! I might actually learn how to do this professionally and earn some money. I mean, and help people. Obviously. And that's good, isn't it?"

"It's definitely not *bad*," her friend agreed somewhat more cautiously. "Weird isn't always bad."

"And weird is par for the course around here, right?"

"Damn right it is," Niki agreed—offering a silent, long-distance high five that Leda returned from behind the desk. She reclined back into her original position, foot up and arms sprawled out.

Casually, she asked, "So . . . are you ever gonna call her?"

Leda grinned and sat back down. "Maybe one of these days. Okay, *probably* one of these days." She opened her laptop again and saw three new emails since their unusual guest had appeared. "Wow," she breathed. Then she cracked her knuckles, reached for her mouse, and dived into all the messages from all the hopeful travelers, each and every one of them wanting the reassurance of Puget Sound's most famous psychic, proprietor of Foley's Far-Fetched Flights of Fancy, which might actually get off the ground after all.

Would wonders never cease?

# Acknowledgments

When I first began drafting this book in 2018, I specifically aimed for something lighter and funnier than my usual fare. After all, the world was dark enough already, wasn't it? If I wanted to write something a little brighter than horror, then surely the time had come.

God help me, I didn't know the half of it.

So now I'm composing this final piece at the tail end of 2020. Truly, this year has been an unparalleled horror show in many wild and terrible ways. But for me, it has also been a time of unexpected professional and creative growth. All things being equal, I suppose, I've weathered it as well as could be expected.

But I didn't do it alone. I *couldn't* have done it alone.

That said, I'm always reluctant to compose acknowledgments and thanks for a book—not because I don't have plenty of folks to thank for their support, but because I live in fear of leaving someone out. As you might imagine, this clashes badly with my corresponding (and well justified!) fear of endlessly repeating myself.

With this in mind, please bear with me.

First, I send big ups and undying thanks to my agent, Stacia Decker—who believed in this book, even when I was afraid that maybe I should just stick to airships and ghosts. I am immensely grateful for all her help and guidance; I'm new to her stable of authors, but she's made me feel welcome and valued at every turn. Likewise, a whole ocean of thanks to editor Kaitlin Olson—who beat this book into shape and shined it up like *whoa*. I've been so thrilled with her support and clarity! These two women are a whole new team for me, and it's been nothing short of a joy to work with them both.

Next, the usual thanks go to my husband—J. Aric Annear—who pays most of the bills these days and plays Dog Valet while I'm trying to work. (Do you want inside? Do you want outside? Put that down! Drop it! Oh my God, what are you eating . . . ? What's this on the rug? Oh no. Oh *no*.)

Finally, for now at least, I must thank my Intergalactic Tipsy Lady-Friends in the secret Slack group of unconditional support. Everyone should be so lucky to have such cheerleaders in their corner, especially in times like these.

# About the Author

Cherie Priest is the author of two dozen books and novellas, most recently the Southern horror project *The Toll* and haunted house thriller *The Family Plot*—as well as the hit young adult project *I Am Princess X* and its follow-up, *The Agony House*. But she is perhaps best known for the steampunk pulp adventures of the Clockwork Century, beginning with *Boneshaker*. She has been nominated for the Hugo Award and the Nebula Award, and the Locus Award—which she won with *Boneshaker*.

Cherie has also written a number of urban fantasy titles and composed pieces (large and small) for George R. R. Martin's shared world universe, the Wild Cards. Her short stories and nonfiction articles have appeared in such fine publications as *Weird Tales*, *Publishers Weekly*, and numerous anthologies—and her books have been translated into nine languages in eleven countries.

Although she was born in Florida on the day Jimmy Hoffa disappeared, for the last twenty years Cherie has largely divided her time between Chattanooga, Tennessee, and Seattle, Washington—where she presently lives with her husband and a menagerie of exceedingly photogenic pets.